The Seductress

The Seductress

VIVIENNE LAFAY

BLACK
lace

Black Lace novels are sexual fantasies.
In real life, make sure you practise safe sex.

First published in 1995 by
Black Lace
332 Ladbroke Grove
London
W10 5AH

Typeset by CentraCet Limited, Cambridge
Printed and bound by Cox & Wyman Ltd, Reading,
Berks

ISBN 0 352 32997 1

Chapter One

'*T*he doctor is here, your ladyship.'

Emma, Lady Longmore, put down the leather-bound book she was reading as she lay, decorously arranged, on the embroidered counterpane of her bed. She presented an attractive picture. Her dark-blonde hair was coiled into a casual bun at the nape of her pale neck, and her dress allowed a glimpse of the creamy flesh above her large, shapely breasts. The hands that clasped the book were small and dainty, as were her feet, now exposed in their silk stockings.

'Show him in please, Kitty.'

Doctor Fielding was a young man, fairly new to the area, who had been to dine at Mottisham Hall, country seat of the Longmores, on two occasions. Emma greeted him warmly, holding out a jewelled hand to him as he entered.

'Doctor Fielding, how good of you to come. I fear this is a trifling matter, for I am in excellent health.'

'Nonsense! Sir Henry's concern is a good enough reason. And I can well understand it. Three years of marriage without issue is . . . unusual, in my experience.'

Emma tried to gauge the man's thoughts, but his eyes were grave and his mouth unsmiling – as far as she

1

could tell behind that infernal facial hair. How she detested the current fashion for large, droopy moustaches! Did the good doctor suspect that her marriage was unconsummated? Emma's full lips curved with amusement at the very idea.

George Fielding approached the bed. Emma could tell he was nervous. Small beads of sweat had broken out on his brow, and he would not look her in the eye. He had rather nice eyes too, she decided, warm and brown and often showing a hint of the sensual pleasure he derived from observing beautiful objects. What a shame he couldn't bring himself to gaze upon her now, while she was looking her best.

'You do understand, Lady Longmore, that I need to examine you physically?'

She glanced at his soft hands with their long tapering fingers, imagining them parting the lips of her sex, and her heartbeat quickened. He had better not take my pulse, she thought. Attempting to look coy, she nodded.

The doctor's discomfort was increasing. 'It will be . . . ahem! . . . an *intimate* examination, your ladyship. I do hope you will not experience discomfort. I shall do my best to perform the procedure with care, and I assure you that I am experienced in the handling of female anatomy. I trained under Professor Grant, you know, whose book on obstetrics is the bible of doctors and midwives throughout the Empire . . .'

'Yes, of course. I am sure you will be gentle with me,' Emma smiled, putting a hand to the flounced hem of her skirt. 'Shall I remove my petticoats now?'

Fielding nodded, swallowed, and removed his jacket, hanging it on the back of the chair where he had placed his bag. With his back to her, he opened the bag and took out a small stoneware jar. Emma took off her undergarments and folded them neatly, then pulled up her skirt so that he could see her half-stockinged thighs, adorned with frilled garters. When the doctor turned round she saw that he had greased his right hand, and

2

a thrill of anticipation went through her. No man beside her husband had ever probed her interior before, and she could feel herself growing damply excited at the very thought of it.

'Now, your ladyship, if you could just part your legs for me. Bend them up a little, that's right.'

His tone was cool, restrained, but Emma guessed that beneath the professional manner he was probably as aroused as she. At the dinner table she had often caught him staring at her, his eyes fixed in admiration on her fine breasts, displayed in a low-necked gown. She let her head fall to one side so that she could view his trousers. They were stretched tightly and his form was clearly visible, making a distinct ridge at the base of his stomach.

Emma felt her flesh grow as soft and wet as a sucked lozenge. She let her thighs fall loosely apart. He has no need of artificial lubrication now, she thought, with a faint smile. Fielding came towards her and reached towards her sex, lightly brushing her thighs, until he could part her already tumescent labia. His fingers were cool on her warm flesh, exciting her further.

'Just relax please, Lady Longmore. I am about to reach inside. That's right, nice and relaxed now.'

It was hard not to moan with the sudden pleasure as the probing finger first slid between her sleek lips then found her opening and pushed slowly inside. Instinctively Emma raised her hips to a more accommodating angle, feeling the delicious wet contact send dizzying volts of pleasure throughout her lower regions. She noted, with some amusement, that it felt much like the effect of Dr Josiah Ellison's 'patent electric shock machine' that was supposed to improve your health.

'Are you comfortable, my lady?' came George Fielding's voice as he introduced a second digit into her dilated vagina. His tone was hoarse, and when Emma looked at him he averted his gaze, hurriedly.

'Perfectly, thank you Doctor,' she replied, calmly,

although a veritable maelstrom of feelings was building up within.

'I need to palpate the internal structures,' he explained, placing his other hand on her belly.

Now Emma could feel his bunched fingers deep inside her, like her husband's thick member, and she longed to increase the delicious sensations by moving rapidly against him. He was straining to feel her reproductive organs, thrusting so hard into her that she could clutch onto his hand with the walls of her passage. If only he would move it in and out! She shifted her position slightly so that the swollen bud of her clitoris was in naked contact with the man's wrist. Oh, bliss! Wriggling ever so slightly, she felt an onrush of heightened sensation.

'Still quite comfortable?' the doctor enquired, almost in a whisper. He was stroking her belly now, trying to estimate her configuration and, incidentally, giving her the most delightful massage both inside and out.

'Mm.' Emma was beyond speech. She glanced down the bed and saw that the bulge in George Fielding's trousers had increased in size. The sight of one of his arms plunged between her raised knees and the other on her belly caused her to grow still more moist. Was he aware of her extreme arousal? Emma fancied his eyes had a glazed look as they peered vacantly towards the window.

Then, just as she was reaching the height of her desire, he began to withdraw his hand. The slow, sensual retreat of first his wrist, then his palm, then his long fingers passing over her engorged sex proved enough to trigger her. The first spasms caught his fingertips in a fierce embrace, anointing them with her love-juice. He pulled his hand away hurriedly. Finding that the contact with him had ceased, Emma crossed her legs and pressed her thighs firmly together to prolong the delightful sensations.

At last they subsided, leaving her flushed and spent. She lay back on the pillow, wondering if the doctor had

4

noticed. If he had, he said nothing, although his face was as red as hers. Instead, he went to the washstand and gave his hands a very thorough cleansing in the bowl of water. Emma thought she should wash too, but later. Meanwhile, for the sake of propriety, she put her petticoats back on.

'What have you discovered, Doctor Fielding?' she asked eventually, when she felt more composed.

He turned, wiping his hands on a towel. For a split second his eyes met hers, wearing an expression which she found unreadable. Then he turned away to replace the towel saying, 'I am afraid the news is not good, your ladyship. I fear your husband will have to be informed that you are infertile.'

'You mean – I am incapable of bearing children?'

'Alas, yes. Occasionally it happens that a woman's reproductive system is malformed. There is no remedy, as the defect occurs before birth. I had hoped there might be some other explanation. I am sorry to be the bearer of such sad news.'

'I see.'

Fielding closed his bag with a loud click and gave a stiff bow. 'Your husband will be disappointed, naturally, but it is better that he knows at once.' He moved towards the door. 'I shall see him now. Good day, your ladyship. And please accept my commiserations.'

Left alone with her thoughts, Emma found she was neither as surprised nor as disappointed as she might have expected. In her heart of hearts she had never seen herself as a mother. The whole business of child-bearing seemed distasteful to her. She had watched her own mother bring forth four of her siblings in dreadful agony, and now it was a relief to know she would never have to suffer the same fate.

Even so, she couldn't help wondering what effect the news would have on her husband. She knew how much he wanted a son and heir, to take over at Mottisham after his day. If he died childless the estate would go to his nephew Charles, a dissolute youth addicted to gambling and drink. Would Henry blame his wife for that? Already she had seen signs of his impatience at failing to impregnate her.

Emma's lips curved into a naughty smile when she thought of all the ways they had tried to bring about the desired event. Henry had been her one and only tutor in the art of love, and she considered herself most fortunate to have married such an experienced man of the world. They had tried many methods to increase fertility, from a range of different coital positions to having him remain inside her for as long as possible after his emission, with his member plugging the outlet. Sometimes that had resulted in a full restoration of his virility, whereupon they had been able to repeat the performance to their mutual satisfaction.

The thought that all that might now change filled Emma with apprehension. She knew she could not live without physical love. Even on her wedding night she had known that. Her virginal body had been roused to the most passionate heights by her husband's expertise, heights she had never imagined, let alone experienced, before. Her education had been furthered by visits to Henry's library, where his large collection of erotic literature was always open to her inspection. She knew it was not considered proper for well-brought up women to enjoy the act of love, but through her extensive reading she had come to realise that this was merely a peculiarity of Victorian England. People of other cultures held no such censorious opinions.

Now her eyes lighted on the book resting on the bedside table. It was the one she had been reading when the doctor arrived. She picked it up and opened it.

Mating Habits of Some South Sea Islanders by Ezekiel Drew, was a rare limited edition, produced by an anthropologist following the example of the great Sir Richard Burton, whom her husband had once met. Although Mr Drew's literary style left much to be desired, the illustrations were of fine quality. Emma glanced again at the detailed portraits of dusky-skinned women with large, pendulous breasts and extraordinary protuberant behinds being serviced in all manner of ways by men with phalluses the size of cucumbers. Emma felt herself growing wet again as she surveyed the lewd pictures.

Remembering that she needed to wash herself, she lifted up her petticoats then let her hand stray between her legs, fingering her already bulging clitoris. With her other hand she undid several of the pearl buttons that secured the front of her lace blouse and thrust her fingers into the warm, firm cleavage within. Inching down beneath her corset she found her nipple already erect and seized it between thumb and forefinger. Then she proceeded to rub herself rhythmically, both above and below, with her eyes fixed on an open page showing an Islander prodding one woman with his large member while caressing the parts of another. It didn't take long for her to come off in a series of wild spasms that left her breathless. Almost as soon as the sensations faded, however, she heard her husband's heavy tread on the stairs.

Normally she would not have tried to conceal the fact that she had been masturbating. Henry approved of her self-pleasuring, believing that it made her more ready for him at any hour of the day or night. Today, though, she felt more wary, uncertain of how he had received the news of her infertility. Hastily she rearranged her clothing then closed the book, hoping her cheeks were not too flushed.

Sir Henry entered abruptly, without knocking. There was a deep furrow in his forehead and his mouth, within the neatly trimmed beard, was unsmiling.

'I have just heard the terrible news, my dear,' he began, approaching the bed. He seized her hand. 'This is a tragedy for you, for me, for the whole Longmore family. If only I had thought to have you medically examined before we married, but you seemed healthy enough.'

'If you had done so, I would scarcely have counted as a virgin,' Emma pointed out.

'True, but it would have been a small price to pay for the avoidance of this sad mistake. I know it is not your fault, Emma dear, but how are we to resolve it? That is the question now.'

She remained silent, not knowing what to say. Henry paced the room, his hands folded behind his back, thinking aloud.

'If nothing else is done, the estate will go to young Charles. Over my dead body, I say! I would rather see the place sold off, lock, stock and barrel, then have that wastrel bleed the place to death with his infernal debts. Oh, Fate has dealt me a cruel blow today, to be sure! I thought I had a marriage made in heaven, but now . . .' He turned, mindful of Emma's presence. 'I speak no ill of you, dear wife, be certain of that. You have been an excellent partner to me in all respects, save one. But that one requirement is paramount to a man of property like myself. I see no immediate way out of this dilemma, but perhaps one will come to me by and by. Meanwhile, Doctor Fielding has assured me that your health is in no way threatened by this discovery. He has even said that normal marital relations might continue indefinitely, if we should be so disposed.'

'I am relieved to hear it, Henry.'

He came close then, sat down on the bed and kissed her lips. She embraced him, thrusting her tongue between his lips, and for a few seconds their kiss deepened. Then he drew away.

'Forgive me, Emma, I do not feel the urge just now. I hope you will understand.'

'Of course,' she smiled. 'Shall we walk together in the park later? Kitty tells me the daffodils are in bloom down by the lake.'

'Perhaps.' He rose and smiled down at her, then left.

Emma got up and washed between her legs with lavender-scented water, then put on clean petticoats. She rang the bell beside the bed and soon her maid appeared. Kitty was a charming girl, quick-witted and eager to please. She had been with Emma almost a year, and they had grown about as close as mistress and servant could become.

Now Emma felt in sore need of a confidante. 'Sit by me, dear, and let me tell you what the doctor said,' she began.

Kitty drew up a chair and placed her neat posterior on it, with her hands clasped over the white apron in her lap. Her dark curls were restrained by a large blue bow, the same colour as her eyes, and Emma could have sworn that she had rouged her cheeks a little. Not that she minded. She liked her maid to look pretty and well-groomed.

'It seems I am not able to bear children,' she began. 'There is nothing that can be done. I am malformed within.'

'Oh, how terrible Ma'am!' The girl's eyes were full of genuine concern. Then she added, fearing she had said the wrong thing, 'But no one would think it to look at you, I'm sure.'

Emma couldn't help laughing at her maid's discomfiture. 'I am normal in every other way, I promise you. I may even continue a normal married life – if my husband feels it worthwhile, that is.'

The note of bitter apprehension that crept into her voice surprised even Emma.

'Sir Henry must be very upset,' Kitty said. 'I saw him slam the door of his study just now and guessed something was wrong.'

'It is the question of inheritance that bothers him,' Emma sighed. 'Still, that is none of your concern. I wish merely to reassure you that nothing will change here at Mottisham. Not as long as I am alive, anyway.'

Yet as she spoke those words Emma knew it was not for Kitty's reassurance, but for her own.

The best indication that normal relations would continue between Lady Emma and Sir Henry would have been his claiming of conjugal rights. For three nights, however, he abstained, saying he was still in a state of shock after the news. He could see his wife was upset and, on the fourth night, made some attempt. It was such a brief and unsatisfactory coupling that Emma was reduced to tears.

'Henry, I fear you will love me no more,' she moaned. 'You used to take such delight in my body, and now you appear to abhor it. What have I done to deserve such rejection?'

'Circumstances alter cases,' he replied, gruffly. 'Do not make too much of it, my dear. I am sure my desire for you will return before long.'

Undefeated, Emma decided to help her husband's libido along by playing the harlot. It was not the first time she had attempted to rekindle his sluggish appetite. A year ago they had gone through a phase in their marriage where, deeply involved in the business of buying up neighbouring land and developing his estate, he seemed to have no time for the pleasures of the flesh.

Then Emma had taken delight in seducing him with wanton ways and new tricks. She had bought herself new dresses based on the latest Paris fashions, that showed off her fine breasts and narrow waist to perfection. She had taken special care over choosing new undergarments, finding corsets of black lace that pushed her chest up so high that her bosoms overflowed like delicious boiled puddings. She had cultivated the art of innuendo and suggestion, leading his thoughts down lascivious paths so subtly that he grew aroused without knowing why. She had studied his books for obscure sexual practices and introduced some of them into their lovemaking, all with great effect. After that, the couple had never looked back – until now.

Emma took up her new project with enthusiasm. In the back of one of Henry's books were recipes for aphrodisiacs. Some had obscure ingredients, like cantharides, the notorious 'Spanish fly'. Others consisted of straightforward foods such as oysters and almonds, or garden plants such as lady's mantle and maidenhair fern. Easiest of all to find were the kitchen herbs and spices: parsley and rosemary, ginger and cloves. Emma made decoctions of a selection of these and kept them in bottles to be added to Sir Henry's food and drink, as often as opportunity permitted.

Endeavouring to make herself more physically attractive to her husband, and knowing how much he admired a well-moulded *derrière*, Emma began to wear a bustle. These were enjoying a fashion revival, and worn under one of her flounced gowns this 'dress improver', as it was euphemistically called, gave her a becomingly rounded shape. Not that she considered herself lacking in that department, but she was keen to pay attention to every small detail that might re-ignite the flame of Henry's passion.

After dinner, Emma did all she could to ensure that his footsteps wended their way towards her room at bedtime. She brought his books to him, pretending to be puzzled by some reference or illustration, so that he was obliged to talk about copulation. Sitting very close to him, so her delicate floral perfumes wafted straight up his nostrils, Emma made sure her hand touched his arm or her hair brushed his cheek as often as possible. She plied him with wine, both during and after the meal, made sure he was comfortable and fussed over him in many small ways, endeavouring to make him feel relaxed and pampered.

Then, one evening, all her efforts were rewarded. When Sir Henry rose to retire, he took her in his arms and gave her a long kiss on the lips.

'You look so beautiful just now, Emma,' he sighed. 'I fear I have been neglecting you lately. Will you permit me to come to your room tonight?'

'I can think of no greater pleasure,' she replied, demurely.

Once she had him lying on her bed, Emma gradually undressed her husband until she could survey the state of his arousal. His penis was semi-flaccid, but she was confident that she could soon improve upon it. He helped her out of her dress and then she approached him clad only in her corset, petticoats and stockings, wiggling her hips at him like a Parisian whore.

'Would you like to watch me undress?' she asked, teasingly.

Emma had read of the way women performed in low-life society clubs and cafés, slowly removing their garments so as to titillate the men into wanting them. Although she had never seen it done, she had worked out her own way of doing it and rehearsed it many times in front of her bedroom mirror.

First she positioned a chair and put one foot upon it, allowing Henry a clear view as she slowly rolled her garter down one silk stocking. She let it dangle from her toes then playfully jerked her foot so that the ribbon flew through the air and landed on the bed.

'You saucy minx!' he exclaimed, entering into the spirit of the entertainment, much to her satisfaction.

Emma did the same with the other garter, then proceeded to remove the stockings in the same slow, tantalising manner. Smiling, she thrust one of the rolled-up stockings right into her already wet quim. She brought it out and sniffed its musky odour.

'Mm, delicious!' she giggled, throwing it at him. He caught it and pressed it to his own nostrils with a contented sigh.

Next Emma rose with her back to Henry and slowly dropped her petticoats, revealing the pale pink flesh of her shapely behind inch by inch. Her husband groaned.

'This is sweet torment, wife! My fingers itch to clutch at those firm, full buttocks.'

She smiled at him, over her shoulder. 'All in good time, husband!'

Once Emma had stepped out of her cotton undergarments she spread her thighs and sat facing the back of the chair. It had a plush velvet seat which gently prickled her fat labia, making her squirm with delight.

Glancing into her strategically positioned mirror, she saw that her bum cheeks were pushed up well on the seat, making them look nice and squashy. She could see, too, that Henry's phallus was well distended and his face had turned a florid hue. With a touch of malice she thought, 'I'll teach him to ignore my desires!'

The black corset was laced tightly at the front. Emma began to untie the laces, to loosen the garment's hold over her spilling bosom. She let out a sigh of relief as the pressure was reduced and her breasts dropped to their normal position. As she lifted the corset free she glanced down at them. Large and firm, with their pink nipples already puckering a little, they were a pair to be proud of. That was another advantage of being childless; she was in no danger of ruining her figure.

'Emma, let me see you!' Henry pleaded, from the bed.

She shook her head and smiled back at him over her shoulder. 'Not yet.'

Continuing with the unlacing until she felt her torso relax in freedom, Emma pulled the corset off and threw it on the floor. Then, cupping as much of her breasts in her hands as she could and rubbing her thumbs over her stiffening nipples, she proceeded to circle her hips and clench her buttocks, rhythmically rising up and down on the velvety seat so that her wide open crotch obtained the maximum stimulation.

'I cannot bear this, Emma! I want to come over and take you on that chair, right now!'

'Not yet,' she repeated, wondering with sudden amusement whether Mrs Farley, the housekeeper, knew how to remove certain stains from upholstery.

'Why are you making me wait?' he whined. In the mirror, Emma saw his hand stray to his rigid member.

'You should know by now, husband dear, that the greater the desire the greater the satisfaction.'

'I know, but we have not made love in over two weeks and my testicles are near to bursting.'

Emma gazed at him archly, over her shoulder, while

13

continuing to pleasure herself. 'And whose fault is that, Henry?'

'Mine, I acknowledge. But I could not help it if my desire was absent. It has returned now, however, and in full force.'

'Then let it continue to grow a while, Henry. No, do not touch your member! I want you fully roused when I finally let you approach me.'

It pleased and excited Emma to talk frankly to him. It suited her well to be in control of the situation, too. In the early days, when she had known nothing, inevitably her husband had been her mentor. Gradually, though, she had come to discover not only what pleasure she and her husband might derive together, but also how to please herself. Now the rough caress of the velvet on her tumid nether lips, through which her hardened bud protruded, was giving her the most exquisite thrill and she wanted to prolong it as far as possible.

'Turn around then,' Henry pleaded. 'Let me see you playing with your lovely breasts, my dear.'

'All right. But you must promise to just lie there and not touch yourself. Otherwise, I may have to tie your hands behind your back.'

She knew he would like that.

'I am not sure I can trust my fingers not to stray,' he replied, slyly.

Rising, Emma picked up one of her discarded stockings and approached the bed. He made a playful grab at her pubis, but she caught both his hands and secured them with the silk pulled tightly round. Her gaze fell to his fine erection and she couldn't resist taking it momentarily between her lips and kissing its purplish engorged tip. As she withdrew her mouth a single liquid pearl appeared in the slit.

Returning to the chair, Emma re-positioned herself facing front. She placed her bare heels on the rungs at the side, so that her thighs were spread and her gleaming pussy was fully exposed to view. The mild stimulation of the velour seat was no longer enough for her. While she toyed with one large, pink nipple her other hand dropped down to delve within her open labia. She trailed her forefinger along the wet groove, dipped momentarily into the opening, then brought it out, glistening, to lightly caress her bursting bud. She knew it had come from beneath its sheltering hood and was sticking right out, like a pea in an open pod. Henry couldn't keep his eyes off it.

'You look wonderful, my dear,' he murmured, thickly. 'But surely you can let me do that for you?'

'All in good time.'

Emma began alternately rubbing her little knob and dipping into her streaming quim: rub and dip, rub and dip, until she felt herself right on the edge of coming. Then she stopped. It was always better if you waited. She rose slowly from the chair and sidled up to the bed, a knowing smile lighting up her grey-green eyes.

'Are you ready for me, husband?'

'You can see that I am. Damn you, tormentress!'

'I wish only to give you pleasure,' she smiled, sitting on the edge of the bed just out of his reach and lifting both of her breasts up. They were large enough for her to reach the nipples with her tongue. She licked first one, then the other, watching Henry all the while. His prick was straining to be inside her, huge and an angry red. Emma knelt on the bed and sucked each of his big toes in turn, letting them slide in and out of her mouth just as if they were his sex organ. When he groaned she laughed at his frustration, clambering up until she could lower herself onto his erection. Still she would not indulge him but hovered with her nether lips just touching his glans, enjoying the raw, naked desire in his eyes. She had wanted him to want her again. Well, now he did, and with a vengeance!

Slowly, slowly Emma inched her way down his extended stalk, letting her sleek walls enclose him bit by bit. Henry gasped, wriggling to free himself from his bonds. She leaned forward and untied the hosiery that bound his hands. At once he grabbed her breasts and thrust one in his mouth, gobbling upon it greedily. Emma squeezed his shaft, enjoying the solid feel of it filling her up inside. She knew that either of them could come in an instant once she increased the pace, but as long as she kept her hips still and stopped him thrusting he would maintain his erection without coming.

How she loved making those tiny muscular movements that pushed her ever closer to the brink! Henry's sucking of her breasts was taking her there quickly now, making her little button throb intensely, sending radiating warmth down her thighs and up across her stomach and buttocks. She gave a guttural groan as the first spasms hit her, then rippled up and down his pole like greased lightning. Excited by her coming, Henry began to buck his hips furiously and soon he was spurting ecstatically, filling her already liquid chasm with yet more hot fluid.

Emma's orgasm outlasted his, although she had been the first to start. The blissful sensations just went on and on, longer than ever before. When at last she lay back, utterly satiated and contented in her husband's arms, it occurred to her that perhaps she had enjoyed love-making all the more because the risk of pregnancy had been removed forever. Although it was never foremost in her thoughts, she realised that it had always been there in the back of her mind, the unknown, to be secretly dreaded. Well, now she was free of all that.

'Henry, dearest, tonight you have given me the reassurance I needed,' she told him, with a smile. 'I was beginning to fear you had quite lost interest in me in that way.'

'Then you have had proof to the contrary, I hope.' Henry gave her a proprietorial kiss on the forehead.

'Yes, indeed.' Emma paused, then spoke her mind. 'So you are now reconciled to the fact that you cannot have a son and heir?'

'I accept that *you* cannot give me one, Emma. But the

future of Mottisham is my business. Please do not speak of it again.'

His gruff tone puzzled Emma, but she resolved to do as he asked. It was an unpleasant subject as far as she was concerned, and one she was happy to forget.

Chapter Two

*T*he satisfactory resumption of normal marital relations in the Longmore household did not last. In fact, after that one glorious night of love, Henry grew distant and seemed to be avoiding his wife, much to her distress. He refused to discuss it, however, and Emma was left wondering what she could possibly have done wrong. In public they were, as ever, the perfect couple. But as soon as the door of Mottisham Hall was closed to the world they were like strangers. Often Henry was away on some business or other, sometimes overnight, and if Emma had not had the company of her maid she would have been very lonely.

One evening she asked Kitty to join her in her room after dinner. The two women sat sewing, Kitty engaged on the mundane task of darning her underwear, while Emma worked on a tapestry cushion cover. Suddenly she flung the stuff down on the floor in disgust.

'Oh Kitty, why am I engaged in such useless and trivial occupations as this?'

The girl looked puzzled. 'Why should you not be, Miss Emma? Needlework is surely a suitable occupation for a lady such as yourself?'

Emma sighed. 'Forgive me, I am overwrought. But sometimes I feel that women are undervalued in our

18

society. In other lands, different cultures, they are the equals of men. Here men pretend to regard us as angels, but they treat us like fools.'

'No man shall treat me like a fool, Ma'am! But then I never intend to get under any man's thumb.' She clasped her mouth, afraid she had said the wrong thing. 'Beg pardon, Miss Emma. I didn't mean to suggest that you were under Sir Henry's thumb!'

Emma sighed. 'It is all right, Kitty, you may think or say what you like for all I care. The fact is, my husband has abandoned me.'

'Abandoned you?' Kitty repeated.

'Oh, we still share the same roof, and he provides me with all my material wants. But I am his wife in name only, and I cannot bear it.'

Feeling the tears well up, Emma buried her face in her hands.

Suddenly she felt Kitty's gentle touch on her shoulder. 'Is it because of you not being able to bear children, Ma'am?'

Emma lifted her tear-streaked face and nodded. Kitty took her mistress into her arms, pressing Emma's head against her apron so that her firm bosom nudged her temple. To Emma's surprise, a slight shiver went through her and she pulled away. Experienced in the reactions of her own body, Emma knew the nature of the *frisson* that had passed through her and it made her blush. Although she had read accounts of Sapphic love in Henry's books she had never dreamed of experiencing such desires herself before.

'Are you all right, Ma'am? Shall I fetch the salts?'

Embarrassed by her reddened cheeks, Emma rose quickly. 'No, I am perfectly fine thank you, Kitty. I am upset about my husband, that is all. I think perhaps I shall retire early tonight. Will you prepare my bath?'

'Of course, Ma'am. Will you have me wash your back for you?'

'No!' Emma realised that she had snapped at the girl

and added, 'Thank you, Kitty. When my bath is ready you may go off duty.'

Only when Emma was lying in her rose-scented bath did she feel safe to explore the new feelings that had so suddenly overtaken her. She had been made aware of the fact that, beneath the black dress and white apron of her maid's uniform, Kitty had a female body like her own. Or, perhaps, unlike. There was an inequality between them, since Kitty had often seen her mistress naked, but Emma had only ever seen the girl fully clothed. She recalled how often her corset had been laced for her, those busy fingers brushing her nipples as they worked. She'd also had her back scrubbed, her hair washed, her hands and feet manicured – always when she'd been in a state of *deshabille* or entirely nude. Well, now her curiosity had been awakened, and Emma suspected that curiosity was in some way sexual.

It had been a pleasure, she had to admit, to be gently handled by the girl, but a *sexual* pleasure? Emma frowned, smoothing her breasts with soapy hands and noting the voluptuous feelings that enveloped her. If her husband could arouse her, if she could give herself similar feelings, why not another woman? The thought excited her greatly, but she knew it was dangerous. Kitty was an excellent lady's maid: efficient, kind, thoughtful and extremely loyal. And she was, in her unassuming way, a better friend to her than most of the prissy and snobbish women in the area. If she upset Kitty by making any unwanted suggestions or advances the girl would give in her notice, and then Emma's life would be miserable indeed.

No, she must quash all such thoughts and feelings that had surfaced tonight. Kitty must not know of them. No doubt she would not have felt like that at all if she had not been so frustrated by Henry's indifference, but she must bear her husband's coldness as best she could. They had been somewhat estranged twice in the past and their reunion had, on each occasion, been crowned with glorious love-making. They were going through a difficult patch in their marriage, that was all.

A few days later, Emma was heartened by the prospect of a ball at Mottisham. Henry had decided it was high time they repaid the hospitality they had enjoyed over the past year, and the best way was to invite everyone to the Hall at once. So they began preparations to receive 60 guests, which was the maximum that the great hall would accommodate for dancing. Emma was promised a new gown, and began looking forward excitedly to the event.

Henry gave his wife leave to travel to London and buy a ball gown in the latest Parisian fashion. She wondered whether he were sorry he had neglected her lately, and was trying to make it up to her, but his manner was still cool. She took Kitty with her on the long coach journey and they arrived in Bond Street in the afternoon.

Inside the elegant salon of 'Madame Suzette' Emma was shown several beautiful dresses designed by Monsieur Worth of Paris. Kitty recommended a style in powder blue and ivory satin, which she said would suit her mistress's colouring very well. They retreated behind a curtain and Kitty helped Emma to disrobe.

'You know, I would be pleased to purchase one of Charles Worth's fashions,' Emma smiled, as she surveyed the gown. 'He was born in Lincolnshire, you know. Although he works in Paris, he is an Englishman through and through.'

She raised her arms so that Kitty could slip the magnificent garment over her head. It had a stiffened bodice that contained her breasts so well she scarcely needed a corset. The low, square neck was rendered more modest by the addition of some creamy lace, and the skirt was filled out behind with a bustle – the device that had not only become Worth's trademark but was now copied by all the other designers.

When Emma stood before the full-length mirror, Kitty gave a sigh of admiration.

'Oh, it suits you beautifully, Ma'am, and really shows off your figure. Especially your fine bosom.'

Her words sent a shiver down Emma's spine, which she did her best to ignore. But then Kitty approached her, frowning a little. 'I think the lace is caught up a little, here . . .'

The maid's deft fingers plucked at the lacy trim, brushing against Emma's deep cleavage. She felt extraordinarily keyed up, and knew that her breasts were becoming flushed with pink. A wanton desire arose to have the girl fondle her, kiss her, plunge her busy fingers under that teasing lace and find her hardening nipples to play with. There was a burning in the cleft between her thighs, a familiar tingling that was urging her perilously near to speaking of her forbidden lust.

Instead she said, sharply, 'Do not mess with it now, Kitty. The gown suits me well, I shall take it. There will be plenty of time before the ball to primp and fuss.'

Kitty stepped back, downcast by her mistress's harsh tone, but Emma did nothing to appease her. She felt irritated with the girl. Didn't she realise how intolerable it was for her to be pawed and mauled by her maid, when her husband would not come near her?

On the way home, though, she realised she had been unfair. The girl was acting as she always had, and could not be held responsible for her mistress's unfortunate position. She took out the packet of bonbons she had bought and shared them with Kitty, so the two women were soon friends again.

It grew dark when they were an hour from home, and Kitty fell asleep in the corner of the carriage. Left alone with her thoughts, Emma told herself that her predicament could not be allowed to continue for much longer. Either her husband must resume their marital relations, or he must agree to her taking a lover. She would not do so behind his back. They had always been open with each other, and she valued that. They had also talked of 'free love', and Henry had always maintained that if a man or a woman were unhappy sexually

22

with their partner then to seek satisfaction elsewhere was their right, provided no real harm were done. Henry was in favour of licensed brothels for this purpose. Unfortunately, however, there were no convenient arrangements for women seeking sexual relations – not in their part of the world, at least. So Henry would just have to allow his wife to take a lover, or be exposed as an hypocrite.

Half dozing, Emma began to consider the local candidates. Most of the men in the neighbourhood were excluded on the grounds of being too old, too ugly, too boring or too stuffy. It was a shame they did not live in the capital, Emma decided. During their brief visits to London she had noticed many handsome and bright young men, some of whom had given her the 'glad-eye'.

But there were one or two hopeful prospects nearer home. Doctor Fielding, for a start. Who better to understand her present predicament than the man who had, by his professional diagnosis, inadvertently plunged her into it? She recalled with pleasure her last 'examination', remembering how his long fingers had plundered her insides while he caressed the sensitive skin of her stomach, causing her juices to flow and eventually bringing her to orgasm. If he could do that to her unintentionally, think what he might achieve on purpose! Yes, she decided, George Fielding was her best hope. In his early thirties and as yet unmarried, she could not hope for a better candidate. Perhaps she would invent some mysterious ailment, a pain in her breast or abdomen, for instance, that would necessitate many 'treatments' . . .

When the day of the ball dawned, Emma felt an excited flutter of anticipation as she put on her new gown, aided by her maid. George Fielding had been invited, and had accepted. She must make sure he danced with her at least three times. As Kitty adjusted her dress, her thoughts were all of George's flashing brown eyes, handsome figure and gentle touch. She felt

23

her breasts swell and her nipples harden at the thought of him, and soon her private parts became wet and open. Tonight she would be scintillating, irresistible, so as to make him want her even more than he did already. If she could possibly lure him somewhere private she would try to get a kiss out of him. The library! That was the perfect place. She would tell him about Henry's literary collection, hinting that it would be in accord with his professional interest in anatomy. It would surely not take long to achieve her goal. Then, when she was sure of George's desires, she would approach Henry.

Descending the main staircase on her husband's arm, Emma knew she looked wonderful. Envious female and desirous male eyes were fixed upon her fabulous gown, the heirloom sapphires at her throat, the subtle beauty of her face and the sensual grace of her figure. She looked around the crowd waiting to be greeted and was relieved to see George Fielding amongst them. She directed a dazzling smile in his direction, but then a slight frown creased her brow. Who was that young woman with him? Some distant relative or acquaintance wheeled in for the occasion, no doubt. One thing was certain: she was no competition. With her fresh-faced look and unfashionable clothes she appeared positively dowdy.

The line shortened as the couples, having paid their respects, moved off into the ballroom where the band was already quietly playing. Now it was the turn of the Doctor to shake Sir Henry by the hand.

'Good evening Sir Henry, Lady Emma,' he smiled. 'May I present to you Miss Margaret Dunning-Brown? We were recently betrothed.'

'Well done, my dear chap!'

Emma let her husband's loud congratulations wash over her as she stood with glazed eyes and gritted teeth. She shook the girl's limp hand, then George's firm one, muttered insincere congratulations, and was relieved when they moved on. It was a blow to her plan, she decided, but not an insuperable one. There were plenty more fish in the sea. And she gave the next eligible bachelor such a warm and dazzling smile that he wandered off in a complete daze.

Determined to enjoy herself, Emma danced with everyone who took her fancy that evening. She hadn't had so much fun since before she was married. Having men hold her close in the waltz and whisk her round in the polka was exhilarating, arousing. She fancied that she could tell, from the way they held her and the bulge which appeared in their trousers, which of her partners would be keen to take their acquaintance further, and before long she had singled out two hopefuls: John Taylor, whose wife had died the previous spring and who owned the neighbouring farm, and Charles Macintyre, a dashing young squire and Master of the Hunt, who was probably the most eligible bachelor around. Surely either of them would welcome an *affaire du coeur* with the eminently desirable Lady Longmore?

During the evening she noticed her husband dancing several times with Catherine Best, a young widow and mother of two sons, who was only recently out of mourning. For someone supposedly still grieving for her late husband she was certainly enjoying herself, Emma noted sourly. Her face and bosom were flushed, and she seemed to be hanging on Henry's every word. As they danced he held her so close that Emma began to feel twinges of jealousy. She was tempted to go up and claim a dance from Henry herself, but thought better of it. It was considered bad form for a host to dance with his wife except at the end of the evening and, besides, there were far more attractive partners for her to choose from.

When her husband and the pretty widow disappeared from view, however, Emma grew suspicious. Surely they were not having an affair? Yet she knew that Henry was not one to forego sexual pleasure for long. She remembered how frequent his absences had been of late and her suspicions grew. Taking the opportunity of a lull in the dancing she slipped out of the hall and up the stairs, pretending she was on her way to the bathroom.

Her husband's bedroom was round a bend in the first-floor corridor, out of sight of the main staircase. Cautiously Emma put an ear, then an eye, to the keyhole. She could hear vague sounds within, but something hanging behind the door obscured her view. Gently she turned the handle. The door was unlocked. Carefully she eased it open a crack and squinted through.

The scene which confronted Emma made her gasp. Her husband was lying on his bed, stark naked, while the 'merry widow' as she was nicknamed, was paying lip-service to his extended penis. She could see the hussy's fat white arse quite plainly, with her wrinkled brown nether lips protruding below. Emma was suffused with rage. It spread through her like a forest fire, accelerating her pulse and raising her temperature to fever pitch. She clenched her fist, wanting to dash in there and slap those disgusting buttocks mercilessly.

But something held her back. Partly through fascination, partly through prudence, she decided to remain watching awhile. It would do no good to disturb her husband *in flagrante delicto*, when he would be in no mood to discuss the matter rationally. No, she would confront him with it later, when the guests had gone and she'd had time to consider how she might turn the situation to her advantage.

Meanwhile, once she had recovered from the shock and her anger had tempered, Emma rather enjoyed the spectacle. Her husband murmured something and the woman stopped fellating him, moving round so that Emma had a good view of her naked breasts. They were flat and pendulous, with rubbery dark-brown teats – nowhere near as pert and full as her own. As if to prove the point to herself, she plunged her hands into her lace-filled décolleté and succeeded in pulling out her breasts so that they jutted over the stiff top of her gown, the pretty pink nipples already semi-aroused. Emma tickled them softly with her nails, enjoying the delicious warmth that curled lazily up from her loins.

Catherine Best was preparing to mount Sir Henry now, lowering her sagging posterior towards his upright member. What she could not see from the door, Emma could clearly view in the wardrobe mirror. The trollop was rubbing the tip of her lover's glans against her own vulva, preparing herself for his entry. Emma could hear the low moans that Henry was making and a burst of anger hit her again. But she was feeling lustful, too. Lifting up her voluminous skirt she pulled her petticoats down until they were bunched round her thighs with her pubis exposed, then thrust her right forefinger deep inside her vagina. It was warm and wet in there, just like that bitch-queen Catherine's, no doubt!

Soon the adulteress was riding Sir Henry hard, bouncing up and down at full gallop while his fingers were on her button. She was groaning too, and muttering beneath her breath but it was impossible to hear what she was saying. Emma worked herself just as hard beneath her skirt, feeling the intense sensations rise towards their peak as her stiff forefinger rubbed away. Her bosom was thrust up high by her corseted bodice, high enough for her to flick her tongue across her nipples if she bent her head, greatly increasing her arousal. She kept her eyes on the woman's jiggling buttocks and flopping breasts, thinking how she would love to slap them, and only directed her gaze towards Sir Henry's contorted face from time to time. Her fury with that harlot was fuelling her own desire, for as her hatred quickened so did her frantic race towards orgasm. She would beat that witch to it, by God she would!

Then came the familiar sound of her husband in the final throes of his pleasure. Emma could tell he was there by his heavy gasps and the fierce convulsions of his legs. Just as if she had been fornicating with him herself, Emma was pushed over the edge by Henry's climax. She came in a series of shuddering contractions that would have swept her off her feet had she not steadied herself with one hand against the door jamb. When she had recovered her wits she drew up her petticoats again and was about to leave the scene when she heard Catherine's complaining voice say, 'But I am not yet finished, Henry dear. Will you not suck me off, as you did last time?'

Emma almost exploded aloud. So the pair had been at it before! She was so angry she was tempted to storm into the room.

Then her husband's voice came in reply, 'I am sorry, my dear, but we have been absent long enough. People will be wondering where we are, especially my wife.'

For safety's sake Emma pulled the door to, but she couldn't help smiling as she eavesdropped on Catherine's next words.

'Oh, you are so cruel! I am left all high and dry, while you are thoroughly satisfied.'

'It cannot be helped. I must dress quickly now, and go downstairs. And you must do likewise, or your partner will begin to suspect that your excuse about visiting the ladies' room was a ruse to escape him.'

'And so it was, the tedious old fool! Oh, when shall I see you again, my love? I count the hours between our meetings.'

'Whenever I can get away, I may say no more at present. Shall I help you with your gown, my dear?'

Emma crept away, unable to suppress a smile. The thought of Catherine burning with frustrated desire for the rest of the evening was extremely satisfying. However, she must not forget that her husband had deceived her with that woman on more than two occasions, and was planning to do so again. With mixed feelings swirling away inside her Emma did her best to compose herself, slipping into her room to repair her hair and wash her hands before facing the throng – and her husband – once again.

When the last guests had left, husband and wife faced each other in the drawing room.

'Husband, I must speak to you,' Emma began, rather nervously.

'Can it not wait?' he snapped, irritably. 'I am quite exhausted.'

She gave him a long look. 'Yes, and not merely from the task of entertaining our guests, I think.'

'What on earth do you mean by that, Emma?'

She decided to come straight to the point. 'I know you are having relations with Catherine Best.'

At first Henry feigned innocence. 'Mrs Best? The young widow?'

Emma despised him for prevaricating. 'The very same.'

'You accuse me of – '

'I saw you with my own eyes, Henry. Tonight. In your bedroom.' His face was incredulous but she felt cool and perfectly in control. 'Through the doorway I watched the pair of you. First she performed upon your instrument, then she mounted you and rode you until you came. I saw it all, Henry. I even heard her beg you to finish her off, but you said there was no time. I know you and she have made love on other occasions, too. She is your mistress, Henry.'

Shamefaced, he nodded. 'I cannot deny it. But it is for the good of Mottisham, Emma. I must have an heir, and she has already produced two boys. She has had no other lover but me since her husband died, so I know that if she conceives the child will be mine. It is the only solution to my problem.'

'*Your* problem! I can see you have given no thought to me in all this. So I am to be cast aside, am I? You shall continue ignoring your wife while you dote upon your mistress?'

He came towards her, hands outstretched, but Emma

29

brushed him away. She could scarcely bear to look at him.

'I am sorry it has come to this, my dear. Believe me, if you had been fecund I should not have looked at another woman. Catherine is jealous, and made me promise not to continue relations with you. That is why I have been distant lately. But once an heir is produced and safely ensconced at Mottisham I shall drop her, I promise you.'

'What do you say?' Emma could scarcely credit his words. 'That woman's brat to live here as your son?'

'Of course. That is the whole object of the exercise.'

Emma felt physically sick at his presumption. 'The way you are talking this might be some business venture, Henry. It is the lives of human beings that you are dealing with so carelessly.'

'Hush, Emma dear, you are understandably disturbed. We may continue this discussion in the morning, if you so wish. Now I beg you to sleep upon it.'

Emma hurried from the room, as anxious as her husband to terminate the proceedings. Kitty noticed her mood as she helped her out of her gown, and enquired gently, 'Is anything the matter, Ma'am?'

Emma heaved a great sigh. 'I cannot speak of it now, Kitty. I long for my bed.'

Once in bed, however, she could not sleep. The very idea of her husband's bastard being raised at Mottisham was anathema to her. Did he intend to pass the child off as theirs? And would Catherine ever consent to such an arrangement? The more she thought about it, the more intolerable the plan seemed. All her earlier thoughts of taking a lover seemed naive and irrelevant now. Yet she had sensed Henry's determination, and knew that he would plough his own furrow regardless of her feelings. Mottisham meant more to him than she did, and that was a fact. She simply could not continue to live there under those conditions.

Next morning, tired and fraught, Emma faced her husband again.

'You need not fret you know, Emma,' he began, more kindly. 'Once a son has been born and brought here you need have nothing to do with him. And I shall ensure that Catherine makes a good match, so she will trouble me no more.'

'You think you can buy her silence, do you?'

'Catherine understands my terms. She is a wealthy widow, and has many admirers. Once she has borne my child she will want to choose a husband and start a new life.'

Emma stared at him, unbelieving. 'And you think I can accept all this?'

'You will grow to accept it, in time. Otherwise . . .' Henry heaved a sigh. 'You will have a miserable life I fear, my dear.'

'Not necessarily.'

Emma faced him squarely, her green eyes glinting with new hope. 'I have been thinking, Henry, of an alternative. If I were to leave you, to make my own way in the world, would you support me?'

He was flabbergasted. 'What on earth are you saying?'

'I am educated, and could perhaps find employment as a governess, as unmarried gentlewomen do. I would find that preferable to living under the same roof as that woman's child, Henry.'

Henry paced up and down with his hands behind his back, and Emma began to feel a cruel delight in his perturbation. He had thought she would be cowed by his proposal, accept it meekly. Well, he had underestimated her!

'You wish to leave me, Emma?' he repeated, wanly.

'Only if you persist in this plan.'

'But I must! It is possible that Catherine is already with child. Yet I do not wish to lose you. Is there no other way?'

'I can think of none. Your behaviour is unacceptable

to me, the possible outcome more so. I shall leave with or without your blessing, but I would rather leave with it.'

'I believe you need to think this through more carefully, Emma. Why not go to your cousin Anne, in Hampshire, for a while? That will give us both pause to reflect.'

Emma thought this an excellent idea. She wrote at once to Anne, announcing that she would arrive in three days' time. Not that she believed she would change her mind. If anything, the taste of freedom that she would gain through being away from Mottisham would merely confirm her desire to leave it forever.

Already the idea of being her own woman was exciting Emma. She could travel to foreign parts, take as many lovers as she pleased, and be accountable to no one. Her whole body tingled with excitement as she envisaged herself, Emma Longmore, in the rôle of adventuress. If Henry would only agree to provide her with a modest income, which he could well afford, and she could find some way of supplementing it by means of some genteel employment, then she was sure her new life would prove most satisfactory.

Chapter Three

Cousin Anne lived with her husband, two young sons and her eighteen-year-old sister, Louisa, in a pleasant old house near Chichester. She greeted Emma warmly, since the two women had known each other from their childhood and had many shared memories. They took tea in the drawing-room then Anne showed Emma to her quarters herself.

As Kitty unpacked her mistress's clothes in the pretty guest room she said amiably, 'This is what you've been needing, Miss Emma, if you don't mind me saying so. A nice holiday. The change of scene will do you good, I'm sure.'

Emma sighed, gazing out over lawns in which the first daffodils were appearing. She knew now was the time to break the news to her maid. 'I needed more than a change of scene, Kitty. Henry and I have agreed to part, and I have left home for good. I intend to go abroad for a while, passing as a widow. If you wish me to find you another post, I shall – '

'Oh no, Ma'am!' Kitty's face was filled with horror. 'I want to stay with you. If you want me to, of course.'

Emma gave her maid a warm hug. 'Thank you for being so loyal, Kitty dear. Well, it is only right that you should know of my plans. I thought we would stay here a week or so, then go on to Dover where we shall take the ferry to Paris. I should like so much to see France.'

'Oh, Ma'am!' Kitty's eyes were bright as she clapped her hands together in delight.

Yet Emma was secretly afraid that her plans might come to nought if Henry did not keep his side of the bargain. Before she'd left Mottisham Hall, Emma had persuaded him to send an allowance to her, care of banks in Paris and Montreux. In return he had insisted, tight-lipped, that their marriage should be declared null and void.

'Doctor Fielding will declare that our marriage was unconsummated,' he'd told her.

'But he has examined me!' Emma had gasped, blushing as she remembered how well she had demonstrated her sexual experience to the good doctor.

Sir Henry had given a wry smile. 'True, but he owes me a large favour for getting him out of some gambling debts that I always knew would come in handy some day.'

Emma had quickly agreed to his plan. Ludicrous as the deception was, she would be far away from Mottisham by the time the annulment was granted. Soon after that, she imagined, Henry would take the widowed Catherine to be his wife and start his wretched dynasty in earnest. Emma knew she would not feel completely free until the whole matter was behind her.

By the time she descended for dinner, Emma was in a carefree mood. Anne had invited several local people to join them in her cousin's honour. At first glance, the men and women were not a very prepossessing bunch, but then she spied a young man loitering gauchely on the edge of the company. His face was handsome, despite its diffident expression, with clear blue eyes, a long straight nose and a wide, sensual mouth. Emma also liked the look of his dark brown hair, which curled most attractively about his ears.

'Ah yes, that is Robert Earnshaw, our local curate,'

Anne smiled, drawing her cousin aside. 'He is interested in our Louisa, and we're hoping to be able to make an announcement soon.'

She took Emma over to him. 'Robert, may I present my dear cousin Emma?'

After his perfunctory bow, the curate eyed her nervously. The lad looked hardly more than twenty, and it was clear that he was unused to female company so he would be a totally inept lover. Poor Louisa! Surely that spirited young woman deserved better?

Emma decided that she must act quickly. If she were the first to pluck the sweet flower of his virginity, Louisa would be assured of a more satisfactory wedding night. She would be doing her young relative a favour and enjoying herself at the same time.

'Have you been at Arnford long?' she began, gazing into his eyes with mesmeric intensity.

'Er . . . no, Miss . . . er . . . Mrs . . .'

'Just call me Emma,' she smiled. 'And I hope I may call you Robert?'

'Oh, well . . . Emma . . . I have been at Arnford for approximately six months now.'

'Tell me, Robert, are there any pleasant walks hereabouts? I do so like exploring the countryside, don't you?'

'There is an agreeable walk by the river,' he volunteered. 'When it has not been raining, of course.'

'And has it been raining lately?'

Emma was enjoying the faint flush of embarrassment that was colouring the young man's cheeks. Her supposition had been correct – he was clearly unused to conversing with women, let alone having any other form of intercourse with them.

'Not of late, M . . . Emma. I think it would be quite dry. Providing it does not rain overnight, of course.'

'In that case, I wonder whether you would escort me tomorrow afternoon, Robert? If you have no other business to attend to, I should be most grateful.'

His blushes deepened, and Emma noticed with

35

satisfaction that he was afraid to look at her. 'If you wish Miss . . . ah . . . Emma. Shall I call for you here at three?'

'That will suit me very well,' she smiled, as the dinner gong sounded.

Next morning Emma bore her cousin's trivial conversation as best she could, but her mind was elsewhere. When Robert finally appeared, punctually at three, it was hard for her to hide her excitement. She was wearing a pretty blue cape and bonnet, and knew she looked her best, as Robert's admiring gaze proved.

'Will you be back for tea?' Anne enquired.

Robert coughed, turned crimson and shuffled his feet. 'Er . . . I should like to invite Emma to take tea at the vicarage,' he mumbled.

Soon the pair were walking along the river bank, admiring the wild flowers that were raising their timid heads to the spring sunshine.

'That bank of daffodils over there reminds me of William Wordsworth's lyric,' Emma said. 'Do you read poetry, Robert?'

He shook his head. 'To me, the finest poetry is to be found in the good book, Miss Emma. The psalms, for instance.'

Emma smiled. 'Or the "Song of Solomon", perhaps: "Let him kiss me with the kisses of his mouth, for thy love is better than wine".'

Robert cleared his throat and stared hard at the path. 'Yes, quite. The poem is an allegory of spiritual love, of course.'

'Is it?' Emma feigned surprise. 'I had always thought of it literally, as a beautiful tribute of a lover to his beloved.'

'Of course physical love may be beautiful,' Robert went on, pompously, 'provided it is pure and holy, sanctified by the sacrament of marriage.'

'Ah yes! My late husband and I greatly enjoyed celebrating that sacrament over and over again. I was fortunate that my husband was experienced in the ways of love, since he had made love to many women before he met me.'

Robert's eyes widened in astonishment. 'Are you saying your husband was . . . a degenerate libertine?'

Emma smiled. 'No, just an experienced lover. There is a difference. A libertine cares nothing for the pleasure of women, only for his own. My Henry always made sure that his partner was as satisfied as he.'

Robert looked decidedly uneasy. His pace quickened, suggesting he wanted to get back to civilisation as soon as possible. 'I think one should not talk of such things,' he muttered.

'What, of women being satisfied? It is not fashionable, I know, to admit that women also have desires. However, I can assure you it is true. And if a man does not recognise that fact and try to please his partner, you may be sure she will find another who does.'

'I think a woman may be pleased with a virtuous and chaste husband, Miss Emma.'

'Do you intend to marry, Robert?'

'Perhaps. When I can get a living.'

Emma could feel her pulses quickening, and decided to press home her advantage. She was aware that while the curate was extremely embarrassed by her talk he was also filled with curiosity. She took his arm as they came to the bridge over the river, pressing close to his side.

'Perhaps you should start "living" a little more yourself, Robert!'

He drew back from her, his cheeks scarlet. 'I took you for a modest woman, Miss Emma, but our conversation so far has been very immodest. Shall we change the subject?'

'If you wish,' she sighed. 'What shall we talk about – the weather?'

'I fear you mock me. Perhaps we had better cut short our walk and postpone your visit to the vicarage.'

Emma sighed. 'I see that you are afraid of life, like too many of your fellow clerics.'

'Afraid of life? How absurd!'

'You fear the vital urge, Robert, that wonderful wellspring of ecstasy that is the province not only of saints but of ordinary men and women, if only they would throw off the shackles of so-called civilisation. Church doctrine has labelled sex sinful to deprive us of that right to pleasure.'

'I repeat, love is not sinful within the frame of marriage.'

Emma realised that all this argument was futile. A more direct approach was needed to break their impasse. There was a small copse nearby, and she drew him into the shade of the trees on the pretext of gathering some early bluebells.

'They wilt in a day or so,' she sighed. 'But they are so delightful while they last. Like love.'

He was watching her, obviously excited by the sight of her bending low so that her rump was thrust into the air. She knew he wanted her, but he would never make the first move. She must be bold. Bringing the flowers to him she invited him to smell their delicate scent.

'They were created for us to enjoy,' she said, smiling, 'like our bodies.'

So saying, Emma stood on tiptoe and pressed her mouth to his. She perceived that conscience and curiosity fought in him for a few seconds, but then curiosity won. Roughly he pulled her close, thrusting his mouth onto hers with a low moan, and she pushed his lips apart to allow access to her questing tongue. She could feel his soft lips tremble, fluttering like the wings of a nervous butterfly, as she ran her tongue lightly between them, tasting the violet scent of a cachou he had been chewing earlier. He did not pull away but moaned, softly, so she reached down and felt his hardness through his trousers, making him moan all the more.

'Pray stop, temptress!' he gasped at last, pulling back.

'I would not be a temptation if you did not desire me,' she murmured.

'It is true, I do desire you, wretched woman! But tempt me no more, I beg of you!'

She pushed him away from her. 'Well, that is enough for now, Robert. Perhaps we should walk on?'

Smiling to herself, and filled with elation at giving the man his first kiss, Emma let him lead her back onto the path. She knew she had him well aroused, and this delay would work to her advantage.

'I do not know what came over me,' Robert declared, in a daze, as they resumed their progress.

'It is quite natural. I think you will be more compassionate towards your fellow men and women when you understand the true nature of their desires. After all, passion and compassion are close bedfellows, are they not?'

'So are sex and sin!' he retorted.

They walked in silence until the spire of the church and the slate roof of the vicarage were in sight. Once the maidservant had left the tea things and Emma had him alone in the drawing-room, she realised that she must again make a bold approach. Ignoring his small talk she began unbuttoning her blouse, watching his flushed, stunned face all the while. Soon the naked bulge of her cleavage was clearly visible and Robert's eyes fastened on it helplessly. She knew she could take complete command of him now. He was in thrall to his own desires, forced, for the first time in his restricted life, to acknowledge that he wanted a woman. She took his hand and placed it on the cleft, murmuring encouragement.

'Feel how soft my skin is, how warm and inviting. You may kiss me there if you like.'

Impelled by sudden hunger the curate plunged his face between her breasts and began to kiss them greedily.

Emma gave a soft laugh. 'That's right, they are made for your delight. And oh, how delightful it feels to me, to have your sweet lips upon them. This is your first lesson in pleasuring a woman, dear Robert. Mutual satisfaction, you see?'

Panting, Emma drew him down onto the chaise longue, where he knelt and grasped her bosom at once, kissing her there frantically and burying his long nose in her abundant flesh. Soon he was opening more buttons, exposing her loose-fitting camisole. Emma had purposely left off wearing her corset that day, so her heavy breasts swung free beneath the covering of white broderie anglaise and blue ribbons. His clumsy fingers fumbled with the drawstring until the flimsy garment was revealing almost all of her torso. Smiling, she pulled out the objects of his desire. Robert moaned at the sight of them as they spilled over the camisole, their pink nipples rearing provocatively at him.

'Oh, what beauties!' he sighed. 'I have never gazed upon a woman's nakedness before.'

'Then look your fill,' she said, smiling, but as his hands reached out for them she suddenly rose and went over to the table where the tea-tray was arranged.

'I am thirsty and this tea is going cold. Shall I be mother?'

He was on his knees still, looking up at her with an expression of adoration more appropriate to a religious painting than an erotic encounter. As Emma bent to pour the tea her breasts swung forward like a pair of ringing bells, and his eyes followed them, full of frustrated longing. She handed him a cup of tea and he took a few sips, then set it down in a daze.

After she had drunk her own tea, Emma reached out and opened one of the scones. It was filled with cream and jam. Smiling seductively at him she smeared a finger with the sweet mixture and wiped it on each of her turgid nipples, then returned to lie in a languid pose upon the chaise longue. Sticking her finger into her mouth she licked off all the residue, slowly and appreciatively.

'This is excellent strawberry jam and fresh cream, Robert. Why not taste it?'

Holding up one of her breasts invitingly, Emma used the other hand to pat the velvet seat beside her. Robert needed no further encouragement. He leapt up and was soon sucking wildly on her sweet teat, groaning and rubbing his thighs together. While he suckled at her nipple and stroked her distended breast, Emma took his other hand and placed it between her legs, squeezing against it rhythmically, and giving herself some intense stimulation where it mattered most.

Suddenly Robert let out a series of gasps which Emma knew could only mean he had climaxed. She cradled his head against her sticky bosom, not wishing to embarrass him further. At last, when he had calmed down, she gently removed his head and sat up.

'More tea, Robert?' she asked, casually, as if nothing had happened.

He made an inarticulate noise which she took to be assent. On her way over to the table she tied up her camisole and buttoned up her blouse so that she was soon the very picture of a respectable woman. Robert's first lesson had been a great success, but she knew when it was time to stop. The man had been overwhelmed by his first encounter with naked, tumescent female flesh and must only be introduced to further pleasures by stages.

As they drank their tea, Emma tried to make him feel better about what had happened.

'You have nothing to be ashamed of, dear Robert,' she said. 'What has occurred between us this afternoon is our secret and shall remain so.'

'But I have sinned in the sight of God!' he moaned, rolling his eyes heavenward.

'Then you must ask his forgiveness. But I truly believe you will be more understanding of the peccadilloes of others now that you have succumbed to temptation yourself'

Cousin Anne's carriage called for Emma at six, as arranged, and by then she was more than ready to leave. The thrill she had experienced at seducing the pious curate had worn off somewhat after his guilt-ridden maundering, but she knew that for all his self-recrimination seeds had been sown that would soon clamour to be harvested.

Emma called Kitty to her room directly she returned and asked the maid to run her a bath. As she did so Kitty enquired about her visit to the vicarage, and Emma had a sudden urge to tell her the truth. 'What do you think of young Master Robert?' she enquired.

'I think he is most handsome, but a little shy.'

Emma let Kitty undo her buttons and remove her blouse, relishing the light touch of the girl's fingers on her naked skin. Her breasts still smelt faintly of strawberries. She stepped out of her skirt then removed her petticoats until she stood stark naked. Kitty's eyes swept briefly over her mistress's body then looked away as she turned off the taps.

'You are right, my dear. He is certainly unused to talking with women.' Emma lowered herself into the lavender-scented water. 'But I fancy he may be a little more bold in future.'

'Why is that, Ma'am?'

Kitty reached over for the loofah, then began to apply it to her mistress's back while Emma soaped her own breasts.

'I have given him a little lesson in how to please a woman.' Emma looked into Kitty's innocent eyes and saw a flicker of interest there. She smiled. 'Perhaps he will not be so quick to condemn other men's desires, now I have acquainted him more thoroughly with his own.'

Faint alarm showed in the girl's eyes. 'What are you saying, Ma'am?'

Emma let her slippery hands move over her stomach and down to her thighs, enjoying the warm thrills produced by the combination of hot water, sensual massage and wicked confession.

'I am saying that I let him kiss me, Kitty. A true lover's kiss, such as he had never experienced before.'

'Oh, Miss Emma! I should not have believed it of a man so . . . upright.'

'He is a man like any other, and with normal instincts. Put him in the company of any attractive woman for half an hour or so and he will lust after her. Give him the opportunity, and he will act on it.'

'And you gave him that opportunity?' Kitty's eyes were alight with wonder, and she could not resist a giggle as she added, 'Shame on you, Ma'am!'

Emma laughed too. Kitty's amusement showed that she had distinct possibilities. The girl was proving to be a very promising confidante.

'It is true, believe me. It is the sweetest thing, my dear, to introduce an innocent man to the pleasures of the flesh. I hope you may enjoy a similar experience one day.'

Emma dismissed her maid with a smile, and set about pleasuring herself with a soapy finger. As she worked herself up into a fine lather, she began to plan what she would do at her next encounter with the naive curate.

On Sunday Emma insisted on going to church, much to Anne's chagrin.

'Oh Lord, the sermons are so dreary, especially when poor Mr Earnshaw is in the pulpit. That man is so nervous he stutters and stammers his way through what is always an indifferent sermon, making it ten times more tedious!'

'And is it his turn this Sunday?'

'Yes. Would you think me terribly impolite if I excused myself with a headache? You may go with Louisa, if you wish.'

So at ten o'clock Emma and Louisa were driven to church in Anne's carriage. They sat in the second row of pews, where Emma could get a good view of the pulpit. Robert had not expected to see her in church and when his eye lighted on her he gave a sudden start and blushed scarlet. She smiled pleasantly at him, enjoying his discomfort.

When the time came for him to mount the steps of

the pulpit Emma could tell that he was really anxious. He rubbed his sweaty palms on his cassock, and ran a finger around his dog collar in a vain attempt to loosen it. When he began to speak he studiously avoided her eye.

'My t . . . text t . . . today is taken from the gospel of St Matthew, verse 46: "For if you love them which love you, what reward have you?"' Robert cleared his throat and launched into his sermon, although his face was a bright pink. 'How easy it is for us to love . . . to love our f . . . friends and family . . .'

His theme was the familiar Christian doctrine of 'Love Thine Enemy' but he made heavy weather of it, and Emma preferred to think of love in the carnal sense. To love one's enemy was to wallow in one's own humiliation, as she had read some women liked to do. The time Henry had always spent in preparing her for the act of love had been almost as satisfying as the act itself. To be forcibly taken, to submit to love from a man one disliked, could surely not be pleasant.

Yet the idea had an odd fascination for her. Sometimes, in the dreamy state before sleep, she had imagined being ravished by some strong and handsome warrior and had become so aroused that she was obliged to pleasure herself before she could rest. Even now the thought of a man's hard tool being thrust straight into her, without preliminaries, was causing her private parts to throb and moisten, so that she wriggled a little against the hard wooden pew.

'So, my friends, n . . . next time you make an enemy of s . . . someone, consider your r . . . reward. Are you h . . . harvesting hatred, or love?'

As the sermon wound painfully to its conclusion, Emma grew excited at the prospect of carrying out her plan, and her thighs shifted restlessly on her seat until they had to kneel and pray.

When the last blessing had been uttered and the congregation began to file out, Emma turned to Louisa. 'Would you mind going back in the carriage by yourself, my dear? I wish to speak with Mr Earnshaw about a spiritual matter.'

At the mention of the curate, the young girl's eyes widened. 'But how shall you get home, Emma?'

'I shall walk. It is a fine spring day.'

Louisa was reluctant and Emma suspected she had been hoping for an encounter with the curate herself. But she was an obedient girl and went off in the carriage without demur. When the last few loiterers had left, Emma approached Robert at the church door.

'May I congratulate you on your sermon?' she began. 'It caused me to reflect on the nature of love, and there is something I would like to discuss with you in private. I thought we might retire to the vestry for a few moments.'

It was obvious that he was both fascinated and repelled by the idea of being alone with Emma once again. As he stood there gaping like a stranded fish, she added, 'My soul is troubled and I need guidance.'

So Robert had no option but to follow Emma down the aisle. She entered the musty-smelling vestry and looked about her. The vicar's robes were already hanging on their peg, and there were a few spare chairs and a *prie-Dieu*, facing a table on which a simple wooden cross was arranged. The place seemed perfectly suited to her purposes.

'What do you want of me?' Robert asked, once he had closed the heavy door behind him and drawn the baize curtain across.

There was a note of desperation in his voice so Emma tried to put him at ease. 'Just a few moments of your time. Shall we sit down?'

He drew out a couple of chairs. Emma sat facing him, aware that she was looking her Sunday best. His eyes skimmed her torso in the figure-hugging dress. 'You m . . . mentioned something in my sermon . . .?'

'Ah, yes, the question of love's reward. I was reminded that the chief reward of love, as we ordinary mortals know it, is pleasure. And yet the church seems to frown on the pleasures of love. Surely there is an inconsistency there?'

Robert frowned. 'As I mentioned before, love sanctified by marriage . . .'

'But how can you say that, when the average husband has no idea how to express his love by giving pleasure to his wife? And, likewise, the average wife has no idea how to pleasure her husband.'

'I know not what you mean.'

'I am concerned only for you, Robert, and for any future wife you might have. I am aware that you are interested in my cousin Louisa, and I would not wish her to remain ignorant of the joys of love for the rest of her life.'

'Whatever affection is between myself and Miss Louisa is pure and unsullied,' he said, haughtily.

'But she will want to serve you in any way she can. And if you do not know how a woman may serve a man, how can she oblige you?'

Emma knew she had him almost in the palm of her hand. He was backing away towards the *prie-Dieu*, looking flushed and confused. When he was standing with his behind against the little shelf designed to hold a prayer-book, she made her move.

'Allow me to show you some of the good service a wife may perform, Robert.'

Emma looked down at the plump hassock, smiling as she read the text embroidered upon it: '"The unbelieving husband is sanctified by the wife".' She knelt upon it and lifted up his black cassock. He seemed paralysed, unable to prevent her from opening up the buttons of his fly and pulling out his already stiffened member. It was long and slim, with a shiny pink bulb on the end. When Emma gripped it the shaft jerked in her hand and Robert gave a groan of mingled shame and desire.

'Such a fine member!' she murmured, taking its tip between her lips. She felt eager hands clutch at her bonnet as she worked her mouth slowly down the rigid shaft. Robert's breath was coming in loud pants, his hips writhing as she reached in and felt the loose sac that contained his seed. She continued to play gently with his scrotum while she licked and sucked, lightly tickling the hairy skin with her nails the way Henry had liked her to do.

'Witch! Demoness!' she heard him moan, as she accelerated her efforts and felt the balls tautening ready to shoot their load. At last the hot stream seared its way down her throat and she gulped appreciatively. It was so long since she had tasted sperm and Robert's was fresh and copious, the sweet sacrament of carnal love.

'God forgive me!' Robert gasped, turning to the small altar and flinging himself onto his knees.

'What for?' Emma asked, softly. 'For being a man, with a man's desires?'

'Get you behind me, creature of Satan!' he snarled.

Emma decided to leave him to his self-abasement. After wiping her lips with her lace handkerchief she stepped out of the vestry and, enjoying the spring sunshine, began to walk back to cousin Anne's house.

Next morning Emma found Louisa alone in the drawing room and decided to take the bull by the horns. She noticed that her young cousin seemed somewhat wan, almost lovesick, and guessed at the reason. She entered quickly, closing the door behind her.

'Louisa dear, what is the matter? A young woman like you should be full of the joys of spring!'

'Oh Emma, indeed I should be if only I were safely betrothed. In two weeks' time I shall be nineteen, and practically on the shelf!'

Emma laughed. 'Nonsense! I was twenty-one before I married. And at your age I had no one in mind.'

'But I *do* have someone in mind. The trouble is, I am not at all sure if he and I are of the same mind.'

'You speak of Robert Earnshaw, do you not?' Louisa smiled shyly. 'I am quite sure he looks upon you favourably, Louisa. I have mentioned your name in conversation several times and he has always showed, both by looks and words, that he regards you most highly.'

'Then why does he not come forward?'

'He is a reticent man, a little shy of women I feel. Besides, he probably thinks he should be made vicar of a parish before he proposes marriage.'

'There is no need. Papa will see that we are comfortably off until he has a good enough income. Oh, I am so tired of living here Emma! Anne is very good to me, but it is not like having a home of your own, is it?'

Emma looked thoughtful. 'I think we may be able to make him realise how strong your feelings are. Perhaps I could deliver some little *billet doux*? Nothing too forward, of course. I will help you write it.'

'Oh Emma, would you? You're such a dear!'

At once Louisa's face took on a lively aspect as she hunted out pen and paper. Emma racked her brains for a suitable approach, then began her dictation. 'Dear Robert . . .'

'Is that not too familiar, Emma?'

'Not at all. The intimacy is appropriate in the circumstances, I am sure. "Dear Robert, I hope you will not think me too forward for writing to you, but I should like to congratulate you on your sermon last Sunday. I found the section on the rewards of loving most apposite. I have often reflected that in my heart there is an abundance of love, but few people to share it. Perhaps you may advise me on how this might be remedied? Yours affectionately . . ."'

'Are you sure he will take this well?' Louisa asked, doubtfully.

'Quite sure, providing you will let me deliver it. Then, if there are any misunderstandings I can rectify them directly.'

Emma took the letter to the vicarage that afternoon. She found Robert alone, it being the servant's afternoon off, which suited her purposes perfectly. However, he did not invite her in straight away but looked decidedly mistrustful.

'I have come with a letter from Louisa,' she began.

Stiffly he held out his hand for it, but she shook her head. 'Will you not ask me in?'

The curate frowned. 'For a few moments only, then. It is not seemly for me to be entertaining you unchaperoned.'

Emma almost laughed aloud. It was rather late to be concerned about proprieties! He led the way into the hall and would have asked for the letter there, but Emma boldly went up to the drawing-room door and opened it. Only when they were both inside the room with the door shut would she produce the missive.

'Emma, give me the letter,' Robert said, crossly.

She eyed him saucily then undid some buttons and placed the folded paper in her cleavage. 'Come and get it, Robert dear!'

'Do not play games with me, I have not the patience.'

'Then come, take it, and be done with it.'

He tried to snatch it out of her bosom, but she caught his wrist and kissed it, making him stroke her bare breast. The curate groaned, allowing the letter to fall to the floor as he came under her spell once again. Crushing her lips with his, he proceeded to lift up her skirt until his fingers were feeling the warm flesh of her naked thigh, above her stocking tops.

'Vixen! I have had no sleep since last I saw you! You have me on fire and I know not how to extinguish the flames of my desire. They consume me, night and day!'

'Tut, tut Robert! You know very well how such fire may be dealt with. Put your hand higher up between my legs and you shall feel another conflagration raging. Shall we not fight fire with fire?'

His fingers were creeping beneath her beribboned petticoats, reaching the hairy lips of her quim, and his groans increased in volume. Emma put her hand down and felt his hard member struggling within its tight confines.

'One moment, Robert,' she whispered, moving away from him just long enough to remove her skirt and hooped petticoat, so that her body was more accessible to him.

Robert threw himself down onto his knees and buried his face in the soft cotton of her undergarments. Emma knew that the musky scent she was emitting would be inflaming his already overheated desire, and she wriggled her buttocks beneath his clasping hands so that her pubis was thrust into his face. Her fingers fumbled with the ribbons of her chemise and soon she had pulled out one ripe breast, fondling the nipple to a long, stiff peak.

'Come, Robert, let us lie down,' she urged him, throwing some cushions onto the Persian carpet and settling back with her body seductively displayed. It was too much for the curate. Furiously he struggled with his trousers until he had pulled them down and his tumid organ sprang to attention. Emma smiled, but slapped his wrist when he tried to fumble with her pussy.

'Not so fast, Robert! Pretend I am your blushing bride and this is our wedding night. You would not wish to cause a poor virgin pain when deflowering her, would you?'

He swallowed and shook his head then muttered, hoarsely, 'Tell me what I must do.'

'That's better. First you may kiss and stroke my breasts, which helps to get me wet down below.'

He obeyed with relish, and was soon rolling her nipple confidently between his finger and thumb while he planted soft kisses all round. Emma encouraged him with sighs and murmurs, then directed him to remove her under-petticoat gently. He gasped when he saw the tightly-curled hairs that hid her private place, and declared he had never seen anything so exquisite.

'M . . . may I see what lies within?' he faltered.

Chuckling softly, Emma opened her thighs wide and spread her labia apart with her fingers. Robert gave it an earnest perusal, his face flushed and his breathing heavy.

'You may touch it, if you like,' she encouraged him. 'But be gentle.'

Tentatively the curate stretched out a hand and probed her folds with his forefinger. Emma felt her wetness increase as he found her hole and penetrated to the depth of half an inch or so. He pulled his finger out and licked it, wonderingly.

'If you like the taste you may suck at my parts directly,' she told him.

Robert knelt down on all fours and put his lips to her privates. At first he was cautious, licking her very gently, but he soon acquired a taste for it and began gobbling away at her, so hard that the sensitive tip of her clitoris began to be sore.

'Wait! Let me show you something.' Emma sat up and pointed to the tiny erect bud at the top of her labia. 'This small knob is the source of a woman's greatest pleasure, but it must be treated with care. Do not rub it directly, but just above. Then it will cause a woman to become very wet and aroused. Try it with your tongue or finger, and see what happens. I shall tell you if you are too rough.'

Robert proved a quick learner and soon had Emma dancing on the edge of orgasm. But she didn't want to come yet. Taking his slender tool in one hand she softly squeezed his balls with the other until she felt them tighten.

'Now, Robert, this is the moment of penetration. It requires great self-control if you are not to tear the woman's delicate membrane and cause her pain. Place the tip of your member at the entrance to my cunny, and let my juices bathe you awhile.'

He did as he was told, but was clearly impatient to thrust into the warm, wet chasm. Emma caressed his glans with her inner lips then bade him slowly enter, an inch at a time. He did his best to hold back, but when he was about halfway in he was overcome by fierce lust and pierced her mercilessly, up to the hilt. Emma gave a cry of joy and clasped him with her internal walls. It seemed an age since she'd had a man probing deep inside her and, even though Robert's organ did not fill her as well as Henry's shorter, thicker one, she revelled in the intimate mingling of his flesh with hers.

Fearing that he might eject his sperm too soon, Emma held him immobile for a while then began to move her vagina slowly up and down his shaft, urging him to do likewise. They soon had a gentle rhythm going, despite Robert's urge to plunder her treasures with wild abandon, for as soon as he tried to speed up she whispered notes of caution in his ear. 'Make it last, Robert dear. Easy does it! That's the way.'

But eventually not even her mild admonitions had any effect. The curate's fire began raging and he pinned down her arms, put his mouth greedily to her nipple and thrust away like fury until all the hot seed had been spilt from his taut, aching balls. Feeling the delicious fountain springing up inside her, Emma also climaxed with a long satisfying series of pulsations that left her spent and breathless.

'Dear God, if I am to be damned, let me be damned for such a sin as this!' he sighed, resting his head on her breast.

They lay for a while then Emma gently removed his head and sat up.

'I must be getting back, or they will be wondering what has become of me. Read the letter from Louisa, Robert, and tell me if there is to be a reply.'

'Louisa?' Robert said, vaguely, as if there could be no other woman in the world for him right then.

'Yes. The poor girl is in love with you, did you not know it? She longs to know your mind.'

Dazed, Robert picked up the discarded letter and read it. He stared at Emma in disbelief. 'She wishes to lavish her affection on me?'

Emma smiled, buttoning up her blouse. 'Yes, and I am sure she could find no worthier object of her devotion.'

'Yet I am not in a position to make an honest woman of her. Please advise me, Emma. You have opened my eyes to a whole new world, one which I long to explore more thoroughly, but I cannot make Louisa my wife. Not until I am well established in my profession.'

'Nonsense! If you are sincere in wanting to wed her I am sure her father will help you financially. He may even be able to secure a living for you, since he is a man of influence. Now, dress yourself and come over to the davenport. I shall tell you what to write to poor Louisa that will set her mind at rest.'

It pleased Emma to dictate the reply that would seal her young cousin's fate. Now that her own desires had been satisfied, and she was sure that Robert would be a considerate husband, she was content to move on to pastures new.

Chapter Four

*E*mma felt disinclined to tell Kitty any more about her seduction of the curate. Perhaps she wished to protect the reputation of her cousin Louisa, who had received Robert's proposal with rapturous assent. The happy couple had been blessed by Emma's Uncle Joseph who, as Emma had predicted, promptly obtained the promise of a post for his future son-in-law at a fashionable London church.

Since the affair had ended so well, Emma felt no misgivings about the way she had behaved. Neither did she feel obliged to stay any longer. Although Anne begged her to come to her sister's wedding, she had declined.

'I plan to visit our distant cousin Mathilda,' Emma explained. 'You know she has an academy for young ladies in Montreux. First, though, I would like to see something of France and Italy.'

'Then I wish you well, dear,' sighed Anne, who now knew about the annulment of her cousin's marriage. 'I suppose life is one great adventure for you again, as it was when we were girls.'

Emma smiled, knowingly. How much of an adventure it would prove to be was anyone's guess, but she was sure of one thing. Whenever she had the opportunity to initiate some young innocent into the joys of love she would be sure to do so.

Anne generously offered the use of her carriage as far as Dover. After a night at the Whitecliff Hotel, the two women waited on the quayside next morning for their ferry to arrive. Emma sat daydreaming about Paris. Henry had often described it to her, and now she would be able to see for herself the famous sights such as the Arc de Triomphe and the Eiffel Tower.

A tapestry began to form in Emma's mind, comprising all the things she had heard about the French capital. There were the bold new trends in art and design, called 'Impressionism' and 'Art Nouveau', the excitement of that naughty dance the 'cancan', and that enchanting actress Sarah Bernhardt, 'the Divine Sarah', whose fame was spreading throughout the whole world.

It was a city of music too: Bizet's wonderful 'Carmen' performed at the Paris opera; the extraordinarily subtle strains of Ravel and Debussy which seemed to affect all the senses at once, and supper clubs where people danced to the sensual sound of the brass instrument invented by Adolphe Sax.

Besides being the centre of artistic life Paris was, of course, the foremost city of fashion. Not only home to the great fashion houses but also to exquisite jewellers like Tiffany and Lalique, and even new inventions like the horseless carriage and amazing pictures that moved. Everything that was new and exciting in the world could be found in Paris, in the last decade of the nineteenth century.

But above all, Paris was the city of love. All kinds of lovers had found their fulfilment there, from those who inhabited the 'demi-monde' like the poets Verlaine and Rimbaud, to the artists who frequented the bars and theatres, like that strange little man Toulouse-Lautrec, and the ghost of Chopin haunting the boulevards where he had once strolled with his androgynous lover, Georges Sand . . .

55

Suddenly Emma caught the eye of a matronly woman in black who was sitting nearby on the quay with a young man who looked like her son. He was flushed and eager, his dark brown eyes shining with youthful enthusiasm. Emma smiled sweetly as his mother came over and made their introductions. 'Good morning to you, Madam. I am Caroline Purchase, and this is my son Charles. We have travelled from Oxford, where Charles has been studying. He is to go to the Sorbonne University in Paris!'

Emma smiled at the note of pride in Caroline's voice. After introducing herself, she replied that she would be staying in Paris for a week or so, and was relieved when Caroline did not quiz her but went on to talk about herself and her studious son.

'He is studying the French language and literature,' she said, smiling fondly at Charles. 'Talk to Mrs Longmore in French a little, dear. Show her how clever you are.'

Charles squirmed with embarrassment but nevertheless murmured, in an atrocious accent, *'Voulez-vous parler français avec moi, Madame?'*

'Oui, bien sûr, Monsieur,' she replied, much to their amazement.

'Oh, you speak French too,' Caroline gasped, obviously disappointed.

'A little,' Emma smiled. 'Perhaps Charles would like to have some more conversation *en route pour la France?'*

'Of course he would. Charles takes advantage of any opportunity he has to speak in French, don't you dear?'

'Yes, mother. I should like to talk with Mrs Longmore very much.'

It was already obvious that, clever as he was, Charles was well under his mother's thumb. Emma was surprised to learn that Mrs Purchase did not intend to travel to Paris with him, but would see him off on the ferry boat. She evidently saw Emma as a potential chaperone for her 'dear boy' and, despite the fact that she felt rather used, Emma was pleased to accept the duty. For Charles, despite his diffident manner, was a likeable and well-built young man with a pleasant demeanour, and Emma was looking forward to getting to know him better.

When embarkation began, Caroline Purchase made her emotional farewell. Once his mother was out of the way, however, Charles was a different man. He ordered a brandy in the ship's bar and a coffee for Emma, and began chatting eagerly in English.

'Sorry about Mater, but she does rather idolise me,' he began, with a grin. 'Due to Papa being in his grave, I suppose. She doted on him, too.'

'I thought we were going to talk in French, Charles.'

The cheekiness of his grin increased. 'Poppycock! I shall get oodles of practice in France, shan't I? And I don't suppose your French is up to mine, anyway.'

'No, I suppose not,' Emma answered, with a rueful smile. 'So, what shall we talk about?'

'You,' he said earnestly, fixing her with his soulful dark eyes.

She laughed. 'There is little to tell. My husband died two years ago and I have no children. End of story. Now tell me about you. How long have you been at Oxford?'

'Two years. I shall have a year at the Sorbonne then return to Oxford. Eventually I hope to go into the diplomatic service, if I am good enough.'

'Do you mean good enough at French, or well enough behaved?' she asked, cheekily.

'Oh, I am always well behaved. Mama sees to that!'

He had spoken with a wry self-deprecation that intrigued Emma. 'But surely you have the chance to get up to some healthy mischief sometimes?'

'Not while she makes me live with her in Oxford, spying on me all the time and interrogating me every time I go out.'

'You mean, you do not live in college like the other undergraduates?'

Charles shook his head. 'No, she would not let me.

And she has to approve all my friends. I must return home by nine o'clock each evening if I go out.' He sighed, gloomily, swilling his brandy round in the glass before downing it in one gulp. 'Imagine what a torment it is for a chap to hear all one's friends recounting their exploits while one has been stuck at home!'

Emma smiled to herself, realising that Charles must still be a virgin and quite ignorant of women apart from his dragon of a mother. She declined another drink but he called for more brandy and she realised that, free from Caroline's company, he was inclined to live recklessly. Well, she would help him along the way a little!

'How old are you, Charles?' she asked him.

'Twenty-one, three weeks ago.'

'Then you are an adult, and deserve to be treated as one. At least you will have your freedom while you are in Paris.'

'Yes,' he grinned. 'And I intend to make the most of it, I can tell you.'

It was a mercifully calm crossing. Emma and Charles spent some time in the lounge, drinking tea and chatting, while Kitty remained on deck. The girl seemed to know when to keep out of the way, and Emma was glad of her discretion. Although they talked of nothing in particular, Emma made sure that she revealed a shapely ankle when she shifted her legs, and the top of her generous cleavage when she leaned forward so that Charles had plenty of opportunity to survey her body. She knew from his flushed face, sparkling eyes and animated conversation that he was looking forward to making the most of his new-found freedom, and she was already whetting his appetite.

They completed their journey from Calais to Paris by steam locomotive. Emma had only been on a train once before, when Henry had taken her to London, and she found it exciting to be hauled through the dull countryside of Northern France by such a powerful beast. Charles was excited too, putting his head out of the window despite the warning notices, and ending up with smuts on his face. Emma found his exclamations of delight charming, and knew that he would bring the same youthful enthusiasm to everything he did.

'Come, Charles, let me clean your cheek,' Emma smiled, taking out her handkerchief. Much as she enjoyed playing mother to him, she knew she would enjoy playing another rôle even more.

'We are nearly there!' he exclaimed at last. 'I believe I can see Gustave Eiffel's wonderful tower!'

Emma came to the window, putting her arm around his shoulder and pressing herself against him as she craned to see. When they sat down again, however, she knew there was no time to lose. 'Tell me, Charles, where are you lodging in Paris?'

'In the Latin Quarter, near the University. I shall be sharing rooms with other students.'

'And I shall be staying at the Hotel Beaufort, in the Boulevard Hàusmann not far from the Gare St Lazare. May I invite you to dine with me there, this evening?'

Charles's eyes lit up. 'Thank you, Mrs Longmore! I was wondering what I should do. By the time we arrive I dare say I shall be very hungry.'

Yes, and not just for food, Emma thought wryly.

On arrival in Paris they went straight to the Hotel Beaufort. Since it was nearby they did not see many sights, although Emma was intrigued by the elegance of the wide streets and the height of the apartment buildings. At first she was rather disconcerted by the pace of the traffic, but she noticed that fashionably dressed men and women were strolling alongside the mêlée of hurtling cabs with an air of total insouciance, so she resolved to do likewise.

Emma had already booked a suite for herself and her maid by post. When he was sure they were settled, Charles went off to take his luggage to the lodgings that had been arranged for him, promising to return at nine for dinner. Emma prepared herself well. After a short rest she bathed and dressed in her most alluring gown, a turquoise green taffeta with Chantilly lace at the cuff and around the low neck. With her blonde hair arranged in a loose bun punctuated with pearl-tipped pins she knew that she was looking her formidable best. The scent of lily of the valley completed her armoury, and then she was ready to do battle with whatever remained of Charles's will to resist.

He was waiting for her in the lobby when she descended the main staircase and his brown eyes shone with admiration as he offered her his arm.

'You look very beautiful tonight, Mrs Longmore,' he whispered. 'I am proud to escort you.'

'Bravo! You know how to compliment a lady. We shall make a gentleman of you yet!'

During the five-course meal, Charles could not take his eyes off her. He was obviously besotted, and Emma was getting more and more excited at the thought of the sport to come.

'Perhaps you would let me escort you round the sights tomorrow,' he offered, as their meal neared its end.

'That would be very nice,' she smiled. 'Do you happen to have a plan of Paris?'

'Yes, I have.' He produced a map from his pocket and proceeded to unfold it.

'No, not here Charles. I need to return to my own room, so perhaps you could bring it there? We could spread it out on the bed and have a good look at it.'

'I'm not sure if Mama would approve of that.'

Emma saw a faint flush creep up from his collar and knew she must be firm with him.

'Charles, your mother is many miles away and has put you more or less in my charge. I am staying in room fifteen. I shall expect you in five minutes.'

Once she left the restaurant, Emma made her way excitedly to her room and called Kitty to help her out of her clothes. 'I shall put on my negligée,' she told her maid. 'That young man will be coming here soon, with a map of Paris to show me.'

'Oh Ma'am!' Kitty giggled, her dark curls bobbing

beneath their cap and her blue eyes gleaming with mischievous glee. 'And shall you treat him the same way you did that curate fellow?'

'Who knows? He is very handsome and amenable, although still tied to his mother's apron strings. But if I cannot untie those strings, nobody can.'

Soon Emma was arrayed in her pretty dressing-gown of sprigged cotton, its lace trim barely covering the upper moulding of her breasts. She lay on the bed and awaited his knock, her body beginning to anticipate the pleasure which she hoped to be enjoying soon. The taut thrust of her nipples beneath the soft material, the warm relaxation of her thighs and the secret moistening of her parts all testified to her arousal. When at last his knuckles rapped tentatively on her door she called to him quietly, 'Come in, Charles!' and he entered, map in hand.

'Oh, Mrs Longmore . . .' he began, poised in the doorway and about to retreat. 'I am sorry. I did not know you had retired . . .'

'Not at all, I was expecting you of course. Don't be shy, Charles. Shut the door behind you and come here. Oh, and do call me Emma in private, please.'

As he walked towards the bed she could see the promising bulge in his trousers. He handed her the map and she spread it out over the counterpane, tucking her legs under her as she perched against the pillows.

'Sit here beside me on the bed, Charles, then you can help me find all the interesting places.'

He was nervous, very nervous, but he did as she asked. Emma made sure her hand brushed against his as she pointed out various monuments, and she watched with amusement the way he kept trying to sidle away from her and move the map over his lap to disguise his increasingly obvious arousal.

At last she folded it up and lay back with a smile. 'Now Charles, tell me some more about yourself. Where did you go to school?'

'Harrow. My name was put down for the school when I was born. Papa went there also.'

'And you were a boarder, I take it?' He nodded. 'Were you much tormented by the other boys? Did you become someone's "fag"? Do tell me. I am fascinated by the strange things men get up to when there are no women present.'

Charles blushed, looking decidedly uncomfortable. 'Oh, only the usual sorts of things,' he replied, vaguely.

Emma recalled a book she had once read which described in graphic detail exactly what sorts of things those were. 'Please be more specific, my dear. You need not be afraid of shocking me. Did you perhaps get a beating from an older boy?'

'Well, yes.'

'Tell me about it.'

'It was when I was in the second year. There was a boy in the Remove, called Ferguson. He said I was staring at him insolently and should come to his study at teatime. When I got there he said he must punish me, but if I bore my punishment like a man I should get my reward.'

'Really? How then did he contrive to both reward and punish you?'

'First he told me to take down my trousers. I was too scared to refuse, because he was much bigger than me. Then he made me bend over a chair and take six lashes with a cane on my bare behind. It stung me dreadfully and when I looked later there were nasty red marks.'

'But did you find the experience in any way rewarding?'

Charles turned his puzzled brown eyes towards Emma, taking care not to let his gaze drop onto her half-exposed bosom. 'Not exactly. I mean, it hurt like the devil. But afterwards there was this rather nice glow. I didn't mind that at all.'

'But what of your reward?'

Charles looked away, bashfully. 'I think perhaps I should not speak of that.'

'Why not? I have told you that I shall not be shocked or upset by anything you say. Did he play with your naked parts, is that it?'

'Not he with mine, no.'

'Then you with his, perhaps?' Charles nodded. 'Ah, I see. The act of caning you had no doubt aroused this Ferguson fellow's manhood, and he wanted the urge satisfied. Is that how it was?'

'I believe so. He told me that he had a very fine organ and that many boys would give a whole week's tuck money to be allowed to play upon it.'

Emma did her best to hide her smile, since Charles looked so embarrassed. She squeezed her thighs together under the bedclothes, enjoying the sudden surge of desire that coursed through her lower regions at the thought of that 'fine organ'.

'And did he show it to you?'

'Yes. It was very long and thick, with a red tip. It made me feel very . . . inadequate. He made me kneel down in front of him and take it . . . Oh, I cannot speak of it.'

'Do not be afraid, Charles.' Emma spoke softly, taking his hand and squeezing it. 'There is little you can tell me that I do not already know, and I am sure nothing you need be ashamed of. Did he ask you to take his member in your mouth?'

He nodded. 'Yes. But this is very strange. I should die rather than speak to my mother of these things, and yet with you it is quite different.'

'That is because I know the ways of the world, Charles. But pray continue. After you took his member in your mouth, what happened?'

'He told me to lick and suck at it. I found it distasteful at first, and when he shot his load down my throat I gagged. But I soon got used to it.'

'You mean, there were other occasions?'

'Yes, many. Sometimes Ferguson would get me to do it for other fellows while he beat them on the buttocks.'

'He sounds an odd sort of fellow.'

Charles hesitated, shifting his thighs uneasily, then continued. 'I believe he was one of those who prefer men to women in later life. We encountered each other again at Oxford and he was mixing with . . . those sorts of chaps.'

'I see. And do you count yourself amongst them, Charles?'

'Oh no!'

His reply was so vehement that Emma laughed aloud. 'So you prefer women to men, do you? How do you know?'

'Because I have feelings towards women that I do not have towards men.'

'Can you describe these feelings?'

Charles looked bashful. 'I would rather not.'

'Oh Charles, have we not already established that you need hide nothing from me?'

'Perhaps, but you must be tired after your long journey, so I shall say goodnight.'

He rose from the bedside and Emma stared up at him for a few seconds, wondering what to say. She could see the conflicting desires mirrored strongly in his young eyes, knew that he longed to continue their conversation and hoped that it would lead on to something more exciting. It would certainly not be difficult to lead him down that path, and her own body yearned hungrily for it. But perhaps it would be best not to go too fast.

'Very well,' she sighed. 'But will you not give me a goodnight kiss, just as if I were your Mama?'

He came back towards her diffidently. Emma sat up higher, letting her negligée fall open at the front to half reveal her prominent breasts. She held out her arms to him and he fell into them with a soft groan, their mouths instantly meeting. Emma revelled in the fresh sweetness of his lips, which parted tentatively to allow her tongue access. She savoured the kiss for a few seconds only then withdrew, leaving Charles open-mouthed and stunned.

'Goodnight, dear boy. Tomorrow we shall explore Paris together,' she smiled, snuggling down beneath the bedclothes. 'Come here to the hotel at ten.'

He turned like a somnambulist, and left the room. Emma extinguished the bedside oil lamp with a smile, settling for sweet dreams of seduction.

Next morning Emma and Kitty arrived in the foyer after their late breakfast to find Charles already waiting for them.

'Good morning, ladies!' he smiled, cheerily, giving a slight bow. Emma thought how fine he looked and, for a moment, imagined what it would have been like to have a son of her own. Maternal feelings seemed inappropriate for what she had in mind, however, so she took Charles's arm and began to walk towards the exit chatting excitedly about where they should go first.

Just as she approached the swing doors, Emma noticed a man staring at her. He was tall and dark-haired, with a neat moustache and penetrating black eyes that were looking straight at her. She had seldom been looked at so boldly by a complete stranger, and something mesmeric about the quality of his gaze set her pulses racing. She could feel a flush rising in her cheeks, and hurried through the doors before Charles, breathing a sigh of relief when she found herself out in the busy Parisian boulevard.

Before the small party had quite disappeared, Daniel Forbes approached the clerk at the hotel desk with a conspiratorial air and nodded in Emma's direction.

'*Bonjour, Monsieur,*' he began. '*Cette femme, qui est-elle?*'

The clerk shrugged and shook his head. A note discreetly changed hands. The hotel register was produced and opened casually at the right page, with the clerk's finger pointing to a name. Daniel muttered, '*Merci,*' and followed cautiously through the doors muttering under his breath, 'Now I wonder, delightful Emma Longmore, who can your young companion be?'

65

Outside, Daniel was just in time to see the party getting into a cab. He took the one behind and prepared to play the sleuth, a role which he had often taken in his time. The two carriages set off down the Boulevard Hausmann, eventually turning right at the Rue de Richelieu with the great palace of the Louvre rising majestically at the far end.

Chapter Five

*E*mma approached the great palace of the Louvre
with awe. She had never been inside such a splendid building before but the treasures within were, if
anything, even more magnificent to her eyes. For a long
time she stood before Leonardo's portrait of *La Joconde*,
otherwise known as the 'Mona Lisa', and at last she
said to her young companion, 'I have heard that there
are many forgeries of this famous painting, Charles. Do
you suppose this one to be genuine?'

Before he could answer she heard a woman's voice
behind her say, in English, 'Do not let any of the
curators hear you say that, Madame!'

Emma turned in amazement to see a woman standing
there with a smile on her lips. She was fashionably
dressed, if in rather too bright a shade of magenta for
Emma's taste, with her blonde hair in an elegant bun.
Inclining her head politely, she held out her hand.

'Allow me to introduce myself My name is Lily
Merchant. As an English expatriate in Paris I like to
avail myself of every opportunity to converse in my
native tongue. I hope you do not mind.'

'Not at all,' Emma smiled, taking her gloved hand. 'I
am here with my maid, Kitty, and . . .' she blushed a
little, realising she did not know quite how to introduce

Charles with propriety. However, he stepped into the breach like a proper gentleman.

'Charles Purchase, at your service Ma'am! Just arrived in this wonderful city to pursue my studies at the Sorbonne.'

Lily's pretty face broke into a smile. 'Oh, how delightful – a "Merchant" meets a "Purchase"! Perhaps we should do some kind of business together.'

Charles blushed and hastily withdrew his hand from hers. Emma was amused by the rapport between the pair, but she felt a twinge of jealousy too. Charles had been earmarked for her own pleasure. Perhaps she had better move faster if she were to be the first to taste the sweet fruit of his virginity.

'Have you seen the special exhibition of religious paintings in the next room?' Lily asked.

Emma thought 'How dull!' but she followed the pair dutifully, unwilling to let them out of her sight.

When they entered the room two adjacent paintings caught her eye at once. They both showed a pale-bodied woman with an outstretched arm, adorned by fantastic jewellery and diaphanous drapery. In one of the pictures she was pointing to a disembodied head that floated in the air in front of her, surrounded by a halo of light.

Seeing her interest, Lily explained, 'Those paintings are both by Gustave Moreau. They are of Salomé.'

'Extraordinary! How white her skin looks against the dark background, and how exotic her attire. It makes me feel quite strange to look at it.'

Lily smiled, knowingly. 'The subject is one beloved by today's artists. I believe they are attracted by the mixture of innocence and decadence that she represents. In my opinion her character was supremely portrayed by that tragic Irishman, Mr Wilde.' Lily gave a sigh. 'His play about Salomé is sublime, whether rendered in French or English. When I heard how that dear man had been persecuted by my own countrymen I wept bitter tears of shame!'

Emma looked at her new acquaintance with renewed interest. Not only was this obviously a woman of culture, but she seemed to share Emma's liberal views. The average Englishwoman had been shocked to hear of Oscar Wilde's love affair with an aristocratic young man, and his recent trial had been the scandal of the century. But Emma, who had read in Henry's books about the pederasts of Ancient Greece and Arabia, recognised that such love had been elevated to spiritual heights by other cultures.

'Tell me, is the poor man's fate yet known?' Lily asked, anxiously.

Emma sighed. 'Alas, yes. Just before I left England he was sentenced to two years of hard labour, for the crime of loving one of his fellow men.'

The two women regarded each other openly, and Emma thought she detected a glow of sympathy in Lily's brown eyes. Could it perhaps be that they were kindred spirits, each despising the hypocrisy and narrow-mindedness of their compatriots?

Charles and Kitty had moved to the other end of the room, and now Lily looked pointedly in their direction with a twinkle in her eye. 'I take it that young Charles is no relative of yours. How did you meet?'

'On the boat, coming over from England. I believe his mother wanted me to take him under my wing until he was settled in Paris.'

Lily gave a quiet chuckle with an undertone of mischievous glee. 'And you were most happy to oblige, I dare say. He is a very handsome young man. I envy you.'

This frank talk took Emma quite by surprise. She was intrigued, too. 'Did you say you are resident in Paris, Miss Merchant? Or is it Mrs Merchant?'

'No, I'm quite free of marital bonds! And yes, I am resident here. Perhaps you would like to visit me at my apartment? I should be very pleased to take tea with you and further our acquaintance. Here is my calling card.'

Emma found that her own hotel was within a few minutes' walk of the address printed in an elegant copperplate hand.

'Do come tomorrow afternoon, if you have no other plans!' Lily insisted.

Once it was arranged, Emma's new friend told her she had an appointment and wished her a pleasant day. While she watched Lily's elegant figure depart Emma suddenly glimpsed a man who ducked back behind the wall of the next room as soon as he caught her eye, ostensibly to examine a painting more closely. Fleeting as the glimpse had been, Emma recognised him as the man who had stared at her so boldly in the hotel foyer that morning, and a tremor of strange excitement filled her veins. She recognised it as similar to the *frisson* she'd felt on looking at the paintings of Salomé, hinting of dark pleasures and forbidden fruits. By the time she walked into the next room with Charles and Kitty, however, the man had gone.

The morning passed quickly as the party visited the cathedral of Notre Dame then explored the area near the Opéra and the wonderful department store of *Le Printemps*. Only the French could call a fashionable store after the most romantic of the seasons Emma reflected, as she and Kitty enthused over the magnificent garments on sale there. After purchasing a delightful pair of kid gloves and a silk scarf, Emma privately vowed to return soon without Charles so that she might try on some of the wickedly seductive corsetry.

They lunched in the Grand Café on the Boulevard des Capucines, where they discovered that the Lumière brothers were demonstrating their wonderful invention, the *Cinématographe*. The waiter seemed most excited as he told them in his broken English, 'It is the moving pictures, Madame. The brothers they show their . . . how you say . . . place of work, at returning home time. All the *ouvriers* . . . the workers, coming from the building, just as real life. It is a miracle!'

'The science of photography is wonderful indeed,' Charles agreed. 'But I cannot see how it will benefit mankind. Whether a picture moves or does not move, it is still only a picture.'

'Come, Charles, have you no imagination?' Emma teased him. 'Think how wonderful it would be to capture youth and beauty forever. Once you would have had to rely on the skill of a portrait painter, but now we may have a true scientific representation of a person's youthful appearance that lasts forever, for they say the camera never lies.'

'I think neither brush nor lens could ever capture your beauty, Mrs Longmore,' Charles said gallantly, although he muttered the words and blushed as he uttered them.

Emma knew she was making satisfactory progress with her young protégé but she was eager to have him to herself. After lunch, the three of them took a cab back to the hotel where Emma said, pointedly, 'Kitty will want to rest now I am sure, but I feel like a walk in the fresh air. Would you be kind enough to escort me, Charles?'

'I should be delighted,' he grinned, as Kitty tactfully retired to her room.

They went to the Bois de Boulogne, where many people were enjoying the early summer sunshine. Couples were strolling amongst the trees and lakes, nursemaids were amusing their charges and occasional riders passed by on horseback. Emma soon led Charles away from the main roads and pathways into a thickly wooded area where they could be alone.

He didn't need much encouragement. No sooner had they entered a secluded grove than Charles seized her hand and, with flushed face and feverish gaze, revealed his feelings in halting phrases. 'Oh, Mrs Longmore . . . Emma! This is the most wonderful time of my life! Being with you in this lovely city is . . . is bringing me more happiness than I ever dreamed of! If only you knew what emotions were in my heart, what desire . . . but forgive me, I should not speak of them.'

'Why not, dear Charles, since they most probably echo my own.'

He stared at her, unable to believe his ears. 'Oh no, that cannot be . . .'

Emma took his hand to her lips and kissed it. 'Dear boy, you clearly have no idea how happy I am to be in your company. I know I am older than you but not, I think, quite old enough to be your mother!'

'Oh, no! Perish the thought!'

Emma smiled to see his discomfort, pressing home her advantage. 'Yet I am older in experience, in the ways of the world. I know only too well what sweet torments a young man such as yourself may undergo when what he longs for is denied him. And there are many young women who, whether from fear or cruelty, will let those torments rage unassuaged in the breast of their suitors. But I am not one of those women.'

She paused, to let the full effect of her words sink in. Charles gazed at her with wondering eyes, scarcely daring to credit what she had just hinted at. 'You mean, you would not have me suffer?' he said, at last. 'But how can you help me? I would not presume to . . .'

'I know,' she smiled. 'But where permission is given, there can be no presumption, no trespass. Come, my dear boy, since no one can see us in this sylvan grove, I think we might allow our mutual feelings a little expression, don't you think?'

So saying she drew him close and placed a delicate kiss on his shapely mouth. Charles groaned and opened his lips at once, pushing his tongue out to meet hers, and his hands fastened hungrily on the padded curves of her bustle. Emma put her hand down between their bodies and felt the strength of his erection through his trousers.

Leaning back from him, she gave a little chuckle. 'Oh, my poor boy! You do want me so terribly, don't you Charles?'

'Yes!' he whispered hoarsely. 'And if I cannot have you I fear for my health, nay for my sanity!'

'In that case we had better do something about it, and soon! I am sure your dear Mama would not wish you to fall ill during your first week in Paris. Shall we return to my hotel and see what we may do for a cure?'

She took his arm and led him out of the wood, burning with secret excitement. They hailed a cab which drove them briskly back past the Arc de Triomphe to the hotel. Although they scarcely spoke during the journey, Emma had hold of Charles's hand under cover of the voluminous folds of her skirt, giving him frequent squeezes of encouragement.

After informing the hotel porter that she was giving her nephew a French lesson in her room, Emma went up the red carpeted stairs with Charles following behind. She could tell he was stifling laughter and she wasn't far off giggling herself. Once they were alone in her sumptuous bedroom, Emma found the small bottle of brandy that she kept by the bed in case of insomnia and offered him a tot in a tooth glass.

'You would do well to drink it,' she smiled. 'It will give you courage, *mon brave*. A man's first time is always somewhat nerve-racking, although I promise you I shall make it as easy and pleasant as I can.'

He swigged the liquor down in one gulp then watched Emma remove her hat and gloves. His face was flushed and his hair dishevelled, making him look far younger than his 21 years.

Emma smiled and held out her hand. 'Dear Charles, let us proceed at a seemly pace. You may sit here on this chair, while I slowly divest myself of my garments. For I believe you have never looked upon a woman's naked form before, am I right?'

He gulped, shaking his head, and she kissed his cheek tenderly. Then, as he sat on the small gilt chair, she lifted her leg onto his lap saying, 'Unbutton my boots for me, there's a good fellow. My feet ache so after all that walking.'

73

He set to work gladly, and soon Emma's delicate little feet were revealed in their silk stockings. She unhooked her skirt and removed it so that she stood in her voluminous petticoats and tight-fitting blouse.

'Now unfasten these buttons, will you dearest?' she asked, coquettishly. Willingly he undid the small pearl buttons down the front of her silk blouse, his fingers trembling as they brushed against the swell of her bosom. Her corset was pushing her breasts up beneath the camisole so that a deep ravine was between them and, before she could stop him, Charles was kissing her cleavage with full-blooded enthusiasm. Emma groaned a little and loosened her stays so that he might get at her flesh more easily, and soon he had pulled down the lace frills and ribbons that hid her beauties from his sight. Emma unhooked a few more stays and then he managed to lever her breasts out on display, gasping as he saw how rosy and erect her nipples were.

'Oh, how lovely!' he exclaimed. 'May I . . . may I kiss them, dear Emma?'

'Of course.' She smiled down at him indulgently, stroking the luxuriant dark curls. Beneath the layers of her petticoats she could feel herself growing hot with lust for this inexperienced young man and eager to initiate him into the art of love. Deftly she wriggled out of her lower garments, except for her under-petticoat and stockings, so that when he at last took a rest from suckling at her tumid breasts he couldn't stop himself from stroking her naked thighs.

'May I . . . take off your garters?' he asked, tremulously.

'Yes. Kneel before me, that is easiest.'

'I will gladly kneel before you, as if you were my Queen – no, my Goddess!' he smiled, making Emma laugh at the extravagance of his metaphors.

Slowly he eased the beribboned garter down her thigh, over her knee and down her calf, finally passing her foot through it. The silk stocking began to fall in lazy folds and Charles rolled it down, kissing every new inch of flesh as it became exposed. He has a charming way with him, Emma thought. Although she believed that he had never been this intimate with a woman before, she had the feeling that he had often dreamed of this scenario, perhaps rehearsing in his mind what he would do if ever he had the opportunity. Well, she was delighted to be making his dreams come true!

'Now, dear Charles, I think perhaps you should remove some of your own clothes,' she said, when she was bare-legged.

Hastily he took off his jacket then his boots and socks. Emma insisted on unbuttoning his fly for him, feeling the huge bulge beneath with a good deal of satisfaction. The lad was well hung, she was sure of it, which would increase her pleasure when the time came. Soon he was standing in his shirt-tails, looking somewhat sheepish, so she suggested that they should move over to the bed. It was a grand affair, with a satin canopy and counterpane under which frilled cotton sheets were spread on a most comfortable mattress.

While Charles lay down on the bed in a state of breathless anticipation, Emma took off her corset and lay down in nothing but a single petticoat. Greedily the young man reached for her generous breasts as if he would stuff them both, whole, into his mouth at once. Emma laughed at his hasty appetite.

'Importunate boy! One thing you really must learn, my dear, is that women prefer their lovers to savour their bodies slowly, and with due respect. Now I realise that in your present state of arousal it would be a kind of torture to keep you waiting too long, so here is what I propose. I shall give you some satisfaction straight away, taking the edge off your desire. Then we may proceed to our mutual content at a more leisurely pace. Will that suit you?'

'Oh yes, anything, anything!' he groaned.

So while he mouthed at her tingling nipples a while longer, Emma delved beneath his shirt and produced his fine and ready member for her inspection. She was delighted to see how thick and strong it was, although a little on the short side. Deftly she began to stroke the hot shaft, eliciting loud moans of pleasure from Charles's lips and feeling corresponding tremors inside her own body that made her shudder with warm excitement. The purplish glans began to swell and seep under her careful tutelage, and she had a sudden desire to place it between her breasts. Squeezing them close together, she massaged his tool with increasing fervour while, bending her head, she managed to take its tip between her lips and flick her tongue over the salty slit.

This proved altogether too much for poor Charles, who discharged his vital load within seconds of Emma's ministrations, sending a hot stream of liquid into her mouth.

'Oh, my dear Emma, I am so sorry!' he cried, abjectly.

Emma dismissed his apologies with a smile, letting his head nestle in the place his phallus had occupied just before.

'A man's spunk is not so terrible a taste,' she explained. 'Many women like it. I cannot say I actively enjoy it, but I do not mind when it happens spontaneously as it did just then.'

'Oh Emma, you are an angel! An angel!'

Charles kissed her lips fervently, re-kindling Emma's previous feelings. She invited him to lift up her petticoat and inspect the bounty within, which he did at once. Seeing the dark vee of rough hair, he exclaimed in surprised tones, tinged with horror. 'Oh, I had no idea that ladies had . . . anything like that down there!'

Emma laughed heartily. 'My poor boy, did you think men and women were so unalike? Of course our parts are constructed differently – just how differently you shall see in a moment – but we have bodily hair in the same places.'

'But no one ever tells a chap,' he said, petulantly. 'When you hear rumours from other fellows you don't know whether to believe them or not. If you're lucky enough to see a painting of a nude woman, or a statue, her belly is as smooth and hairless as a child's.'

Emma stroked his matted hair back from his brow. 'Tut, tut! How we elders do deceive the young! I agree it is scandalous that you should know so little of female anatomy, Charles. Why, some men even marry before they discover that their wives are not so different from themselves down below.' Her voice dropped to a conspiratorial hush: 'You know, they say that even the learned John Ruskin was so shocked by seeing his wife's pubic hair that he could not consummate the marriage!'

'Well, since it is evident that Nature has made men and women alike in that respect I believe it is pointless to deny the fact.'

Emma stroked his cheek affectionately. 'I agree whole-heartedly. In fact, there is so much hypocrisy and untruth in our society that I have often despaired of our so-called "civilisation". When it comes to sexual matters it seems to me we are more ignorant than the poor natives of Africa and other countries that we like to look down on.'

She thought for a minute of Lily, whom she suspected would share her view, but then it became obvious that Charles was eager to further his education and she let him wriggle down the bed to get a closer look at her privates. Parting her already tumescent labia with her fingers, she allowed him to make a close inspection of the folds and structures within.

'I would never have dreamed that female anatomy was so . . . complicated,' he declared. 'When fellows talked of a woman's thingummy I imagined a front passage like the back passage, and that was all.'

'Ah well, you see, a woman may derive much pleasure from the folds and crevices of her parts,' Emma explained. 'Do you see that little knob at the top, for instance? If you gently caress that you will bring me to the greatest joy imaginable.'

'May I try?'

'Of course, but be gentle dear boy. Rough handling will make my little man retreat behind his hood for protection.'

'Extraordinary!' Charles breathed, and set to work with tentative fingers.

Emma encouraged him to dabble in her increasingly wet entrance from time to time and then to plunge further in while she showed him what a tight grip she could get on his invading finger. Everything she showed him was received with a 'Marvellous!' or a 'Wonderful!' so that she began to see herself – and her sex – with new eyes. His adoration of her proceeded apace until it was obvious that there was only one way he could satisfy his desire for full knowledge of womankind and that was to plunge into her up to the hilt, which he soon did.

At first he was clumsy in his approach, pushing rapidly into her then jerking his whole body up and down in the way he imagined it might be done. But Emma was soon able to show him how to use his slender pelvis to good effect, and how to brace himself on his elbows so that he did not crush her with his full weight. It wasn't long before he got a passable rhythm going and Emma was able to lie back and enjoy herself in a relaxed and sensual fashion.

As she had imagined Charles did not last long, but for once Emma was hardly concerned about her own pleasure. It was satisfaction enough to see the look of utter rapture that passed over the young man's face as he understood, for the first time, what pleasures might be discovered within the delicious moist softness of a woman's quim. When he had collapsed on top of her, murmuring extravagant compliments, Emma found she had only to squeeze her thighs together a few times to bring about her own discreet paroxysms of delight. Feeling that Charles had received quite enough startling revelations for one night, she decided to wait for another occasion to let him know that, contrary to popular belief, it was possible for a woman to enjoy similar raptures to that of a man when handled by a considerate and experienced lover.

They dozed in each others' arms for a while until Emma became aware of Kitty moving around in the adjoining room. Tenderly she woke Charles with a kiss and suggested that he might like to douche himself before dressing. When he finally left her room it was with promises to dine with her the following night.

'The time between now and then will be an eternity,' he declared, as he blew her a last kiss at the door.

Almost as soon as he had gone, Kitty knocked at her mistress's door. She looked agog.

'Miss Emma, was that really Master Charles I saw leaving your room just now?'

'I think it may have been,' Emma replied, with a teasing smile.

'Oh, Miss Emma! He is such a fine young man, is he not?'

'Kitty, I do believe you are jealous!'

The girl looked downcast, but Emma went over and chucked her under her pretty little chin. 'I am only teasing, dear! It is quite natural that you should find him an attractive young man, and now he is a very satisfied young man I believe. This afternoon I have considerably furthered his education, I'm happy to say.'

'Oh, Ma'am!' Kitty giggled, her eyes bright as speedwell. 'Did you treat him the same as you did that curate?'

'In a similar fashion. He is so eager to learn, Kitty, that I shall quite have my work cut out "tutoring" him!'

'Will you be seeing him again tomorrow, then?'

'Yes, we shall dine together at night. In the afternoon I shall be visiting Lily, whom we met in the Louvre. She seems a most interesting woman, and I am looking forward to it immensely. Now, I think I shall take a nap before dinner.'

While she lay on the bed Emma reflected on her new beau with some seriousness. He was in love with her – what young man would not be with the woman who first granted him the ultimate favour? Yet their affair must, of necessity, be transient. Much as she would like to spend longer in that wonderful city, soon Emma would have to leave Paris and pass through Italy to Switzerland, where Cousin Mathilda was expecting her. The parting from Charles would be painful, on both sides, but Emma knew that soon he would be caught up in student life and would probably find some sweet Parisian girl to fall in love with. As for herself, the future looked equally rosy.

For a few minutes Emma's thoughts continued to dwell on the future. She was hoping to be given some employment in Mathilda's establishment so that she could be, in part at least, independent from Henry. For it was women's financial dependence on men that caused many of their ills, Emma decided. She was fortunate in having no children, but other women were obliged to stay with their cruel or dull husbands purely from economic necessity.

The following afternoon, Emma went alone to Lily's address near the Boulevard des Italiens. A smiling *concierge* took her up to the apartment, which was beautifully decorated in white and gold. Emma was shown into the drawing room to await Lily. It was an extraordinary room. In the marble fireplace stood a brass fire screen designed as a peacock's tail, inlaid with turquoise stones, and on a small table stood a beautiful glass vase in jewelled colours containing several real peacock feathers. On the floor were exquisite Persian rugs and the long windows were draped with green and purple curtains made from a fabric patterned with sinuous leaves and flowers. Emma noticed two boldly coloured glass lamps in green and purple with carved bronze stands, and several graceful statuettes of nude women. She had never seen such works of art in a private house before and was so absorbed in studying the treasures that she didn't notice Lily's entrance.

'Do you like that vase?' her hostess enquired.

Emma had been looking closely at an opalescent orange vase with a purple iris motif.

'Oh yes!' she enthused. 'I think everything in this room is in the most exquisite taste!'

'Thank you, my dear.' Lily came forward to take her hand. She was wearing a charming loose silk gown in a shade of blue that exactly matched her eyes and, as far as Emma could see, very little underwear. Her fair hair was immaculately coiffed, however, and held in place with tortoiseshell combs studded with what might have been real diamonds. Surrounded by such luxury, Emma was inclined to believe they were genuine.

Lily gave the orange and purple vase a brief caress. 'Here in Paris one can find the most wonderful *objets d'Art*, and the Duke has been kind enough to allow me to furnish the apartment with some of them.'

'The *Duke*?' Emma repeated, flustered. 'Pardon me, your ladyship, but I believed you to be unmarried.'

Lily gave a delightful peal of laughter that echoed round the large room like tinkling glass. 'Oh, my dear, you are so naive! Forgive me, Emma dear, for not making it more plain. I am not the Duke's wife, but his mistress. I thought you would have realised!'

Emma blushed. 'I am so sorry. I know nothing of life in Paris, except what I have read in books.'

Lily gave her a quizzical look, then led her to a chair near a small table. Sitting opposite, she looked thoughtful for a moment then said, 'Perhaps I should start by telling you how I came to Paris. I was just eighteen when I realised that London had little to offer me. I had been working there as a milliner but the wages were so low that I had to find some way to supplement my income as I had a widowed mother to support.'

'It must have been hard,' Emma murmured, but she couldn't help wondering how a humble milliner could have travelled so far up the social scale.

'Naturally I took the only way out, and began sleeping with men for money. You don't mind if I speak frankly do you, Emma?'

'Of course not. I am familiar with such matters.'

'I thought as much when we first met. You may tell me more about yourself soon, but let me continue my tale. To cut a rather tedious story short I did rather well as a "dollymop", entertaining my clients in West End restaurants and theatres and selling the expensive jewellery that my lovers often gave me instead of money. I was able to give my poor old mother a comfortable life in her last days, and a decent burial at the end.'

'Did she know how you . . .?'

'I believe so, although we never spoke of it. But after mother died I realised I was free to go wherever I wished. I also realised that I had come to enjoy my style of life for its own sake. I was beholden to no one, I had wealth and beautiful clothes and, by that time, I could please myself whom I took to my bed. But, most of all, I realised that I loved the act of sex in all its forms. My pleasure between the sheets was not feigned, as with some ladies of the night, but genuine. I believe that goes a long way to explaining my success with my gentlemen patrons.'

Now Emma knew why she and Lily had recognised each other as kindred spirits. Despite the frequent assertions of doctors and churchmen that virtuous women had no 'animal desires' and found the act of procreation thoroughly distasteful, their own experience had taught them otherwise.

'I am sure you are right, Lily,' Emma smiled. She found she was bursting to speak of her own pleasure in seducing young men. It was one thing to talk of such things to an innocent like Kitty, but it would be quite different discussing them with this woman of the world.

'Well I came to Paris and, dressed in my finery, began frequenting the theatres and high-class casinos. My first protector here was an army officer, but I soon progressed to a wealthy financier. It was he who introduced me to Sergei, a Russian Grand Duke. Dear Sergei set me up in this apartment and gave me a generous allowance in return for letting him see me just two nights a week. He is not jealous, and is happy for me to see other men provided I do not entertain them here. So I have a room reserved for me in a select "Maison des Rendezvous" near the Grand Hotel, which is very convenient for the Opéra Balls.'

'You must lead a most exciting life,' Emma commented, enviously.

'Yes, indeed. One might almost say a double life, for I move in circles that people would imagine are very far apart. I am equally at home at an embassy reception and in a bar such as A La Souris which is frequented by those ladies whom our sainted Queen Victoria believed could not exist.'

Emma frowned for a moment but then laughed as the penny dropped. 'Oh! You mean women of the Sapphic persuasion!'

'Yes indeed. Many of them lie with men for payment, you know, while their true affections are for their own sex. There are also bars I know of in Montmartre where most of the "ladies" are men. They fashion false breasts out of sheeps' lungs, would you believe!'

'How extraordinary! You have experienced what I have only read about, Lily. My husband had a collection of books which, being of a liberal cast of mind, he encouraged me to dip into. I had thought of myself as knowledgeable on such subjects, but in comparison with you I realise that the subject of human sexuality is vast and my own explorations have been very limited.'

'Then perhaps we shall remedy that during your stay in Paris,' Lily smiled. 'First, tell me about this husband of yours. He sounds an enlightened soul. Or are you widowed, my dear?'

Emma filled in her background as best she could, finding Lily a sympathetic listener. Then the maid brought in tea on a silver tray laden with fine bone china. As they nibbled at macaroons and madeleines, Emma introduced the subject of Charles.

'I guessed at once that you were lovers,' Lily smiled. 'I have a practised eye, you see.'

'I find a particular delight in seducing virgins,' Emma admitted.

'You resemble many men in that respect. I know of several brothels where defloration is the main attraction and doctors are on hand to supply certificates. The strange thing is, that the same girls seem to be presented again and again!'

Emma looked puzzled. 'How can that be?'

Lily laughed. 'By means of such little tricks as bladders filled with blood and secreted in the girls' vaginas, and vinegar douches to tighten them up. Virginity, real or fake, will treble a girl's value. Fortunately I have never had to resort to such dubious practices. The men who seek my favours do so because they know I am an expert at my profession, not an innocent.'

'This has been an extraordinary afternoon,' Emma announced at last, sensing it was time to leave. 'I have learnt more here, in a couple of hours, than I ever did in Henry's library.'

'Then let me show you Parisian low-life in all its dubious glory,' Lily offered with a smile as they both rose from their chairs. 'I am entertaining Sergei tonight, but tomorrow evening I would be free to give you a glimpse of the Parisian demi-monde, if you so desire. I can promise you will be quite fascinated.'

'I should love that! I am dining with Charles tonight, but I have no further plans.'

'My dear Emma, why not bring young Charles along too, if you feel he would benefit from widening his studies?'

Emma hesitated. Would such a sudden introduction to the hidden side of Parisian life be too much for him to stomach? She would have to think about it. Kissing Lily on both cheeks, French style, Emma left the building and walked back to her hotel in a mood of quiet exhilaration.

Chapter Six

*T*he minute Emma entered the hotel dining room with Charles she feared it had been a mistake. There was that strange gentleman again, sitting at a corner table by himself, fixing her with a curious stare and smiling to himself beneath his moustache. Although she averted her eyes from him at once, Emma felt a tell-tale flush spread over her cheeks and wished that she had taken Charles somewhere more discreet.

Throughout the meal, while they discussed the sights they had seen that day, Emma was aware of the stranger's eyes upon her and it quite put her off her food. What was it about those dark eyes that reduced her to jelly inside? It was impossible to behave in a natural fashion, and even Charles noticed that she was not quite herself, enquiring whether she was feeling unwell.

'Oh no, dear boy, I am a little fatigued after all our sight-seeing today, that is all,' she smiled. Then, seeing the disappointment in his face, she added, 'But I shall be perfectly all right later. One of those Turkish coffees will set me right after our meal.'

They took their coffee in the lounge and Emma was quite disconcerted when the gentleman appeared and settled opposite them with a copy of *Fin de Siècle*. When she caught his eye he smiled and inclined his head, almost as if he already knew her, and she felt herself blush once more. Try as she might to engage Charles in earnest conversation, she was relieved when they had both finished their coffee and could leave the room.

Before dinner Emma had been looking forward to being with Charles again. She had put on the corset trimmed with Chantilly lace that she had bought that afternoon, and doused herself in her new Parisian perfume, which smelled of lilies and roses. Yet now, going up alone to her room after instructing Charles to follow at a discreet interval, she was strangely disturbed at the thought of that dark stranger sitting in the lounge below. She had the oddest feeling that he knew of her liaison with the young Englishman and was somehow amused by it. The idea that she might be the subject of speculation, or even scandal, in that liberal-minded city had simply not occurred to Emma.

Once she was alone in her room with Charles, Emma did her best to build on their last encounter, introducing him to yet more delights. While in a state of *deshabille* herself she slowly undressed him, noting that each time she took off one of his garments, the bulge in his trousers became a little more prominent. When he was naked she told him to lie face down on the bed while she applied one of her satin slippers to his buttocks in spirited style. For Emma had not forgotten his 'tales out of school' and she guessed that he had acquired the taste for what Frenchmen called *le vice anglais*.

From the way Charles was eager to tup her after his thrashing, Emma knew she had been right. He practically tore the lace-trimmed stockings from her thighs, obliging her to restrain him lest he should damage the delicate fabric. He thrust straight in without preliminaries, making her gasp as the root of his thick shaft made instant contact with her already swollen clitoris. Emma gasped again as his actions became fast and furious but she let him have his head, like an untamed horse, knowing that he was fast acquiring a taste for this new sport and needed to explore his own feelings and capabilities thoroughly.

With an almighty groan Charles finally attained his goal, spraying with abandon and then lying limply by Emma's side as his breathing gradually slowed to normal. When he seemed almost recovered she said, 'Let me tell you about a treat that Lily and I have in store for you.'

'You and Lily? You mean, that lady we met in the gallery?'

'Yes. I took tea with her this afternoon and she has invited both of us to join her tomorrow evening on a tour of the Parisian night-life. She promised that it would be a most interesting experience. Will you come?'

Charles's dark eyes glowed assent. 'Oh, I should love that! Imagine what stories I shall have to tell the fellows back home! They will be green with envy.'

'That's the spirit, Charlie boy! Think of your time in Paris as one grand adventure, then you cannot go wrong. But now I am rather exhausted and wish to sleep. I think it would be best if you left the hotel and took a cab back to your quarters.'

'Must I?' he asked, wistfully.

'I am afraid so. We women of the world still have reputations to maintain, and hotel managers cannot afford to be suspected of running a *bordel* . Meet me in the foyer at eight o'clock tomorrow, there's a dear boy.'

His last kisses were passionate and demanding, but Emma gently extricated herself from his embrace. Once he had gone she rang for her maid.

'I think that Charles is growing fond of you,' Kitty commented, as she brushed out Emma's long tresses. 'He will miss you when we leave.'

'Yes, but it is only infatuation. A young man always believes he loves the first woman who grants him favours. It cannot be helped. But Charles is not the languishing kind. I cannot see him lying love-sick in a garret, can you?'

No, Ma'am!' Kitty laughed. Then she sighed. 'Sometimes I wish I could find a young man like him. Not that I am unhappy in your service, Miss Emma,' she added, hastily.

'I understand, dear. It is only natural that you should long to be courted by someone yourself and, one day, I am sure it will happen.'

'There is so much I long to know, particularly about the physical side of marriage. All I know is how babies are made, and I am sure there is more to it than that or men and women would not make such a fuss about it.'

Emma laughed at her maid's ingenuousness. 'You are right, Kitty, and perhaps sometime I shall enlighten you a little more. But now I am quite fatigued and need to rest. Please call me in the morning at eight.'

Once she had bid the girl goodnight, Emma lay down and waited for sleep but it took a while to arrive. Two men preoccupied her thoughts. Charles would be happy in the longer term, she was sure of that, but it would be good if she could find some way of easing the pangs of their parting. Perhaps Lily would know of some suitable girl who would comfort him with her charms.

Then there was that other strange gentleman, who threatened to haunt her dreams and even turn them into nightmares. Emma was not accustomed to being stared at in that peculiarly knowing way, as if the stranger knew more about her than he was letting on. It crossed her mind that he might even have been set to spy on her by her husband, but that seemed incredible. Henry was not the jealous type and she imagined that he had all but forgotten about her by now. Yet she was not sorry that in three days she would be leaving Paris, and then she would no longer be looking over her shoulder all the time.

Daniel Forbes could see into the hotel lobby from the bar, where he was enjoying a nightcap of brandy before turning in. He needed his sleep, he told himself wryly.

Time to recharge his batteries after the interesting night he'd spent at the apartment of a Turkish pasha with exotic tastes in women and generous feelings towards Englishmen. And what a night! Daniel had still not recovered from the sight of three dusky maidens performing the 'Dance of the Seven Veils' and then indulging themselves in Sapphic play as a preparation for the orgy to follow. Cautioned to remain on the sidelines by his Turkish friend until the women were thoroughly aroused, Daniel's self-restraint had been sorely taxed but he managed not to let his friend down when it came to the business. And what business! He could feel the magical resurrection of his male member as he recalled some of the tricks those girls had performed on him as their willing victim.

Tonight, though, he would be glad to abstain. The one thing Daniel feared was becoming like those raddled old roués whose faces could be seen again and again in the exclusive clubs and smart brothels of Paris. Some of them needed whipping with nettles before they could rise to the occasion. Others indulged in various gross and unsavoury practices that even Daniel would baulk at. No, when the palate was jaded fasting was the only cure. After a few days of abstinence food tasted so much more delicious.

Suddenly a figure passed through the hotel foyer and Daniel was wholly alert. He went to the door to make sure it really was that certain young man, then returned to the bar and ordered another brandy. Daniel smiled to himself. So, the little tomcat had been put out for the night, had he? It was scarcely midnight. Perhaps the admirable Emma Longmore was beginning to tire of youthful inexperience and, in keeping with her name, to long for someone more imaginative, more worldly, more adventurous.

Well, he must bide his time. Tonight, when she'd caught his eye in the dining room and later in the lounge, she had seemed agitated. Did she suspect him of spying on her? He must be more careful or he would set up such a resistance in her that a rebuff would be inevitable if he were to approach her. Perhaps he could find some way to ingratiate himself with the woman, make her obligated to him. After all, that ploy had worked before.

For, one way or another, he knew he must have her, before she slipped from his grasp forever.

Emma could scarcely believe she was really there, seated in the infamous Folies Bergère. Charles was excited too, and she noticed him eyeing up the plump, pretty chorus girls with slight pangs of jealousy for she knew she could not compete with their youthful charms. Her attention was soon distracted, however, when Lily began chatting *sotto voce* about the elegantly dressed men and women who were all around them.

'I have not brought you here to see the show, so much as to view the audience,' she began, with a low chuckle, while a couple of acrobats went through their paces on stage. 'You see that woman over there, with a fortune in pearls around her neck and a gentleman on each side? That, my dear, is Cora Pearl!'

Emma looked blank, and Lily looked shocked. 'Don't tell me you have never heard of her? She is the most famous courtesan in Paris, mistress of Prince Napoleon amongst others. Yet she was born plain Emma Crouch and within the sound of Bow Bells, to boot. You should hear her speak, my dear! She swears like a trooper but no one seems to mind.'

'She is very beautiful.'

'True, but you need more than beauty to get where she is. The woman has spirit, I'll give her that. She has been known to dance naked on a carpet of orchids, and bathe in a silver tub of champagne as entertainment for her dinner guests!'

Lily continued to point out various notorious women, or men with perverse tastes, as the show progressed through a conjuror, a man who mimicked the manners and accents of French provincial life, a *chanteuse*, and a performing poodle act. Then came the high spot of the evening. The master of ceremonies announced the first of the famous *tableaux vivants* and the curtain rose on an extraordinary scene.

To the strains of the 'Blue Danube' a real fountain was revealed, with a man dressed as Neptune sitting on a pedestal above. Gathered around him were his 'water nymphs', bare-breasted girls draped with sea-weed and shell necklaces. As coloured lights turned the water display into a rainbow cascade, on came a 'sea monster' with three 'mermaids' riding on its back. Then a huge oyster shell opened up and another semi-nude girl appeared and proceeded to do a graceful dance. Emma was enchanted. She had never seen anything so wonderful in her life.

She glanced at Charles, who was equally struck by what he saw. Naughtily, Emma reached out in the dim light and put her hand over his fly to feel his erection.

'I see you are enjoying the show!' she whispered.

Lily, however, looked a trifle bored. She had obviously seen it all before and, having exhausted her repertoire of gossip, suggested they should move on to another night spot where they might see 'something more interesting.' Emma was slightly disappointed, but she agreed to go and they took a cab to a private club called 'L'Hermaphrodite' where, Lily told them with a smile, you could hardly tell the men from the women.

It was very dark inside and it took a while for Emma's eyes to become adjusted to the gloom. When they did, she realised that there was definitely something odd about most of the clientele. Some were obvious trans-vestites – muscular-looking 'women' with square jaws and a hint of shadow about the jowls, or pigeon-chested 'men' who were obviously wearing wigs and false moustaches – but Emma was relieved to find that there were some fairly normal-looking individuals too. Except that, after a while, she began to wonder: what if those apparently 'normal' ones were simply disguised more successfully than the others? It was strange looking around and being unsure what gender people were. Perhaps Lily, Charles and herself were the only people in the place who were just what they seemed to be.

They sat at small tables and drank wine while a man in a ball gown did an impression of Dame Nellie Melba. Then everything went very dark and on the small stage a round globe began to glow like a full moon with black tree shapes silhouetted against the 'sky'.

A voice from the wings announced, 'Long ago, in ancient Greece, Aphrodite mated with Hermes and produced the Hermaphrodite. Whether we know our friend as a bearded Venus, a follower of Cybele or Sappho, or just as our two complementary selves, we pay our own special tribute to this wonderful creature that we all know and love. Messieurs-Dames, Mesdames et Messieurs, here for your delectation we present the birth and incarnations of our namesake, Hermaphrodite!'

The light on stage grew bright enough to show the figures of Venus and Hermes, she with outsize breasts and he with a huge artificial phallus. They proceeded to mime the act of love, with much noisy enthusiasm until Hermes finished the task and then tore off his dildo, throwing it into the audience amidst cries of glee. The lights went up a little more and Venus came to the front of the stage to show off her grotesquely swollen belly. She strutted up and down until her face contorted with pain and the lights dimmed. There was much moaning and groaning, but when the lights went up again and the figure centre stage could be clearly seen, the offspring of the god and goddess was possessed of both sexual attributes, having pendulous breasts as well as a large penis.

There was much applause, then on came a troupe of 'nymphs' who were obviously men with false breasts, and 'satyrs' who were women with false penises. They carried birch rods which they proceeded to use on the upraised behind of the hermaphrodite, dancing in a circle and each delivering a blow in turn. Soon the naked buttocks of the man-woman were blushing scarlet and the flagellants were increasing the pace, whooping as they did so, until the whole scene became an orgiastic frenzy of beatings. Emma felt uneasy until Lily told her that the unfortunate creature's posterior was a prosthesis also, stained with dye on the tips of the rods.

Even so, it looked very realistic and when Emma glanced at Charles he appeared to be wholly taken in by the illusion. His cheeks were as red as the fake behind, his breathing had accelerated and the mound that rose from his crotch was very obvious.

At last the spectacle came to an end with the hermaphrodite being borne in triumph from the stage wearing a laurel wreath. The house lights went up a little, and Emma could see that many of the audience had been as moved by the performance as Charles had been. Lily said, pointedly, 'I think Emma and I will retire to the ladies' room while you order more champagne, Charles.'

Emma smiled to herself when she realised that some of the company would have difficulty in deciding whether they should avail themselves of the ladies' or the gentlemen's.

When the two women had relieved themselves they sat side by side in front of the large gilt mirrors to make those small adjustments to combs and pins that made their coiffures more secure.

Lily smiled wickedly and said, in a low voice, 'Did you notice how aroused your friend Charles was during the flagellation scene? I would wager any sum you care to name that the boy was whipped by other boys at school and gained a taste for it.'

Emma giggled. 'I believe you are right. Only last night I spanked him roundly on his posterior with one of my slippers and his enthusiasm grew apace. I could hardly prevent him from ravishing me on the spot.'

Lily's eyes twinkled with mischief. 'In that case, my dear Emma, I have something in my place of rendezvous that I am sure he would enjoy. The device requires two

93

operators, however. How would you feel about joining me in giving that young man the time of his life?'

As soon as Lily mentioned it, Emma knew that the answer to the problem that had been troubling her was right there in front of her nose. Surely her friend would be the ideal person to take Charles under her wing when she left Paris? It was something to reflect upon but, for the time being, she would be delighted to join in the mysterious sport that Lily had in mind.

The three of them drank champagne while an androgynous comedian told salacious jokes. Then, when they were all quite merry, they took a cab to the discreet apartment building in the Rue de Clichy where Lily had a room. The concierge, a round-faced woman with horn-rimmed spectacles, welcomed them with a smile.

'Your room is ready for you, Madame,' she said. 'Would you like to see your appointments for next week?'

'Later, Hortense, thank you,' Lily smiled. Emma was struck by how genteel the whole business seemed. The foyer was thickly carpeted and furnished with gilt chairs and a small table, on which was a statuette of a nude girl and some copies of *Fin de Siècle*. The sight of that risqué magazine reminded Emma, briefly, of the stranger in the hotel but she made a determined effort to put him out of her mind.

They walked up the rather grand staircase and Lily indicated the gentleman's cloakroom at the end of the landing. She told Charles to knock on her door in about five minutes, giving them time to prepare themselves. Filled with curiosity, Emma followed her friend into the love-nest where she entertained her illustrious clients.

The room was dominated by an enormous bed, surrounded on three walls by large gilt mirrors. There was even a mirror on the ceiling, much to Emma's surprise. A chaise longue and various chairs occupied the rest of the room, together with a wash-stand, wardrobe and many bowls of fresh-scented lilies and roses. The lighting was supplied by oil lamps and in one corner was an alcove, curtained off by heavy red velvet drapes. On the walls were paintings showing erotic scenes: shepherds toying with the breasts of shepherdesses; an Indian Rajah making love to five women at once; a parody of a Fragonard painting showing a couple copulating on a swing.

It was a boudoir designed for love, but Emma was hardly prepared for what she saw when Lily drew back the red curtains with a flourish and revealed her secret armoury. There was a collection of whips and canes in a rack on the wall, everything from supple rods to thick leather straps. There were dildos too, hanging on hooks as casually as hats on a hat stand. But standing to one side was a kind of trestle with velvet padded rungs, like a ladder. Lily picked it up and brought it out to the centre of the room for Emma to see.

'This is my version of a *chevalet*,' she said, proudly. 'I had it made specially. In London it is called a "Berkley Horse" after that famous Mistress of Correction, Mrs Berkley.'

'What is it for?' Emma asked, wonderingly.

'It is a kind of thrashing-bench. The man is tied to this side, with his genitals projecting through the rungs. While he is flagellated by one woman from behind, his parts may be stimulated by another in front. If one of my gentlemen wishes to avail himself of the treatment, I have to find an assistant. Tonight, my dear Emma, I am sure that both Charles and I would be grateful if you would do us that honour.'

The very thought excited Emma immensely. She could well imagine how Charles would love the idea of simultaneous reward and punishment and after last night, when she felt she had given him short shrift, it would be gratifying to see him so well satisfied.

'Of course, I should be delighted,' she smiled.

'Then we must attire ourselves appropriately,' Lily said, opening the wardrobe.

Emma was amazed to see the variety of costumes contained within. She noticed a nun's habit and a nanny's uniform as well as a fine assortment of wigs and corsets, frills and furbelows. Lily took out a white broderie anglaise camisole threaded with ribbon, a pair of white lace garters and silk stockings threaded with gold.

'I think these will suit you, my dear,' she smiled. 'You need wear nothing else . . . oh, except perhaps these!'

She picked up a pair of silver high-heeled shoes decorated with shiny rosettes. Emma took the clothes eagerly, laid them on the bed then began to undress. Lily brought out a high-necked plain gown and apron.

'I call this my "governess" outfit,' she smiled. Then, seeing Emma naked from the waist up she added, 'Oh, Emma, what delightful breasts you have! And such a tiny waist! You would be such a success if you decided to take up a career as a courtesan!'

Emma blushed, pulling the camisole over her head. Soon she was examining her appearance in one of the mirrors. With her bosom unrestricted beneath the thin cotton, and her light brown muff daringly exposed between her gartered thighs, she certainly looked the part from the neck down. Her coiffure was rather too severe, however, so she took out the combs and pins and let her blonde mane fall to her shoulders.

Immediately Lily came to stand behind her, dressed in the dowdy grey gown. She lifted up the heavy locks in admiration. 'Such beautiful fair hair!' she sighed. 'You are right to wear it down. But I think we should put some colour in your cheeks, my dear, and on your lips.'

Fetching her paint box she proceeded to smooth rouge into Emma's cheeks and on her lips. When she had finished, Lily gave her a light kiss on the forehead. 'Perfection! Charles will die of desire for you, I know it.'

Soon afterwards there came three tentative knocks at the door. Lily threw Emma a wink then went to open it. 'Come in, Monsieur!' she said, with a little curtsey.

Charles entered, wide-eyed, his gaze falling first on Emma in her state of *déshabille*, then on the contraption in the middle of the room. Lily took his jacket and put it on a hanger behind the door, then helped him off with his shoes and trousers. He seemed dazed, passive, but when his shirt was removed and the extent of his erection could be clearly seen, Emma knew that he was more than ready for whatever they had in store for him.

When he was completely naked, Lily came up to him with two silk scarves.

'Someone has been a naughty boy!' she began, archly. 'Someone must needs be punished. Stand against the whipping horse, and let me tie your wrists so you cannot escape.'

Emma took up her position on the stool while his eager penis projected between two of the rungs. His eyes were glazed with a mixture of inebriation and lust, and he hardly seemed to notice her. When the first stinging stroke from Lily's birch rod hit his buttocks, however, he gave a loud groan – not so much of pain as of recognition. He might have been back in the Remove, being punished by 'Ferguson' in his study.

Carefully, Lily pulled his bollocks through the hole as well and began caressing them gently. She could feel her pussy growing wet with excitement as she bent her head to his purple glans and delicately licked it. There was something enormously satisfying in seeing his helplessness, his abject longing, his total submission to the wills of the two women. Lily was wielding the cane with careful precision, now striking his left buttock, now his right, and every time she did so his penis quivered and jerked between Emma's lips like a creature with a life of its own.

Taking more of the salty tip into her mouth Emma fondled his taut balls, watching his face contorted in extreme delectation as pleasure and pain imposed themselves equally upon his consciousness. His shaft was thick and strong as she moved her lips up and down it, her tongue flicking back and forth all the time. She itched to feel that powerful length inside her and hoped that once the whipping had climaxed in his orgasm she would have a chance to satisfy herself, otherwise she feared she would be rubbing herself in frustrated longing in the cab on the way back to the hotel.

Suddenly Charles moaned loudly in response to one of Lily's canings, and his prick spurted hotly into Emma's mouth, almost choking her. She looked up to see the smile of satisfaction on Lily's face and the utter rapture on Charles's, and knew that their efforts had been well worthwhile.

'There, my dear Charles, was that not the most exquisite experience you have ever had?' Lily cooed, as she untied his slumped form from the *chevalet*. Emma helped her to guide him over to the bed where he lay exhausted for a few moments, his limp organ lying against his thigh. She sat down on the bed and stroked his matted hair while Lily took off her plain garb and revealed her buxom figure, clad only in a fine lawn shift. She came to sit on the other side of Charles's supine form.

'Well, my dear,' she whispered. 'And how did *you* enjoy that experience.'

'Very much indeed! Mrs Berkley must have been very practised in the art of pleasing men to have invented such an ingenious piece of equipment.'

'Well as soon as Charles has recovered we shall make him pleasure you also, Emma dear. You have striven hard for his satisfaction and swallowed his spunk into the bargain, which few women care to do. I think you have earned your reward.'

As she spoke, Emma could feel herself tingling in her nipples and clitoris and when Lily placed her arm around her neck and gave her a lingering kiss on the mouth her desire mounted. The other woman began to feel her breasts beneath the thin camisole, sighing softly as she tweaked the hard nipples into greater prominence.

'Take this off for me, my sweet,' she begged her,

hoarsely. 'I wish to see your twin beauties again. Seldom have I seen a pair so full and round and perfectly formed.'

Emma was happy to oblige, being past the stage of caring whose hands or lips titillated her. Yet as she removed the garment she felt Charles stir and, when Lily's hands descended on the firm contours of her breasts he sat up.

'Two lovely ladies . . . Am I in Heaven?' he murmured, still flushed from his former passion.

'You have been there and back, dear Charles,' Lily replied. 'But now you must take Emma there. She has served you well, and deserves the best loving you can give her.'

'Yes, indeed!'

Charles got to his knees, with his stalk already at half-mast, but Lily said, 'First pay lip-service to her honeyed quim, there's a good fellow. I am sure you will enjoy it as much as she.'

Obediently he shuffled down the bed and parted her damp, cushiony labia with his fingers. She felt his tongue explore her crevices and at the same time Lily's lips took her left nipple and mouthed it softly, filling her with the most exquisite sensations. It was wonderful to lie still and simply allow herself to be intimately caressed, feeling her body respond with ever-increasing waves of pure delight.

Her rise to orgasm was steady and swift, taking her to the brink and holding her there for a few seconds while she waited for Charles's questing tongue to find her throbbing love-button. As soon as he did, Lily sensed that she needed more stimulation and with one hand squeezing her right nipple she sucked more strongly upon the left one. Emma issued a loud sigh as the first thrilling ripples passed through her womb, making her vagina convulse briefly. When Charles slipped his forefinger inside her the delicious feelings intensified until she was squeezing him throbbingly with her wet walls, thrusting her breasts upward in frenzied abandon for Lily to caress, feeling the twin centres of her pleasure somehow merge into one mind-numbing swirl of ecstasy, bubbling up from the core of her being.

It took quite a while for her to come back down again. When she did so, she was aware of the three of them lying in a tumbled heap on the satin counterpane. Feeling wonderfully warm and relaxed, she managed to crawl between the sheets without disturbing the others and in a few seconds she was fast asleep.

When she woke in the morning she was alone in the bed. Sitting up and rubbing her eyes, she realised that Lily was performing her toilet at the washbasin. For a while she gazed at the woman's graceful back and slender buttocks, seeing the outline of her heavy breasts as they dangled beneath her armpits. She would make an excellent artist's model, Emma thought, remembering the paintings by Renoir and Manet that she had seen in the Louvre.

Then Lily turned round, saw she was awake, and smiled. 'I trust you slept well, my dear? Charles remembered that he had to register for some course at the Sorbonne at nine, so he rose early. I believe he was well pleased with the night's sport. We certainly introduced him to a few novel diversions, did we not?'

Emma laughed. 'I should say we did!'

'He left this message for you.'

She handed her a note written on the back of his calling card. It read: *Dearest Emma, last night you and Lily had me in thrall with transports of delight but, alas, I must leave now. I shall call at your hotel, 7 p.m. Hoping that will be convenient, C.*

Lily came and perched on the edge of the bed and, placing her arm around Emma's shoulders, kissed her cheek. 'I hope you enjoyed our love play as much as he did, Emma.'

'Oh yes, it was wonderful! I have never made love with a woman before, let alone with both a woman and a man at once.'

'There are many more delights I could introduce you to. Will you not stay awhile? I do believe that Paris is the most accommodating city in Europe for those who truly appreciate the pleasures of the flesh.'

'I am sure you are right, but my cousin expects me in Montreux by the end of the month and I wish to see something of the Riviera and Italy before then.'

'Indeed? The wander bug has never bitten me, I must confess. Now that I am installed in Paris I have no wish to travel elsewhere. I shall be perfectly content to stay here for the rest of my days.'

'My only qualm regarding my departure is the thought that I shall be leaving Charles alone,' Emma sighed. 'I know he will make the acquaintance of his fellow students, but he has come to rely on the regular satisfaction of his sex appetite, and I fear he may have to resort to low-class prostitutes, with all the dangers of disease.'

Lily hugged her close. 'Do not fret, Emma, for I shall personally take charge of those needs of his. He is a personable young man, and I will have no difficulty in finding a girl of sweet disposition with a clean bill of health to take him on.'

'How very kind. I shall be able to give you a lump sum to provide for that – ' Emma began, but was instantly quashed.

'I would not hear of it! Let it be a token of our friendship, Emma dear. If I can find no suitable girl to oblige him from time to time, then I shall be happy to satisfy him personally. I can promise you that his needs will not go unattended when you are gone.'

They kissed for a while, in sweet accord, and it soon became clear that Lily would have taken things further but Emma was worried about Kitty.

'My maid will be wondering where on earth I can be,' she explained, as she rose from the bed.

'But you will not abandon me entirely?' Lily asked, anxiously. 'You will visit me again before you leave?'

'Yes, of course.'

'And maybe, one day, you will return to this *Ville d'Amour*?'

'Maybe,' Emma smiled.

Chapter Seven

*B*eneath the excitement Emma felt to be setting out on another journey in a strange land there was a lingering emptiness. As she waved to the forlorn figure standing on the platform of the Gare de Lyon she had to wipe away a tear. Kitty, ever solicitous, squeezed her mistress's hand.

'Miss Merchant will take care of him,' she smiled. 'And he will soon settle into student life, I am sure.' She sighed. 'It must be very fine for young men to spend their days studying in a foreign city.'

'Of course you are right, my dear.' Emma dabbed at her eyes with a scented scrap of lace. 'And we have a new adventure to look forward to, don't we? I have always wanted to see the Riviera for myself. They say it is so beautiful.'

Even so, she could not help regretting the transience of her affair with Charles. After several years of satisfying marriage she had come to enjoy Henry's companionship as well as their sexual relations, and she secretly longed to find a man who would give her that again. But Charles was not that man. He was far too young and naive, so their relationship could never be much more than a physical one. Although Emma recognised this fact, it was still hard to accept.

They had booked a sleeping compartment for the journey through France, and when Kitty raised the blind next morning the Mediterranean sunshine poured in through the carriage window, instantly raising Emma's spirits. Everything was so bright and colourful. It was easy to see why many of the French artists that Lily had told her about divided their time between the congenial bars, salons and *ateliers* of Paris and the stunning landscapes of the 'Midi'.

On arrival in Nice, the two women took a cab to the Hotel des Anglais which was situated on the famous *Promenade des Anglais* which ran the length of the sea front. Elegance was everywhere, from the graceful palm trees that swayed in the light sea breeze to the architectural splendour of hotels like the *Negresco*, which rose from the promenade like some elaborate pink-iced gateau.

After lunch and an hour's rest, Emma suggested that they should take a walk along the promenade. The sun was hot, so Emma wore her lightest silk blouse and took her parasol. It was very pleasant viewing the vibrant turquoise of the Bay of Angels, on which small white sails were dotted, and she was beginning to forget about Paris altogether. Here was a world altogether more leisurely and sedate, a town built for the simple pleasures of the morning constitutional, the occasional excursion into the fragrant countryside, the flutter at the casino and indulgence in *la gastronomie*.

They had walked for half an hour along the sea front, smiling at the fashionably dressed ladies who were walking pampered poodle dogs with fancy collars, bows and frills to match their mistresses' outfits. There were vehicles passing up and down the dual carriageway beside them and Emma, finding the heat fatiguing, suggested that they should hail a cab to return to the hotel. She walked towards the kerb, looking left, then stepped out into the road.

Everything happened so quickly after that. There was a shout, an alarmed neighing and whinnying, a clatter of hooves. Emma was aware that a carriage had pulled up sharply to her right to avoid running into her. At the same time, strong arms pulled her back onto the safety of the pavement.

Kitty instantly produced a bottle of *sal volatile* and waved it under Emma's nose, but when she recovered her wits the stranger's arm was still about her, and the effect on her senses of his warm, masculine odour was almost as strong as that of the smelling salts. As she withdrew from his partial embrace and turned to thank him her heart, just steadying after her fright, once again began thudding irregularly in her chest. Because the 'stranger' wasn't entirely unknown to Emma. In fact, the face that was now so near to hers was all too familiar. She had seen that same faintly amused expression, those deeply penetrating eyes, many times at their Paris hotel and found the experience disturbing. Now the proximity of the man actually made her shiver, even though the sun was beating down.

'Your mistress requires the salts again,' the man said, in a perfect English accent. Kitty dutifully held the bottle beneath Emma's nose and the man escorted her to a nearby bench. Although she felt quite unable to speak, Emma's mind was racing. Surely it was no mere coincidence that had brought her and this man to the same town, at the same time?

The idea that he had followed her from Paris, however, seemed patently absurd. Emma sat down with Kitty beside her, while the man towered solicitously over them.

At last he said, 'Perhaps I may be permitted to introduce myself. I am Daniel Forbes, an Englishman. I travel in ladies' undergarments.'

Kitty stifled a giggle and Emma found it hard to keep a straight face, hoping that her shaking shoulders would be interpreted as the after-effects of shock.

'Mr Forbes, I am truly grateful to you,' she replied at last, deciding not to introduce herself yet. 'I do not know what came over me. I must have forgotten which way the traffic was going.'

'It is easily done,' Daniel smiled, his expression softening. 'But if I am not mistaken Madame, were we not both staying at the Hotel Beaufort in Paris? Your face seems most familiar.'

Emma inclined her head. 'Yes, I was staying there. How very strange that we should meet again in Nice.'

Her tone was pointed, and she fixed him with a suspicious stare but he appeared perfectly oblivious to her implication. 'Both cities are on my itinerary, Mrs . . .?'

'Longmore,' Emma said curtly, rather put out that she was obliged to give her name to this dubious man. She had decided to drop her title while abroad, being unwilling to call too much attention to herself.

'May I escort you back to your hotel?' Daniel offered. 'I am sure you would wish to rest after your ordeal.'

'That is very kind of you.' She gave him a half-smile that wavered on her lips as their gaze briefly met. Oh, why did she feel so strange every time she looked into those dark, unfathomable eyes? They made her feel that she had no secrets from this man, as if her soul were laid bare to him.

He helped her up and this time they crossed the two roads without incident. Daniel hailed a cab and insisted on sitting opposite Emma and Kitty until they were safely arrived at the Hotel des Anglais. En route, he chatted amiably about Nice.

'It is one of my favourite cities,' he told them with a smile. 'Particularly the area to the North of the town, beloved by Queen Victoria.'

'You must travel a great deal, in the course of your work,' Emma commented, trying to seem polite.

'Yes, indeed. Only last month I was in New York, where I was introduced to a revolutionary new item of underwear. Perhaps I might be permitted to show you, sometime? I can assure you that every woman of fashion will be wearing them soon.'

The idea of discussing intimate apparel with that man gave Emma an odd, but exciting, *frisson*. In her confusion, her reply came out rather more prudishly than she'd intended.

'I do not think that would be proper, Mr Forbes.'

'Oh, I should not dream of embarrassing you, Mrs Longmore!' His brown eyes sparkled provocatively at her. 'What I propose is that I leave a package at your hotel reception. You may then try on the garment at your leisure. It is called "the combination". If you like it, I shall be pleased to allow you to keep the garment, with my compliments.'

'Oh no, Mr Forbes . . .' Emma began, reluctant to be any more beholden to him than she already was. But they had drawn up outside the hotel, and he was already helping Kitty from the cab. He saw the two women into the hotel lobby, then bowed with a smile and bade them *au revoir*.

After he had gone, Kitty said, 'What a kind man, Miss Emma! And how fortunate that he was on hand in your moment of need.'

'You think it was merely "fortunate", do you Kitty?'

'What on earth can you mean?'

'I mean that Mr Forbes has been taking too close an interest in me for my liking. While we were in Paris he saw me with Charles several times, and I often caught him staring at me in a manner that I can only describe as prurient. Now he suddenly appears in Nice, at just the right moment. Was it coincidence that led him to stroll along the promenade at that time, or could he possibly have been following us?'

'Oh, Miss Emma!' Kitty sounded reproachful. 'He seems such a nice gentleman!'

Emma smiled. 'All right, Kitty, I am prepared to give him the benefit of the doubt.'

That evening, Emma and Kitty dined together in the restaurant where a string quartet played amongst the potted palms. Their waiter was a charming young man called Alphonse, and it wasn't long before Emma

107

found herself reading rather more into those soulful glances and soft murmurings than she felt was good for her.

After he had served dessert, she turned to Kitty and asked, in a low voice, 'Am I imagining it, Kitty, or is our charming waiter being attentive to me beyond the call of duty?'

Catching her mistress's drift, Kitty giggled. 'I have been having the same thoughts, I must confess.'

Emma smiled, taking a spoonful of 'Pêche Melba'. 'The question is, should one do anything about it?'

Kitty pretended to look shocked. 'In a public place, Miss Emma?'

'Ah Kitty, you would be surprised what can be achieved with a glance, a touch, an innuendo. Then there is always "room service". If Madame would care for a little late-night refreshment, then surely the ever-willing Alphonse would be only too glad to deliver it in person.'

'What did you have in mind?' Kitty asked, her pretty cheeks pink with excitement. 'Something to fill a hole, perhaps, or to help you to sleep?'

'Kitty! Such talk is not seemly!'

Emma's reproof was genuine. The girl had gone too far. It was all very well to talk lasciviously in private, but in a hotel dining room where they might be overheard she should not be encouraged. There was a time and a place for everything.

Duly chastened, Kitty contented herself with observing what went on between her mistress and the waiter for the rest of the meal. Emma regarded the situation as a challenge to her ingenuity and discretion. When Alphonse returned she placed a lightly restraining hand on his arm as he cleared away her dish.

'Please, Alphonse, do give my compliments to the chef,' she smiled up at him. 'That was the most delicious Peach Melba I have ever tasted.'

'Thank you, Madame.'

The young man had a sweet, gentle face and rather

shy eyes. Even so, he appeared drawn to Emma and she sensed that she had only to press home her advantage and he would succumb to her charms. But it must be done sensitively.

'Alphonse, will you be on duty later tonight?' she asked him, innocently.

He nodded. '*Oui, Madame.*'

'Then I should be obliged if you would bring a nightcap to my room at eleven. I find a brandy and water helps me sleep.'

'Of course, Madame. Room twenty-seven, I believe?'

'Yes. Such a charming room, with a beautiful sea view.' Emma sighed contentedly. 'I believe I shall really enjoy my short stay in your lovely town.'

'I shall do everything in my power to ensure that you are well satisfied by our service,' Alphonse replied, with subtle emphasis. When he turned his back, Emma winked at Kitty. She didn't want the girl to think she was cross with her.

At eleven, Emma sat up in bed wearing the pretty bed jacket she had bought in Paris. It was made of black Chantilly lace with pink ribbon trim and beneath it, instead of wearing the matching night-dress she was completely naked. Surveying herself in the mirror, Emma had delighted in the tantalising appearance of her breasts beneath the semi-transparent lace.

When the soft knock came at her door Emma was almost trembling with excitement and anticipation. The waiter entered with his eyes discreetly lowered, bearing a tray on which was a pitcher of water, a tumbler and a half-bottle of brandy. But after placing the tray on the bedside table, his glance strayed to Emma and she saw his pupils dilate as he took in her torso then caught her eye.

'Thank you, Alphonse,' she said, smiling. Perhaps you would water my brandy for me? Just an inch or so should suffice.'

'Yes, Madame.'

She turned on her side as he reached for the pitcher,

managing to just brush his forearm with her left breast. The contact sent shuddering waves dancing through her body. As he gave her the tumbler with a trembling hand she threw him a dazzling smile.

'Thank you, Alphonse. Would you care to join me? I do so dislike drinking alone.'

'I am on duty, Madame,' he replied. But his eyes told her that he wanted to share *something* with her, very much indeed!

'And when will you be off duty?'

'At midnight, Madame.'

'If you wish you may join me then. I suffer from insomnia and am seldom asleep before one in the morning. I usually pass the time reading, but it would be so much more pleasant to have some company.'

'I am sorry, Madame, but we are not permitted to fraternise with the guests. It is against management policy.'

Emma could see that he was torn between duty and desire. 'I am sure that it is also "management policy" that your guests should be well satisfied with the service offered. Do you want me to tell the manager that I have found his staff uncooperative?'

She had spoken sternly, telling herself that it was for his own good. Alphonse turned frightened eyes on her face, trying hard not to let his gaze drop below her chin. 'No, Madame. Please . . .'

'If you will do me this small favour, you shall have nothing to fear from me,' she smiled. 'On the contrary, I shall speak most highly of you to your superiors. Now, you had better go about your business. Until midnight.'

'Yes, Madame. Thank you, Madame.'

'No, thank *you* Alphonse!'

Emma knew she had him now, but the hour she must endure before he returned would be difficult. Already she had nipples as hard as acorns and a pussy as soft and damp as a wet sponge. After taking a swig of brandy and feeling its warmth course through her veins, Emma's hands strayed beneath the lacy bed jacket to find her breasts rearing hungrily, longing to be fondled. She squeezed them and felt an answering throb in her equally hungry clitoris. One hand continued to stroke the straining globes with their uptilted nipples, while the other played between her folds, making her wetter and wetter at the thought that before long other hands would be doing the same work, preparing her willing flesh for even more acute delights. As she came quickly to her self-induced climax, Emma knew that it was not the last she would experience that night.

By the time that tentative knock came again at her door, Emma was well primed for the delights which she was sure would follow. Alphonse entered sheepishly, still in his waiter's uniform, and Emma smiled up at him.

'Pour yourself a brandy, dear boy, and sit by my bed,' she urged. 'Then you can tell me all about yourself.'

'There is not much to tell, Madame. I came to this hotel at the age of thirteen, under the protection of Gaston, the head waiter.' He shrugged, downing his brandy in one gulp. 'End of story.'

'Surely not. What is he like, this Gaston? Does he treat you well?'

To Emma's surprise, the lad blushed scarlet mumbling, 'Well enough, Madame.'

Her suspicions roused, Emma asked, 'Is he cruel to you, Alphonse? Does he beat you? Do not fear, you may speak freely to me. I promise not to get you into any trouble.'

His eyes were miserable as they met hers. 'He . . . uses me, Madame, that is all.'

'Uses you? In what way?'

'I would rather not say.'

Now Emma was more or less certain that the head waiter was a pederast. He must have had the boy in thrall from a tender age. Her anger rose, but she tempered it to enquire, casually, 'How old are you, Alphonse?'

'Twenty, Madame.'

'And are you walking out with any nice young woman?'

The depth of his blushes and the vehemence of his *'Non, Madame!'* convinced Emma that her suspicions were right. Boldly, she took his hand. 'Then it is high time you discovered the pleasures that may be enjoyed between a man and a woman. Forgive me for speaking so bluntly, Alphonse, but I believe your experience of the physical has been somewhat brutal up to now, am I right?'

Her words acted like a key on his long-locked heart. All the resentments, the pain, the humiliation of the past seven years came tumbling out in one inarticulate gush.

'He forced me, Madame . . . that first night . . . I knew nothing of such things. Then he said I would lose my job if I squealed. My mother . . . three young ones at home – she needed my wages . . . I could do nothing, Madame, tell no one . . .'

'You poor soul!' Emma couldn't resist opening her arms to take him into a motherly embrace. His head nestled against her bosom and she felt the lustful tide rise in her, but first the wretched boy must be healed of his emotional wounds.

'There are men who prefer the favours of other men from boyhood, who never think of women except as mothers or sisters. But I believe you are not one of those, are you Alphonse?'

He shook his head, murmuring, 'Always I dream of one day meeting some girl and marrying her. And of setting up my own restaurant. But I know it is just a dream.'

'We shall see about that. But tell me, do you dream about what you would do when this sweet girl and you are all alone? On your wedding night perhaps?'

'Oh yes, Madame.' Alphonse became positively starry-eyed.

'Then tell me,' Emma coaxed. 'Tell me how you would make love to her.'

'Oh, Madame! I cannot speak of such things. It would not be proper.'

'Then if you cannot tell me, perhaps you can show me. Let us pretend I am your blushing bride, Alphonse, and we have just entered the bridal chamber together. While you were in the bathroom I divested myself modestly of my clothes and slipped into our marriage bed. Let us take it from there.'

He looked at her with flushed cheeks and wild eyes, hardly daring to believe that his dream was about to come true and totally unable to speak his mind. Emma smiled in encouragement then asked, in a sweetly innocent voice, 'Would you prefer me to turn out the light while you get undressed, husband?'

Speechlessly, he nodded. Emma extinguished the bedside candelabra and the room was plunged into semi-darkness. Since the shutters were open and the moon was bright there was sufficient illumination in the room for her to see him take off his clothes. Out of the shadows reared the dark silhouette of his rampant penis, and Emma felt her insides dissolving blissfully in anticipation of the joys to come.

'Now, dear Alphonse, remember that you, too, are a virgin as far as women are concerned. It is only natural that you should be nervous on your wedding night, so do not be afraid. We shall lie in each others' arms awhile, kissing and cuddling, until you are ready to take it further.'

Emma threw back the bedclothes to let him in. With a gasp he noticed the furriness of her bush in the moonlight, then feasted his eyes on the heaving contours of her breasts under their scanty covering. 'You may untie the ribbon at my neck if you wish,' she invited him.

With trembling hands he seized the pink satin and

untied the bow, letting the front of her bed jacket fall right open and the naked mounds of her breasts appear, silvery pale but with their tips stiffening provocatively.

'Oh!' he gasped. 'How I have dreamed of this moment!'

'You may touch them if you so desire, Alphonse.'

He leaned forward, near enough for her to smell the fruity aroma of brandy on his breath, and gently stroked her right breast. Between his thighs the eager instrument of his passion jerked uncontrollably and Emma felt another melting moment occur, deep inside her aroused body. She could see that Alphonse's organ was longer and thinner than Charles's had been, but it promised to be just as effective when wielded with such enthusiasm.

'Please take both my breasts in your hands and squeeze them, Alphonse. We women like to be firmly handled once we are roused, and the sight of your delightful member has certainly made me eager.'

'Oh Madame, you say things that make me feel so . . . wicked!'

Emma smiled, lying back voluptuously as the young man did as he was told. Alphonse bent forward and kissed her fervently, but with closed lips. Gently Emma prised them apart until their tongues were touching and he was murmuring his delight at the new experience. Soon his hands grew more bold, venturing below the tumid slopes of her breasts to her stomach. At every stage Emma encouraged him with satisfied sighs and words until she had managed to lure his questing fingers into the chasm between her thighs.

'Oh, Madame, you are soft as fondant in a hot kitchen!' he declared, with a delighted sigh.

'Then do you not wish to discover whether I taste as sweet?'

His brown eyes looked up at her, filled with the delighted expectation of a child promised a birthday treat. 'Taste, Madame?'

'Yes, indeed. A woman may be savoured like a

114

delicious meal with touch, smell and taste. Why not try kissing my lower lips in the same manner as you kissed my upper ones? You will find they will part willingly, allowing your tongue to enter into my nether mouth and sample its sweet juices.'

Eagerly Alphonse obeyed, and Emma settled back on the pillows once again to enjoy an extended session of cunnilingus. The waiter was tentative at first, tickling her labia almost unbearably with the sparse whiskers of his thin moustache but she said nothing, not wanting to deter him from his pleasant task. After a while his tongue protruded further into her moist channel and she sighed as the entrance to her vagina was filled with warm flesh. By wriggling sensually she was able to brush her clitoris against his full lips and soon she was ready to take the action further.

'Alphonse, dear boy!' she whispered, stroking his thick brown hair. 'Let me see what effect all this is having on your little man!'

Reluctant to take his lips from the new-found delights of her cunny, Alphonse swivelled round to show her his extended organ, now so elegantly long and slender that Emma was filled with a strong desire to stroke and fondle it. The glans was still almost hidden by his foreskin, so she guessed that he might need a little help in that quarter.

'Alphonse, turn around a little more so my lips may pay equal homage to your fine member.'

He willingly obeyed and soon Emma was licking round the edge of his foreskin with delicate precision, gradually easing it back over the glans with the tip of her tongue. Alphonse groaned in pleasurable torment as more and more of the deep pink tip was exposed and a little white liquid emerged from the slit.

'There, that's better!' Emma declared, when the whole of his rosy glans was freed from its covering and could move freely back and forth. She slid her fingers up and down the shaft a few times, enjoying every silken inch of him, then bent her head to take him between her lips again. This time she enveloped as much of his erection as she could, but only three-quarters of the length could be encompassed by her mouth.

'Oh, Madame! Excuse me, I cannot wait!' she heard him cry. Immediately a hot gush swept down her throat making her cough and splutter.

Alphonse withdrew his organ shamefacedly, gasping and moaning as he stuttered out his apology: '*Je . . . suis d . . . désolé, Madame . . .*'

At once Emma gathered him into her arms, cradling his head against her bosom and murmuring, 'Never mind, my dear Alphonse, I do not mind. You could not help it. I understand that you were overcome by passion and I am flattered, truly flattered that you desired me so much.'

'Really, Madame?' He lifted anxious eyes, his face palely illuminated by the rays of the moon. 'You are not disgusted with me?'

'Not at all. In fact, I loved the feel of your penis in my mouth and the salty taste of your fluid. It took me rather by surprise, that is all.'

'Extraordinary!' he breathed. 'You are an extraordinary woman, Madame!'

'Perhaps.' Emma smiled. 'It's true that I am a woman who knows what she likes, and what most men like too. But we have not finished yet. You are young and lusty, Alphonse. In a few minutes you will be quite recovered and your lovely long member will be raring to go again. Then we shall discover even more heavenly delights that a man and a woman may share.'

Alphonse sighed contentedly and cuddled close to Emma, his long fingers stroking her breasts as gently as a babe's. She decided it was a good time to question him more closely about his life at the Hotel des Anglais.

'Tell me, dear boy, did you ever enjoy what you did with Gaston?'

'Never!' he said, vehemently. 'He made me do to his

116

organ what you did to mine, but he was rough and thrust it down my throat. I hated it!'

'You are talking in the past tense. Does that mean it is all over between you now?'

Alphonse's face set grimly. 'It is as far as I am concerned. I had become accustomed to being used in that way, I accepted it as normal. But you have showed me something much finer, Madame, something . . . wonderful. I can never go back to such brutality, such . . . bestiality again! I shall find a new position in another hotel. There are plenty here in Nice. And I shall follow my dream, Madame. That I can promise you.'

'I am so glad, Alphonse.'

The thought that she had helped free this poor boy from his sexual slavery kindled a warmth in Emma that soon turned into desire, and she hugged him close. Between their naked bodies rose his stiff mast, his victory flag. Emma reached down and felt its delicate strength, her quim convulsing at the prospect of shea-thing all that firm flesh.

'Come,' she murmured, throatily, 'I think it is time for the Marquis of Lome to ride in the Berkshire Hunt!'

She had to guide him in, and once he was safely docked he began to ride like a huntsman in full pursuit of the quarry. Emma hadn't the heart to ask him to slow down and, indeed, it was hardly necessary. His keen enthusiasm was infectious, and soon she was panting towards a climax herself, with heaving breasts and bucking hips, feeling the long hardness of him press against her swollen lips as he lengthed her again and again. At last she was wriggling in the throes of an exquisitely fierce orgasm, the thrilling ripples setting him off as they repeatedly clasped his plunging member.

How Alphonse groaned as the first fiery spurts arrived, propelling him into seventh heaven! Amongst his inarticulate cries Emma could hear herself being called his 'sweetheart', his 'darling' even his 'love goddess'! Yet she knew better than to take it personally.

He was overcome by his first experience of a woman's body, and all that it could offer men in the way of sensual fulfilment, that was all.

Nevertheless she was tender with him as they lay together in the big bed, arms about each other. Alphonse repeated his vow to free himself from the tyranny of Gaston forever, and Emma hoped that he would soon find a worthy object for his affections. He was a sweet and good-looking young man who deserved better.

Once Alphonse had returned to his quarters Emma took some more brandy and settled down to sleep, but her thoughts returned to the incident earlier in the day when that strange man, Daniel Forbes, had appeared so opportunely and proceeded to make her acquaintance. Just why did she find his presence so unsettling? He was a fellow Englishman, and she should have been glad of his company, yet her reaction to his physical presence was always disturbing, always puzzling. Well, it was mystery that she did not particularly wish to solve.

After breakfast next morning, however, Emma was reminded of the Englishman again.

'Oh, Madame Longmore!' the clerk called from the desk. 'There is a *paquet* for you!'

She knew at once what it was, but she could hardly refuse to accept it. Frowning at Kitty's giggles she took the paper parcel and returned to her room. With her maid hovering excitedly at her side, Emma unwrapped it. Beneath the tissue paper inside was the neatly folded undergarment with a card that read: *With the compliments of Daniel Forbes of London, Corsetier and Manufacturer of Fine Lingerie for Ladies of Discernment.*

Despite herself, Emma also felt somewhat excited as she unfolded the cream silk and held it up for inspection.

'Oh, Miss Emma!' Kitty exclaimed at once. 'It's so beautiful!'

Suspended from the lacy straps was a delicate chemise that combined with drawers and a small petticoat to form one complete undergarment, evidently designed to be worn beneath a corset. The fine China silk and Nottingham lace were of the best quality, and the needlework was superb. Slowly, Emma's initial misgivings were being replaced by a grudging admiration.

'You will try it on, won't you?' Kitty urged her. 'Here, let me help you.'

Emma allowed her maid to unbutton her dress and strip off the cumbersome layers of underclothing that she was used to wearing. It would be a novelty to wear drawers. Normally Emma wore only petticoats beneath her voluminous skirts. Kitty untied the drawstring ribbon round the neck of the chemise. Emma stepped into the garment, letting her maid pull it up over her waist and breasts.

'Oh, Miss Emma, it does flatter your figure so!' Kitty said in admiration as she pulled the ribbon taut across her mistress's bosom. Emma could feel her nipples stiffening at the slight brush of Kitty's fingers, and the feel of cool silk tight against her thighs and bottom was equally arousing. Then, going over to the full-length mirror, she surveyed her appearance and gave a smile.

'You are right, Kitty. It is a very pretty item of underwear indeed, and so very comfortable to wear.' She sighed. 'What a shame that the demands of fashion dictate that we should constrict our bodies in corsets. If we women could wear such simple garments as this beneath our clothes we should be a great deal happier and healthier, I dare say.'

'Will you wear it today, beneath your corset?' Kitty asked, clearly still excited.

'No, I shall dispense with my corset altogether. Help me put on my dress and underskirts. I shall see what it feels like without stays. You must tell me how I look, Kitty. I shall take your advice and if my figure is sadly wanting then I shall put my corset back on. But it would be wonderful to be free of it, if only for one day, don't you think?'

'Oh yes, Ma'am!'

Kitty was almost beside herself with glee as she helped Emma back into her clothes.

When the dress was on they both studied the image in the long mirror critically. The softly rounded contour of her bosom was a novelty, and the waistband of her dress felt tight without the constricting corset, but Emma rather liked her new look.

'I believe I may be passable, Kitty, but what do you think?'

'I think you look perfectly fine. Maybe you will start a new fashion, here in Nice. That would be one in the eye for those Parisians, wouldn't it?'

Emma laughed. 'Oh, I could never take the credit for such innovation, Kitty. It is Mr Forbes who should be honoured for introducing this revolutionary garment to Europe.'

'It was so kind of him to give this to you, was it not Ma'am?'

Emma was aware that her maid was watching her face closely for signs of emotion. She knew what was going through the girl's mind. Kitty was an incurable romantic and would love to see her mistress married off once more. However, a manufacturer of undergarments was not the sort of man she would ever consider as a suitor.

'Yes, very kind,' she replied, impassively. 'And now, Kitty, shall we go downstairs? I should like to take a cab to Cimiez, and discover just why our dear Queen finds it so pleasant to stay there.'

Emma decided that she would not encourage Kitty to talk of the Englishman again.

Neither would she let her own thoughts dwell on him. Yet as they left the hotel it crossed her mind that she could hardly forget about Daniel Forbes completely as long as she was a walking advertisement for his wares.

Chapter Eight

The foyer of the Hotel des Anglais had a large gilt mirror, conveniently situated, which offered a view from the lounge of all the comings and goings. Daniel Forbes sat, strategically positioned, watching the strip of red carpet between the desk and the door. I could make a second career out of espionage, he thought wryly, as he sipped his whisky and water.

He had already spied on Emma Longmore the day before, and she had certainly been a sight to remember. His practised eye had known at once that she was wearing his undergarment as she walked through the hall with such casual elegance. Her bosom had shown a more natural and, to his eyes, infinitely more attractive line under the cream silk blouse and Prussian blue jacket. As he had watched her walk with easy grace beside her maidservant such a fire had run through his veins, such a stirring in his loins, that he had scarcely been able to bear it.

Yet he knew that Nice was not the place to further their acquaintance. He had already achieved much: his arms had been around that slim waist, her head had rested momentarily on his shoulder, and she had given him a grateful smile despite her obvious misgivings. Then she had received his gift, his *intimate* gift, and honoured him unwittingly by wearing the garment. Daniel smiled to think of that cool silk caressing her warm flesh, the lace delicately tickling her deep cleavage, the long drawers snug over her thighs and open at the crotch to let her sweet pussy feel the air as her petticoats rustled. He smiled again to think how easily she had swallowed his story about being a commercial traveller in lingerie. It was a useful cover, giving him an alibi in whatever city they should happen to meet.

Where would it be, their next rendezvous: in Rome, perhaps, or Venice? In that one respect she was mistress of their joint fate, for the itinerary was hers. In other ways, however, he was pulling her strings, working to his secret agenda. It remained only for him to take a peep at her suitcase when the porter brought her luggage down.

Was that him now? Daniel half rose from his chair as the familiar portmanteau, two smaller cases and two hat-boxes, all in matching green morocco, appeared on a trolley. He emptied his glass, sauntered cautiously into the hall and bade the porter good day, glancing down as he did so. The luggage label clearly stated 'Florence'. Well and good! In that city of Art and Culture there were many fascinating secrets that a gentleman might reveal to a lady if she would only overcome her scruples about consorting with a lowly traveller in ladies undergarments!

On the morning of their departure from Nice, Emma was sitting in the hotel breakfast room drinking her coffee and chatting amiably to Kitty when she noticed Alphonse hanging around the door to the kitchen, laughing and joking with an invisible companion. It was only when the kitchen door swung open and revealed one very pretty waitress that Emma understood what was going on. The boy was actually flirting! Good for him. Soon he would find another position and, if he was lucky, a woman to warm his bed. Emma smiled with the satisfaction of a job well done.

'I believe we shall like Florence very much,' she told Kitty, turning her mind to the exciting prospect of another journey and another country. 'It is full of ancient buildings and the most beautiful works of art. I know a little Italian, so I am sure we shall get by.'

'I think you are extraordinary, Miss Emma!' Kitty suddenly announced, blushing. 'Few other women would undertake such a journey without the protection of a husband.'

'Fortunately, dear Kitty, I do not share the English illusion that civilisation only begins at Dover. I set out believing that a woman of breeding and spirit is respected everywhere in Europe, and so far I have not been disappointed.'

Kitty gave a mischievous grin 'What about that under-wear salesman? Do you think he regards you with respect as well?'

For a moment Emma was caught off guard. She hesitated, thinking that 'respectful' was not quite the word she would have used to describe Daniel Forbes's demeanour. 'Covetous' would be nearer the mark, and yet perhaps there was a kind of respect in that. At the thought of those dark, desirous eyes Emma felt something twitch deep inside her, and once again her discomfort vented itself on poor Kitty.

'I would prefer you not to refer to that man again. I intend to leave his gift behind in our room so that I am not beholden to him in any way, and let that be an end to the matter.'

They travelled along the Côte d'Azur to Monte Carlo, then crossed into Italy. Emma would have liked to break their journey at Genoa and Milan, but she had limited time and had set her heart on Florence. When they finally arrived in the great marble hall of the railway station, she knew her instinct had been right. There was something elevating in the air, in the very faces of the Florentines, a timeless sense of *joie de vivre* that augured well.

'Take us to the Hotel Mantana!' Emma called to the

cabman, who set his horse ambling through cobbled streets, past the domed splendour of the green and white cathedral, across the huge square dominated by the crenellated tower of the town hall, and then towards the embankment of the river Arno where their hotel was situated in a quiet *piazza*.

'It is all very beautiful, is it not?' Emma remarked happily, seeing Kitty's wide-eyed wonder. 'Tomorrow we shall take our guide book and begin to explore in earnest.'

Emma soon discovered what was most to her taste in that city. The dark churches she did not much care for, but the paintings and statues were exquisite! She particularly liked the two 'Davids', but Michelangelo's monumental version, with his heavily muscled torso and hefty thighs pleased her less than Donatello's charming youth, with his boyish hips and languid stance. She tried to justify her preference to Kitty by saying that Michelangelo had made his David too athletic, too much of a match for Goliath, and that Donatello had made him seem more vulnerable.

'Or perhaps, Ma'am,' the girl said smiling slyly, 'you just prefer slender youths!'

'Kitty!'

Emma pretended to be shocked, for form's sake, but she knew her maid was right.

It was hot at midday and although Emma found the churches too gloomy for her taste their cool interior was welcoming. She decided to visit the church of Santa Croce and view the monuments. After seeing the tombs of Michelangelo, Dante and Machiavelli she was walking past a confessional box when a tinkling bell caught her attention. She saw a hand appear from a curtain, beckoning her, and a low voice said in English with a strong Italian accent, 'I am ready to hear your confession, Signora.'

There must be some mistake, Emma thought. She had said nothing to any of the black-robed priests who moved in shadowy corners like dark ghosts. Should she just walk on and ignore it, or pause to explain?

Kitty giggled, but then Emma realised that she was actually rather attracted to the idea of the confessional. Although brought up in the Protestant faith, she had often thought that it must be a sweet relief to confess one's sins and receive absolution. Not that she regarded any of her recent seductions as sinful, of course, but it would be amusing to talk about them to some anonymous priest, to imagine how he might struggle to suppress his lustful responses. Remembering how much she had enjoyed her encounter with Robert, the young curate, Emma smiled to herself then whispered to Kitty that she was 'going to confession' and her maid must amuse herself for the next few minutes.

Emma entered the wooden kiosk that smelt of incense, and knelt on the hassock provided. Before her was a perforated screen with a shadowy figure beyond. The priest began by asking if she was sincere in wanting to confess her sins.

'Oh yes, Father!' Emma replied, fervently, squashing an urge to laugh.

'Then proceed, child,' came the response in a deep, throaty accent.

'My sins are those of the flesh, Father. I have been unable to resist the opportunities I have had to lead young men astray.'

'Indeed? And how many of these poor unfortunates have you debauched, daughter?'

'Three, Father. All of them innocent virgins.'

'Shame on you! But you shall not be absolved until you have told me in detail how you abused these wretched young men. Describe your first act of indecency.'

'It was with a curate, Father . . .'

'A man of the cloth! Double shame upon you, wicked woman! But . . . tell me more.'

Emma found herself growing hot below as she recalled her first encounter with Robert. 'As soon as I saw him I knew that I could not resist his charms. I asked him to walk with me and we talked lasciviously until he was fully roused. Then I made him give me a kiss. He resisted me at first, but when I visited him at the vicarage he was too enamoured of me to spurn my advances.'

'You seduced a man of the cloth in his own vicarage? Why next you will be telling me that you defiled him at the altar!'

'Not quite.' She smiled to herself, squeezing her hand between her restless thighs. 'Only in the vestry.'

'The *vestry*!'

'Yes, Father. It was there that I showed him how a woman might pleasure a man without fear of consequence. I thought it might be useful to him if he did not wish to father too many children.'

'Dear God, have I not heard enough? You encouraged him to go against our Lord's decree to "go forth and multiply"?'

'I showed him how he might spill his seed into a woman's mouth, Father, instead of into her woman's place. It is a practice that many men enjoy and which I do not believe to be sinful.'

The voice of the anonymous priest was hoarse. He was breathing faster, and there was an underlying eagerness that he could scarcely disguise. 'I think your confessor is the best judge of that. But pray continue. It is good for one's soul to contemplate the full extent of one's sin.'

'I discovered that this man of God was so ignorant of the ways of the flesh that he needed educating further. My own cousin was betrothed to him, so I felt he should know how to behave on his wedding night. I taught him to pleasure and satisfy a woman to the fullest extent, and I satisfied myself that I had helped to make his life, and that of my cousin, a good deal happier.'

'You believe happiness lies in debauchery, Signora? Shame on you! True happiness lies in leading a chaste and holy life.'

'I am sure that is true of a holy man like yourself, Father. But if you have carnal desires I believe it is better to indulge them than to become frustrated, so long as you hurt no one.'

'Saint Paul said, "Better to marry than to burn". But *nota bene*, Signora, he did not advocate promiscuity!'

'I agree that happiness may be obtained within marriage, but that is not possible for everyone. My second lover was a student with many years of hard work ahead. As a lusty young man, with natural desires, he could hardly be expected to live a continent life. The introduction I gave him to the joys of the flesh certainly helped to further his education.'

'And where did this "education" take place, Signora?' The priest's tone was guttural, and Emma could hear his robes shuffling. Was he as titillated by her 'confession' as she was? She was pressing hard against her vulva with her fingers now, rubbing the hard nub of her clitoris which she could feel even beneath her petticoats.

'In my hotel room, in Paris. And in another establishment in that same city.'

'I presume you refer to some house of ill repute?'

'In a manner of speaking. Although I think he was duly chastised for his sins . . .'

'Chastised?' He sounded eager, as if she had strayed into familiar territory. 'With the whip, perhaps? Or did you employ some other ingenious device?'

'Yes Father, he was strapped to a *chevalet*. But his torments were sweet, I can assure you.'

'As, perhaps, are the torments of hell. I have often wondered whether guilty seducers rejoice when their flesh is scourged by demons, their bodies lashed with whips. Could it be that those who languish in the eighth circle of hell are also in seventh heaven? But I digress. Do continue, Signora. You said you had three violations of youthful innocence to confess.'

Beneath her clothes Emma could feel her heart thudding wildly as she squeezed with her thighs and rubbed with her fingers, bringing herself ever closer to her consummation. She pictured the shy face of Alphonse then his long, eager penis and her arousal increased.

'Ah, yes!' she gasped, more fervently than she had intended. 'The third of my encounters was, I believe, truly an act of salvation.'

'Salvation? You dare to refer to the rape of a young man's virtue as his *salvation*?'

Emma stopped the friction for a moment. It was becoming impossible to speak normally. 'Yes, Father, compared to what he had known before. You see, this particular youth had been repeatedly sodomised by his employer and had never known the tender embrace of a woman. I gave him hope, Father, and a new life.'

'Hm. Perhaps your intentions were generous, but you are still guilty of fornication and must convince me you are sincerely repentant. Do you vow never to seduce a young man again?'

Emma hesitated. Maybe she would let the next 'young man' seduce her, instead! 'Yes, Father.'

'Then you must perform this penance. Tonight, on the stroke of midnight, you will come to this church and prostrate yourself in the cloister. Leave off your finery, Signora. A simple shift befits a penitent. There you will prostrate yourself and say six "Hail Mary's" allowing nothing and no one to distract you from the act of contrition. After you have completed it, you may return to your bed with a light heart.'

Emma felt that same heart race at the thought of putting herself in such jeopardy, yet she was excited too. There was a strange, conspiratorial atmosphere in the confessional booth that intrigued and aroused her. It was as if she were making a lovers' tryst with this man of God. While the priest intoned his last blessings she pressed her forefinger hard against her pulsating little button and jiggled it furiously until she felt the hot spasms come fast and furious, giving her relief at last.

When she stepped out, somewhat giddily, into the spacious nave, Emma craved fresh air. She found Kitty and they left the sombre building at once, blinking as they emerged into the brilliant afternoon.

'I know what would be perfectly wonderful right now,' Emma declared. 'An ice-cream!'

They were enjoying a delicious combination of coffee and fig flavours in a nearby café when an English voice suddenly called, 'Mrs Longmore! What an extraordinary coincidence! It seems we meet again.'

Emma looked round. She gripped the edge of the table as a heady draught of something very like euphoria swept through her. 'Oh, Mr Forbes! What on earth are you doing here in Florence?' She had spoken in a series of gasps but she forced a smile and added, nonchalantly, 'Don't tell me you have been following us all the way from Nice!'

He gave a hearty laugh. 'Certainly not! I have been on business in Rome. But it seems we are fated to follow in each others' footsteps. Do you mind if I join you?'

It would have been impolite to refuse. Emma told herself that as soon as they finished their ice-cream they would make their excuses and leave. But she felt strangely excited by the Englishman's sudden appearance. He was almost like a friend, and yet she had the peculiar feeling that he was in some way her enemy. The confusion acted like opium on her mind, making her feel fuzzy-headed and distanced.

They began to chat politely. Fortunately Daniel made no indecent reference to his gift of underwear and since their conversation was entirely about travel Emma began to relax. He seemed to know Florence very well, and offered to show her the sights.

'I am leaving in three days' time,' she told him. 'But until then I hope to see as many of the art treasures as possible.'

'Have you visited Santa Croce yet?' he asked.

His darkly enquiring eyes were piercing hers in a way Emma found most disconcerting but she gave a brave smile. 'Yes, just a short while ago. Magnificent tombs.'

'Indeed. I am not religious, yet whenever I enter that

129

church I fall into a penitent mood.' Emma looked at him sharply, wondering if he could possibly have seen her enter the confessional, but his face was impassive. 'All those famous men, the magnificent achievements of Dante and Michelangelo . . . they make one regret one's lost time, lost opportunities.'

'Well, I intend to lose neither time nor opportunity here, Mr Forbes,' Emma smiled, rising briskly. 'Come, Kitty. We have to see the Duomo and the Baptistery this afternoon.'

Daniel met her eye with a hint of urgency in his. 'Perhaps we might dine together tonight, Mrs Longmore? I should like to hear your impressions of this beautiful city and perhaps suggest another itinerary for tomorrow.'

'That is most kind of you,' Emma began, unsure whether to accept his invitation or not. Perhaps to dine with him would do no harm. She might even overcome her initial reservations and find him pleasant company. 'If you call at the Hotel Mantana around eight o'clock I shall be ready.'

'Oh, Miss Emma!' Kitty whispered, as soon as they had walked away. 'So you do like that gentleman, after all.'

'I'm not sure Kitty, but I am prepared to give him the benefit of the doubt. If I have any misgivings about his manner or behaviour tonight, however, I shall shun him forever more, you may be sure of that.'

After their sightseeing the two women returned to the hotel for a brief siesta. Kitty had ordered hot water to be sent up and as she sponged her mistress with scented lather, Emma related what had happened in the 'confessional' and described the strange penance.

'But you'll not go to the church so late, and all alone, will you Miss Emma?'

'It may be that Mr Forbes will accompany me to Santa Croce.'

'But surely you cannot take that instruction seriously?

I had never thought of you as a religious person before, Miss Emma. Not to take it that far, at any rate.'

She was right, of course. Emma had no time for the tedious rituals and hypocritical doctrines of the church. Yet there was something about that priest's voice which had been extraordinarily persuasive. He had made the idea sound like an adventure, a rather naughty one at that. A midnight tryst, perhaps? Emma's loins shuddered a little at the thought. Had that faceless priest hoped to make an assignation with her? The more she thought about it, the more likely it seemed. He had been aroused by her confession, perhaps had even felt the waves of sexual heat that had emanated from her stirring loins. It was not impossible that he had longed to be seduced by her, just like those 'innocent youths', and this was the way he had chosen. Well, she might just go along with his fantasy!

'Fetch me clean underwear please, Kitty,' she said, changing the subject.

Kitty opened one of the smaller cases and gave a gasp of surprise. 'Oh, Miss Emma! I thought we had left this behind in Nice!'

She held up the 'combination' garment that Daniel had given her. Emma frowned, sure that she had given her maid orders not to pack it. 'Did you put it in by mistake, Kitty?'

'Oh no, Ma'am. I left it neatly folded on the wash stand, still in its parcel as you told me.'

Emma did not doubt the girl. The garment must have been transferred to their luggage by a well-meaning chambermaid, since her name had been on the parcel. She was not altogether sorry. Perhaps it had been from a sense of false propriety that she had attempted to leave it behind her. Well she would wear it that evening, and to hell with the consequences!

It gave Emma a secret thrill to be wearing only flimsy silk beneath her rose pink gown and midnight blue cloak. She had behaved ungenerously before, she decided. There was no harm in acknowledging that the

131

undergarment was a charming innovation and that she welcomed the increased freedom it afforded. When Daniel Forbes arrived with a carriage, she decided to tell him that she was wearing his gift. The prospect gave her unexpected pleasure.

He certainly cut a dashing figure himself that evening as he offered her his arm. The thought crossed Emma's mind that they made a handsome pair. Not since her marriage had she ventured forth in public on the arm of such an apparently eligible beau, and yet her feelings for this strange man were mixed. She was attracted to him, she had no doubt of that, yet there was something she saw in the mysterious depths of his eyes that profoundly disturbed her.

'We shall go to Florio's, Mrs Longmore,' he announced as he helped her into the carriage.

'Oh, please, do call me Emma!' she insisted, unwilling to be reminded of her former marital status.

'I shall be delighted,' he smiled and, bringing her gloved hand up to his mouth he pressed his lips to it.

In the cosy intimacy of the enclosed carriage, Emma felt bold enough to mention his gift.

'I found the garment most comfortable,' she told him, 'and I am sure that it will prove a great success.'

Daniel gave her a relaxed smile and she felt her heart unexpectedly lighten. 'It is very kind of you to say so, Emma. You see, I have my own philosophy of underwear, particularly where it concerns the fairer sex. I believe that we have held our women in shackles for too long. It was not always so. Consider the loose gowns of the Empire period, or even the charming styles of Renaissance Florence which you may see depicted in the paintings of Botticelli and others. They flow with a graceful line, revealing the natural shape beneath rather than distorting it into a parody of the feminine form.'

'I had no idea that any man thought so deeply upon the subject, Mr Forbes.'

'Daniel, please. Well, I confess to being a lover of

female beauty and I hate to see it despoiled. In my opinion there is nothing so wonderful as a woman's body totally without adornment of any kind.'

Emma felt her cheeks flush at his outspoken words. Suddenly the cab seemed very small, and he was very close. Her chest was burning and her heart was beating rapidly. She almost swooned at his proximity, and fumbled at the bow beneath her chin to loosen her cape.

'Too hot, Emma? Here, let me.' His large hand closed over hers, firmly pulling at the ribbon until her neck was laid bare. 'Since there is no Kitty to hand with the salts, you must rely on me if you feel faint. Excuse me, I shall roll up the blind a little.'

'Thank you.'

Emma sat looking out for a while, letting the cool night air fan her cheeks while he watched her solicitously. At last they arrived at the restaurant and, in the midst of company, Emma felt safe again. They talked of what Emma had seen in Florence, of the cultural differences between the French, the English and the Italians, and before long her reservations about Daniel Forbes began to disappear. When he grew animated his features lost their severe cast and his expression became handsomely amiable. He was an entertaining conversationalist and a man of the world, recommending dishes and choosing wines with impressive confidence. He made her laugh several times with stories of his exploits in foreign lands, and also touched her heart once or twice when he spoke of his struggle to make a success of the family firm after his father died almost bankrupt.

Time passed quickly, and Emma felt so relaxed that she almost forgot about her midnight tryst. They left the restaurant at eleven and Daniel suggested a stroll down the fashionable Via de Calzauoli, where the sellers of leather goods had their shops. They passed into the square of the Signoria, where they stopped for a night-cap, but just as Emma was finishing her camomile tea the great bell of the town hall began tolling midnight, and she leapt up in alarm.

'Goodness, is that the time? I must be going! Please, Daniel, hail me a cab I beg of you.'

He gave an infuriatingly lazy grin. 'Why such haste, Emma? In a few moments I shall accompany you to your hotel. On such a fine night a walk would be pleasant . . .'

'No, no! I . . . I prefer to go alone. There are some cabs in the corner of the square. Please don't trouble yourself, Daniel, finish your drink. I have some Italian, and will instruct the cabman myself.'

'I would not hear of it,' he insisted, downing his *grappa*. 'Come, take my arm. If you insist on taking a cab, at least let me hire one for you in a dignified manner.'

Emma's heart was thudding mercilessly in her chest as she hastened across the cobbled square. She did not wish to seem ungrateful, but she had to part from Daniel now if she was to keep her appointment in the cloisters. Climbing into the cab she held out her hand saying with firm emphasis, 'Goodnight, Daniel, and thank you for a delightful evening.'

'Are you sure you wish to return alone?'

'Quite sure.'

'Then may I call for you tomorrow morning at your hotel, so that we may follow that itinerary I mentioned?'

'Certainly,' Emma smiled, relieved that he was not going to delay her further. 'But now I really must be off. Forward, driver!'

'Where to, Signora?' the man asked, but she pretended not to hear him until he repeated himself at the edge of the square. She directed him down one of the alleyways which she knew led towards Santa Croce and at last they came out into the piazza in front of the church.

'This will do!' she called. 'Please wait here, driver, until I have finished my business.'

Slipping from the cab, Emma hurried up to the door

at the right of the great façade. Finding it open, she quickly entered the silent quadrangle with its green lawns and cloisters.

In the privacy of the covered walk Emma took off her gown and laid it down on the cold stone so that she could rest upon it. Penance was one thing, but she had no intention of catching pneumonia and ruining her travels. The air felt deliciously cool on her bare legs and the soft material of her dress caressed her silk-covered breasts. Racking her brain to remember the '*Ave Maria*' that she had learnt from her Roman Catholic governess, who had sought to indoctrinate her under the guise of 'classical education', she began to repeat the Latin phrases.

'*Ave Maria, gratia plena . . .*

What was that? Emma was sure she had heard a sound, like a latch opening. She continued to recite, but with her ears pricked. '*Dominus tecum: Benedicta tu . . .*'

Yes, it was plain to hear now. Footsteps on the stone flags, as clear as anything. '*. . . in mulieribus, et benedictus . . .*'

He was right behind her now, viewing her prostrate body. Emma held her breath. But the priest had warned her she must continue in her recitation no matter what. '*Fructris ventris tui . . . Jesus!*'

The last word flew from her mouth as an expletive. Warm hands had begun stroking her buttocks through the fragile silk, pinching the fleshy mounds and then passing down over her thighs with soft caresses. Emma felt her nether parts soften and moisten at the insidious assault upon her senses.

'*Ave Maria . . .*' Emma began again, convinced now that it was the priest who was taking advantage of her penitential position to impose some further mortification upon her flesh. She could hear his heavy breathing, feel his fingers probe into the opening in her drawers, finding her labia already shamelessly swollen and the hard centre of her desire fully aroused.

'Gratia plena . . .' she gasped, as one thick digit found its way right in through her entrance and dabbled around in her juices.

'Dominus tecum!' came the harsh voice in her ear as she felt thicker flesh take the place of his finger. With a groan she moved her pelvis to allow him to penetrate her, clasping the substantial member with her inner walls as it slid further and further into her. This was congress without any of the tender preparation she was used to, a sudden thrusting into her innermost being that should have left her feeling violated. Yet Emma found she was thrilling to the unequivocal directness of the man's approach. Something in her answered to his need, the basic hunger of a man driven to the edge by lust, and her own body was mirroring that hunger, wanting him as much as he wanted her, needing the rapid rise towards gratification that only the most urgent of longings could provoke.

Then there was the delicious sense of wickedness. While she uttered the holy words in half articulate gasps, the man of God was engaged in what he regarded as a most unholy act, damning himself as well as her. Emma had never known a man deflower himself with such desperation, such uncompromising passion. She felt she had little part in it, she was simply the instrument of his self-abuse, and yet they met as naked souls, each swept along by the same tempest like leaves in the wind.

His shudders ripped through her with a force she'd never known before, triggering her own intense climax and subjecting her body to wave after wave of fierce convulsions. Dimly she felt him slip out of her, felt the cool air fan her parted lips, knew that he was retreating back into the darkness, creeping back into his night of shame like a nocturnal creature fearful of the light of day.

For several minutes Emma lay, utterly spent. The fatuous pretence at penitence was over. The 'sins' for which she was supposedly atoning had been cancelled out by that rogue priest's actions. He had condemned her for stealing young men's innocence, but now he had used her in the same way. Except that this time she had not been in control. This time she had been taken, summarily, as a horse takes a mare, and it disturbed her greatly to find that she had enjoyed it.

Chapter Nine

*E*mma returned to the hotel in a state of semi-shock. She paid the cab driver in a dream and entered the quiet foyer, ignoring the curious glances of the night porter as she took the key to her room. Only when she was alone could she examine her feelings. After lighting the lamp she took off her dress and, still wearing the combination shift, stared at herself in the mirror for almost a minute, examining her features for signs of the inner transformation that she had undergone.

Something irrevocable had happened to her that night, and it both elated and frightened her. Emma thought about how her marriage had been, a period of initiation by Henry and then a kind of equality where each felt at liberty to follow his or her whims and desires, confident that the other partner would share in the game. She thought about the seductions she had performed since, enjoying the sense of power over her willing victims, revelling in their newly-discovered pleasures almost as much as she had in her own. Yet what all her previous *amours* had had in common was a sense of play, a light-hearted exploration of erotic stimuli and a joyful gratification of the senses.

What had happened to Emma in the cloister of Santa Croce was of a different order. She could not call it rape, for she had been ready and willing for the priest's carnal knowledge of her. When his finger had first insinuated itself into her private place she had felt a welcoming surge of desire, a longing for the act that was to follow. His sudden dive into her had been a kind of victory, for her as well as for him, and she had wanted it whole-heartedly. But then everything had changed. Suddenly she was no longer only the seductress but also the seduced: Eve the serpent's dupe, as well as Adam's temptress.

The stark reality of the man's need had mocked her feeble repetition of the sacred words, rendering them null and void. At the same time Emma had been overcome by a different sense of holiness, a bending of their petty human wills to the greater law of Nature, which all must obey. What could a virgin goddess tell her about the glory of a man and a woman discovering each other, body and soul, for the first time? Nothing! And perhaps, in the pure fire of their conjunction, that wayward priest had felt the same.

Anyway, she would never know how he felt, never know what became of him, and that was how it should be. They had met as archetypes, not as individuals, and whatever each had taken from the encounter was theirs alone. Sighing, Emma removed her undergarment, pulled on her nightdress and got into bed.

Next morning, when Kitty asked about her mistress's midnight assignation Emma shrugged it off. 'Oh, I said my six "Hail Marys" and that was all,' she lied.

Promptly at ten Daniel Forbes arrived at the hotel, ready for their tour. Emma was pleased to see him, for she was looking forward to their visit to San Marco and the exquisite frescoes of Fra Angelico. He offered her his hand when they met in the foyer, and Emma was struck by the particularly keen look he gave her. Had he been wondering what opinion she had been forming of him? Well, today at least she was relieved to be with a fellow Englishman with whom she could discuss art

139

and history. It would take her mind off the disturbing events of the previous night.

Emma was charmed by the old monastery with its rows of tiny cells, each containing a faded fresco. She could imagine the devout monks kneeling before each portrait of a saint or biblical scene, lost in contemplation. Many of the paintings struck her as crude, however. Only those attributed to the master, Fra Angelico, had the power to move her. She loved the simple pure lines of his Annunciation scenes, the figure of the androgynous angel distinguished from that of Mary only by the beautiful rainbow-coloured wings.

When she viewed the artist's painting of the 'Last Judgement' at first all appeared to be light and joy, with a triumphant Christ enthroned and a circle of dancing angels. Then Emma looked at the right-hand section and found the mood totally altered. It showed the damned in hell, each section providing new torments for its hapless victims.

Emma looked more closely, in morbid fascination. Evil-looking demons were torturing their charges in various ways: boiling them in a giant pot, feeding them to ravenous beasts, tearing them limb from limb, even – or so it seemed to Emma – forcing them to drink urine and eat excrement. She shuddered as the full horrors of the scene became clear to her.

Daniel was right behind her, his breath warm on her neck, his voice strangely excited as he murmured, 'I have often wondered whether the guilty rejoice when their flesh is scourged by demons, their bodies lashed with whips.'

Emma turned in alarm. What was he saying? His words frightened her, but his smile was reassuring as he explained, 'I only mean to suggest that, if they feel guilt and remorse, they should be glad that they are being punished for their sins. And if they are glad, how can their torments be a punishment? I am no theologian, Emma, but the curious lengths to which devout Christians will go to justify their doctrines never fails to amuse me. Sometimes I like to beat them at their own game.'

For a moment Emma was reminded of her own delight in engaging Robert Earnshaw in theological debate, and was tempted to respond to Daniel's ingenious sophistry. But then she reflected that it was no fun unless the other party truly believed in what he was saying. If Daniel were merely acting as 'Devil's advocate' there would be no sport in it.

'Look closer at the faces of the damned,' Daniel urged her, as she vacillated. 'Do they really look like souls in torment?'

When Emma surveyed the painted faces she noticed surprising evidence to support his theory. None of their expressions was particularly anguished. Indeed, quite a few were definitely smiling while they were being tormented by demons, as if it were all a huge joke.

'One might attribute it to Fra Angelico's lack of skill in depicting facial expression,' Daniel continued. 'But an alternative view might be that, as a Dominican monk familiar with the practice of self-flagellation, he recognised that some people find pleasure in pain.'

'You really think so?' Emma frowned, looking closely at the painting again.

'Just a thought, Emma. As you get to know me better you will realise that I love to speculate and the wilder, the more outrageous the theory, the better.'

'Then you are an extraordinarily perverse man,' she told him, with mock disapproval.

'Sometimes perversity is just a willingness to tolerate the socially unacceptable. What, for instance, is "normal" behaviour? Little more than the suppression of one's natural instincts for the greater good of society.'

'Is there any harm in that?'

'Perhaps not – if it works. Take the sex instinct, for example. If it were possible to repress it entirely in a man would there be any need for prostitution? I think not. Or take the consumption of alcoholic beverages. In America the Anti-Saloon league is so powerful that I believe they may eventually succeed in prohibiting the manufacture and sale of alcohol altogether. But what would be the result? Take my word for it, the stuff will be produced illegally, and there will be a great traffic in it. There are certain habits and instincts in the human species that can never be totally eradicated.'

'You seem to have firm opinions on a great many subjects,' Emma smiled.

'That is because I engage with life. I do not accept received wisdom, I dare to ask questions. I examine my own motives and impulses and assume, from my observations, that others experience similar feelings. I am interested not only in the smiling face of Time, Emma, but in the hidden clockwork.'

While he spoke Daniel was regarding Emma solemnly, giving her the impression that he was divulging his creed. She began to realise that there was a great deal more to Daniel Forbes than met the eye. 'Then you must find life a good deal more interesting than the average man,' she commented, wryly.

'More interesting? Yes, indeed. But also more frustrating, since it's hard to find others who share my interests. Still, I am more or less resigned to being a lone seeker after truth.'

The title certainly suited him, Emma reflected as they moved out of the dark monastic buildings and into the sunny square. She had seldom met a man who seemed more self-contained, more sure of himself. Yet there was a pall of loneliness about him which she found half attractive and half repellant. Any woman who formed a liaison with Daniel Forbes would have a hard task ahead if she wished to come to some understanding of him.

They strolled down to the Arno and spent some time on the Ponte Vecchio, admiring the jewellers' shops, then Emma said she would like to return to the hotel for a siesta. At the door of the Hotel Mantana, Daniel paused. 'Will you do me the honour of joining me for dinner again this evening, Emma?'

She hesitated. Was she seeing too much of this man?

But since she was leaving Florence soon Emma thought she might as well make the most of congenial company while she had the chance. On the arduous journey through Northern Italy and Switzerland there would only be her maid for companionship, and Daniel Forbes was certainly proving a most interesting and knowledgeable escort.

'I should be delighted, thank you,' she smiled.

'And perhaps, after we've dined, you would accompany me on a visit to a part of Florence that tourists seldom see,' he went on, arching his thick eyebrows with an enigmatic smile.

'Really? How intriguing. And where might that be?'

'Not far from Florio's, where we shall dine,' he replied airily. 'I shall call for you at eight. Until then, *dorma bene!*'

But Emma was far too excited to sleep. After chatting for a while to Kitty, who had amused herself that morning by crossing the bridge over the Arno and watching an old lady feed dozens of feral cats, she lay down on the bed in her shift and fell to speculating about the mysterious Mr Forbes. He seemed remarkably erudite for a man of commerce. It seemed he was a free thinker, too, and therefore someone that Henry would have been pleased to meet. Emma gave a long sigh. For the first time since leaving England she began to long for what she had left behind, for the easy familiarity of her marriage and the sense of a shared destiny that had been shattered in a few short weeks. Once her excursion to Europe was over, she might well begin searching for someone with whom to share her life.

But until then there were more adventures ahead, she was convinced of it.

Emma and Kitty took a stroll in the late afternoon in the magnificent Boboli gardens, admiring the grottoes and statues, lake and fountains. After a while the girl tried once more to draw her mistress on the subject of her English acquaintance.

'He is a fine figure of a man, and seems most

143

gentlemanly,' she observed, when Emma mentioned his dinner invitation. 'I expect you shall miss him when we have to go.'

Emma tried to sound nonchalant. 'It is true that he has been a most interesting guide, and our chance meeting here was perhaps fortunate. Yet I do not believe our acquaintance will be furthered once we leave Florence, Kitty. People who travel often strike up quite intense relationships of a transient nature that are all but forgotten once they return home.'

'If it were me, Ma'am, I should at least find out where he lived in England.'

'That is enough, Kitty! My interest in Mr Forbes extends only to his considerable knowledge of Florentine art, history and related matters.'

'Such as . . . ladies' underwear, for instance?'

'You go too far, Kitty. I have warned you against such talk in public. A lady must guard her reputation at all times, and her maid must be just as vigilant in upholding the proprieties.'

Although Emma felt somewhat hypocritical, she knew she must curb the girl's youthful propensity to overstep the mark. She must learn that in private they could talk more freely, but in public they must act with decorum at all times. No matter how many young lovers Emma took to her bed she would always insist that they treated her with respect. For that was perhaps the essential difference between a high-class courtesan and a low-class whore.

That evening Kitty spent a long time over Emma's toilet, sweeping her hair up into a more becoming style and dressing her in the purple taffeta robe and diamond earrings that Henry used to say presented her at her most 'majestic'. The answering light in Daniel's eyes when she first saw him in the foyer convinced her that it had been worth the trouble. His gaze dipped to her bosom and she wondered with some amusement whether he was assessing the nature of her underwear. Tonight she was wearing a full corset that pushed up her breasts and cinched in her waist. It was worth some discomfort in order for her figure to do full justice to the elegant gown.

'You look like a princess, no – an empress!' Daniel declared, giving a slight bow and kissing her lilac-gloved hand. 'The young Victoria to the life, I do declare!'

Emma laughed. 'Then you shall be my Albert for this evening, my princely consort.'

Daniel offered her his arm. 'I am honoured, Ma'am!'

At Florio's the waiter remembered them from the night before and gave them the same table. This time Daniel ordered champagne, and soon Emma felt quite light-headed. The conversation turned to the subject of English society, but Emma became increasingly embarrassed as the talk became more personal.

'As a widow, my dear Emma, you must have often found yourself in tedious social situations,' Daniel commented. 'In my experience a woman who has lost her husband invariably finds herself paired off at gatherings with some crusty old bachelor or beardless youth.'

'Well yes, I suppose you are right,' Emma replied, uneasily.

'I believe you deserve better. A lovely young widow needs more entertaining company. Yet an eligible young man is believed to be interested only in virgins, while husbands are supposed to be interested only in their wives. Do you not find the situation tedious, Emma?'

'I confess I have not attended many social occasions since . . . since my marriage ended.'

'Really? That is more tragic still. Have you never considered re-marriage? Pardon me if my question seems indelicate. It is kindly meant.'

'For the moment I am content as I am,' Emma answered, primly.

He did not pursue it, but from the sceptical look on his face Emma deduced that he had not been deceived by her replies. She knew he had seen her in the

145

company of the first of her young lovers, and possibly the second also. Had his quizzing of her been a kind of mockery, or a test of her nerve? Well, she had come through it without mishap.

She decided to turn the tables on him. 'And what of yourself, Mr Forbes – are you married?'

'Good heavens no!' he sounded quite shocked. 'I thought you had surmised as much from what I said to you before. Marriage, Emma, is for those who wish to toe the line, who desire a safe and predictable life, free from the challenges and stimulations on which I thrive.'

'But have you never wanted to produce offspring?'

'Never! The thought of another little Daniel Forbes being brought, kicking and screaming, into this world attracts me not at all. No, I am afraid that being a "confirmed bachelor" is my calling.' His dark eyes began to twinkle. 'Of course, that does not necessarily imply a life of monk-like sobriety and celibacy.'

Emma felt daring. Was it the champagne that made her bold? She looked at him over the top of her glass and murmured, 'You might say the same of certain "widows". They say even our dear Queen has a constant companion in the form of her gillie, John Brown.'

Daniel smiled wickedly. 'What are you implying, Mrs Longmore?'

'Only that a woman who has become used to close male companionship through marriage often finds it hard to relinquish, Mr Forbes.'

He smiled, inclined his head and remained silent. To Emma, he had the air of a barrister who has just proved his point in court.

Emma enjoyed her meal but, once it was ended, her curiosity grew about where Daniel might be taking her. He resisted all questions, merely responding with an enigmatic smile and a 'wait and see, my dear'. Outside the restaurant he offered her his arm and they began to walk down the Via de Pucci. Suddenly he stopped outside an imposing building with a stone coat of arms over the door. He pulled at a bell rope and a face looked out from behind a window grille. At once the ancient door creaked open and Emma was ushered inside.

'Signor Forbes, how nice to see you!' gushed the porter. 'I heard you were in Florence again. Mimi will be delighted.'

Ignoring Emma's raised brows, Daniel led her across an open courtyard where a fountain played and in through a door opposite. It took her eyes a while to get used to the gloom, but eventually she realised that she was in a large room full of tables with a black curtain at one end. It was lit only by torches, held in sconces on the walls. Soft music was playing and the place was full of people, but the atmosphere was hushed and expectant as if they were awaiting the start of some entertainment. A waiter led the pair to a table on which two glasses and an ice-bucket containing champagne were already standing.

'Thank you, Giovanni,' Daniel whispered to the ageing waiter, slipping him a coin as they took their seats.

'Where are we?' Emma whispered, rather nervously, looking around at the eerily lit faces.

'In the Jockey Club,' he replied, tersely.

Emma was mystified. The place did not have the air of a sporting club. As he poured the champagne she edged closer, wanting to know more. 'Are you a member?'

'An honorary member, yes. Now no more questions, Emma. You will find out soon enough what goes on here. Meanwhile, your very good health my dear!'

After another couple of glasses Emma found she was viewing everything with a hazy perspective, but even if she had been sober the people round about would have appeared strangely attired for an evening indoors. Many of the women were dressed in riding habits, carried crops or wore studded collars. Some of the men had spurs on their boots and one eccentric fellow was wearing blinkers.

The woman called 'Mimi' loomed up and kissed

Daniel rather too familiarly on the mouth, smiling cattily at Emma when she was introduced. She wore the most extraordinary clothing – or rather, underclothing. A tight black satin corset was laced just below her breasts, which spilt over the cups openly displaying their nipples. She wore elbow-length gloves to match, and around her waist was an elaborate leather harness. Her pelvic region was entirely naked but her stockings were held up with silk garters and she wore knee-high boots of shiny leather, all in black. From her forehead rose a sable plume, similar to those that adorned funeral horses.

'When you perform tonight, will you think of me?' Daniel asked her, in a low insinuating tone that sent shivers down Emma's spine.

'Of course, *caro*! I often think of you, whether you are present or not. You know that!'

The strange woman kissed him once again and was gone. Seconds later a fanfare was played and everyone sat up, craning their necks to see what was happening as the curtain swung back to reveal a small stage. Emma had a good view and saw that two couples were coming on in an extraordinary fashion, one woman holding a man by the ankles and making him walk on his hands, while another man did the same to the other woman. All four were in a state of undress, but when the two 'human wheelbarrows' were lowered to the ground Emma saw that they were saddled and bridled like horses, ready for their partners to ride upon their backs.

'How diverting!' she murmured, feeling the strangest thrill of anticipation.

Each 'rider' made a show of mounting their 'steed', amidst much cheering encouragement from the crowd. Emma glanced at Daniel. He was leaning back in his chair sipping his champagne with an amused expression in which there was a tinge of boredom, indicating that he'd seen it all before. She looked back at the stage. Much to her surprise she saw that the female rider had lowered her quim over the pommel of the saddle and was now jerking back and forth with enthusiasm. The male rider, however, had a large erection which he nurtured with one hand while he wielded the reins with the other. Their mounts were now bucking and rocking with gusto, the breasts of the 'filly' wobbling as they dangled while the 'stallion's' penis was visibly stiffening with the excitement. Through it all members of the audience were shouting, '*Va! Va! Fa presto, presto!*' as if they were at a real horse race.

Emma was reminded of the club she had visited with Lily. She had the same odd feelings of being aroused against her will and perversely enjoying the experience. Down below she was already wet and could scarcely resist pressing her open labia hard against the tickling plush of her seat. Surreptitiously she wriggled around, getting herself into the best position for stimulating her clitoris and all the while feeling deliciously guilty, just as when she had been taken clandestinely from behind by the priest.

The riders on stage were using their crops on the bare buttocks of their steeds now, making them revolve so their blushing cheeks could be observed. Emma found she was almost riding on her chair like a saddle, mimicking the rhythmic actions of the performers. And she was sure that Daniel must have noticed too, for his lips had curved into a secretive smile, but she was beyond caring. It was impossible to sit there detachedly and view the frantic proceedings on stage without becoming stimulated herself.

Suddenly the male rider gave a loud groan and Emma saw his seed shoot from his organ onto the back of the woman he was riding, who gave a series of moans herself and shuddered violently. The other couple were behaving in a similar manner, with the female rider dropping the reins in order to rub her ample breasts and pull at her large brown nipples, giving her the extra stimulation she needed as the rise to a climax began in earnest. She was soon thrashing around in the throes of her pleasure while the male beneath her swiftly brought himself off with a series of rapid strokes.

Tumultuous applause followed, during which Emma was conscious of Daniel's eyes upon her. Although she had not come herself, she knew that her cheeks must be flushed and it was hard to look him in the eye. Eventually he leaned across the table and said, casually, 'Did you enjoy that, Emma?'

She didn't want to admit that she had, yet she had no idea what else to say. 'It was very . . . peculiar,' she managed at last.

'I suppose so, if you have seen nothing like that before. Those of us who are well acquainted with these hidden byways sometimes forget that to other eyes such displays are shockingly strange. Forgive me if I have exposed you to unpleasantness, Emma. I had hoped you would regard the activities in this club as little more than a freak show, but if you are offended . . .'

'Offended? Oh no!' Emma realised she did not want to be thought a prude, least of all by Daniel. Neither did she wish to be regarded as naively inexperienced in such matters. 'As a matter of fact I visited a similar establishment in Paris, where many of the men were dressed as women and vice-versa.'

'Really? Not the Hermaphrodite Club, by any chance?'

'Yes, I believe that is what it was called.'

'Then it is mere chance that we did not attend on the same evening, for I am a member there too.'

His dark eyes were glistening at her, observing every small nuance of her expression, and Emma felt dangerously exposed. On the one hand she did not want him to regard her as a debauched woman but, on the other, she wanted to appear reasonably sophisticated in these matters.

'You seem to frequent such places often. Are you a student of the Underworld?' she asked him, with a quizzical smile.

'You could say that.'

She wanted to tell him that she also had a fascination for such things, initiated by reading Henry's books. She debated with herself for a few seconds: it would probably be unwise to reveal too much to a man she knew little about. Yet tomorrow she would be leaving Florence and it was unlikely they would ever meet again. For some reason she felt impelled to confide in Daniel, to reveal the secrets of her past to a man who would not be shocked to hear them. It would be a kind of relief to talk openly of such matters and perhaps to learn from him. Emma was about to take the conversation further when her attention was diverted. Another fanfare sounded and all eyes swung towards the stage. Mimi came forth, dressed in the same lewd costume as before and wielding a long whip. She held up her hand for silence and then addressed them in a strong, commanding voice.

'Signore e Signori, Mesdames et Messieurs, Ladies and Gentlemen! Tonight we present an exciting spectacle for your eyes only! Single-handed, and armed only with this . . .' she gave a loud crack of her whip, 'I shall attempt to break in a wild young stallion who has never before worn a saddle or bridle.'

A cheer arose, and Daniel threw Emma a wide smile. She felt the warm urge rise once more between her loins, and hoped he did not suspect her of profligacy. Yet a part of her also wanted him to know that she was a sensual woman, wanted him to share in her secret excitement. Why was it that he filled her with such contradictory feelings?

A naked man with long, wild hair and staring eyes leapt onto the stage and crouched at the front, surveying the audience and pretending to neigh, his long penis dangling between his thighs. Emma felt her excitement grow as Mimi cracked the whip and advanced upon him with confident strides. The man saw her out of the corner of his eye and leapt up with a whinny, galloping around the stage while she followed on, letting the tip of the lash fall upon his buttocks from time to time.

Mimi's other hand held a coiled rope and eventually she managed to throw the lasso over the man's head and bring him to the ground. He kicked and struggled, but she forced a bit between his teeth and lashed him until he stayed still at her command, with just one hand pawing at the ground.

Applause rang out, but she held up her hand. 'Please, not yet! We have cowed our magnificent stallion, but we have not mastered him.'

Mimi got him onto all fours and tried to put a saddle on his back but he bucked and twisted until it fell off. By now Emma could see that the man's prick was erect and a fine thick one it was, with two fat bollocks swinging below. Emma gave an involuntary sigh. The sight of his naked lust was evoking an echoing response in her pussy, and she rearranged her skirts so that her naked pudendum could rub against the plush once more undetected.

'A fine specimen!' Daniel murmured, with a smile in her direction. 'Does he meet with your approval, Emma?'

'As a stallion he is certainly well hung,' she replied, scarcely believing that she could speak so boldly in public.

'Then would you like to ride him?'

'Perhaps.'

Emma retreated from a conversation that was getting rather too close to the mark with a demure smile. She was far too hot between the legs to continue talking in a detached fashion, and with a man whom she sensed would not hesitate to take advantage of her if the occasion arose. Perhaps she had already gone too far, but provided she kept her head she should be able to return to her hotel without mishap. For one thing she was sure of: she did not want to be seduced by Daniel Forbes. He was a fine man to flirt with, but that was as far as it would go.

Even so she was uncomfortably aware of his strongly masculine presence while she watched the licentious goings-on between Mimi and her wayward steed, and felt herself growing more and more inflamed down below.

Now the intrepid horsewoman had her stallion saddled and bridled and was attempting to mount him. Three times he threw her, amidst raucous laughter and sporadic applause, but at last she succeeded in keeping her seat and made him trot docilely round and round while she tapped his flank with her crop. The great rod between his thighs bobbed and his balls swung as she made him break into a trot. Emma thought every woman in the place must be half faint with desire for him – she certainly was.

Mimi brought him to the front and made him stand still while she found him some sugar lumps. 'I will reward my wonderful horse with two sugar lumps,' she told the audience with a smile. 'But I shall hide them, and he will have to find them. Where shall I hide them, *Signore e Signori*?'

Various improper suggestions were called out and then, to Emma's surprise, Mimi thrust the two small cubes right into her pussy. She lay down beside the man with her knees apart, so everyone could see the hairy folds of her vulva, and invited him to search for the sugar. When he began mouthing her, putting his tongue right inside her sugary quim, Emma could hardly contain her lust. She pressed her thighs together, worked her secret muscles rapidly and wriggled surreptitiously on her chair until she felt herself beginning to come.

Just as she was at the point of no return Daniel leaned towards her and said, 'From now on, when my friend Mimi invites me to tea and enquires "one lump or two" I shall scarcely know where to put my face!'

Emma exploded into laughter, a laugh which just happened to coincide with the onset of her climax. The relief of being able to hide her paroxysms of pleasure with those of mirth was intense, and the result was a long and satisfying orgasm that was all the more memorable for being the first she had ever experienced in a room full of people. When it finally faded, and her heart-rate had almost returned to normal, she realised that Mimi and her steed were in the throes of similar convulsions, accompanied by rapturous applause.

'More champagne, Emma?'

Daniel's face was close to her own and smiling wryly, suggesting he knew exactly what had been going on beneath her voluminous skirts. She was still trembling and her voice shook a little as she replied, 'Just half a glass, thank you. Then I think I should be returning to the hotel. I have a long journey ahead tomorrow, and must rise early.'

'And where will you be travelling next, on your European odyssey?' he asked.

'Oh, to Milan,' she replied, airily.

It was partly true. They had to go to Milan before they crossed the border into Switzerland but Emma had no intention of staying there.

'Then we may meet again, since that city is on my itinerary too. I shall be there at the end of the week.'

Emma didn't tell him that by then she would be in Montreux. They had met three times 'by chance' and if it happened again she would no longer believe it was an accident. The idea that Daniel might he following her around disturbed her, and if that was the case she had no wish to encourage him.

They left the club just after midnight. As he hailed a cab, Daniel looked at her quizzically. The carriage drew up and he helped her inside then said, 'And how shall I instruct the driver, Emma – shall he take you to Hotel Mantana, or to Santa Croce?'

'Santa Croce?' Emma felt her pulse race. How did he know?

'Well, it is past midnight and I thought you might have another moonlight tryst in the cloisters.'

Dear God, had he followed her there? Panic seized

Emma as she wondered what he might have seen whilst hovering in the shadow of the church. She tried her best to sound unconcerned as she said, 'I do not know what you mean, Daniel. I told you I wished to return to my hotel.'

She heard him call out the name of her hotel then he swung himself inside and sat down beside her. In the close confines of the carriage Emma felt agitated by his proximity. She prayed that he would not talk to her, but soon his low insinuating voice began again.

'I had no idea you were so devout, Emma. To visit a church by day is quite enough for me, and then I can only bear a few minutes of all that stuffy piety. I confess I am impressed by your desire to loiter in draughty cloisters in the dead of night. Were you performing some rigorous penance?'

'You were spying on me!' she said, coldly, her body rigid with anger and something less identifiable. Could it be fear?

'Forgive me, Emma. I was merely ensuring that you were in safe hands. You insisted on departing alone and I could not, in all conscience, have allowed you to travel in the opposite direction from your hotel at that time of night and not watched over you, even from a distance.'

Emma needed to know if he had entered the cloister but she dared not ask him directly. Just how much had he witnessed? 'I was perfectly safe, in God's house,' she replied, feeling hypocritical as she mouthed the first words that came into her head.

'Of course.'

He was silent for a while, much to her relief. She watched the ancient walls of Florence drift by as they neared the square where her hotel was situated. Then, when the cab began to slow, he leaned close to her and whispered, 'I shall miss you, Emma dear.'

His hand squeezed hers, but she dared not turn her face to his. Steeling herself to speak with stiff formality she said, 'It has been pleasant meeting you, Daniel.

And I am very grateful for your kindness in showing me around Florence.'

'I should like to know where it was that you found your greatest pleasure, Emma. Was it in visiting the monastery of San Marco? Or the Church of Santa Croce? Perhaps it was tonight, in the Jockey Club. Or even last night in those cold cloisters, where you made your penance and received your sweet absolution?'

Emma faced him in horror, unable to help herself or utter a word. His eyes were piercing through her with the intention of scrutinising her very soul and, in that instant, she knew the identity of the 'priest' who had heard her 'confession' and later kept his nefarious appointment with her. Emma's heart jolted painfully with the shock. Feeling sick and faint, she scrambled from the cab and, nearly tripping down the step, managed to stumble towards the door of the hotel where she grabbed frantically at the porter's bell rope. Behind her she heard Daniel call out in a confident tone, 'Back to the Jockey Club, driver!'

His laughter was carried back to her on the draught from the cab and continued to haunt her for the rest of the night.

Chapter Ten

*T*he Simplon Pass ran for 40 miles, from Domodos-
sola in Italy to Brig in Switzerland, passing over
more than six hundred bridges and offering some
spectacular Alpine scenery. Emma and Kitty sat, well
shrouded in furs, inside the cab they had hired. The
coachman had assured them that it was possible to do
the trip in a day if they set out early so they had been
on the road since dawn.

As they rose further and further into the clear mountain air Emma began to feel pure and whole again, for
the first time since leaving Florence. The trip to Milan
had been a nightmare, with Kitty chatting eagerly all
the while, asking innocent questions about Mr Forbes
and generally making it difficult for her mistress to
forget her ordeal. Time and again Emma cautioned
herself not to take her feelings out on her maid, remind-
ing herself that it was not the girl's fault, but in the end
she had pleaded a headache and asked to be left in
peace.

Emma soon found that the silence was worse, since it
made her more aware of her own thoughts and feelings.
She could not forget the way she had felt when she was
so summarily, and powerfully, taken in the cloister of
Santa Croce. Yet if Daniel Forbes had made a direct

advance to her she was sure she would have rebuffed him. Had that cunning man been aware of that fact and engineered the situation deliberately, so he could have his wicked way with her in the guise of a fallible priest?

Then there was the visit to that licentious 'Jockey Club' where she had spoken with him intimately, flirted almost. Now, with the benefit of hindsight, she felt both shame and anger. It was clear that the Englishman had intended to seduce her all along, one way or another. He had followed her through France and into Italy, seeking his moment, and she had fallen for it like an April Fool. He was a Don Juan of the worst kind, an evil libertine who dared not even approach his victims openly but employed subterfuge and disguise, under cover of darkness. A very devil!

Still, she was well rid of him now. Confident that she would never see him again, Emma sat huddled in the corner of the carriage as the road wound its way through a white fairyland, and drifted into a doze as the first flakes of snow began to fall outside.

When she awoke, around an hour later, Kitty was pulling gently at her arm. 'Miss Emma, wake up, please! We are stuck in the snow!'

It was true. The carriage was stationary at an odd angle and, as she looked out of the cab window, all that could be seen was a whirling mass of white. She could hear the coachman grunting as he unshackled the horses and, in a short while, he opened the door still puffing.

'My apologies, ladies, but this is as far as we get tonight. The road is blocked.'

'What?' Emma started up and grabbed his arm. 'But what on earth are we to do? It is freezing cold and getting dark.'

'I know, I know. But there is a hut nearby where you may spend the night, Madame, if you wish. I shall take the horses on to shelter – they are worn out, poor things. In the morning we shall discover how bad the fall is and, with help from the local people, I shall clear it.'

Emma was flabbergasted. She was also angry with the cabman for not warning her that this might happen, but there seemed little point in scolding him when they were at his mercy.

'Come, ladies!' He held out his hand to her. 'The hut is used by mountaineers. It has a stove and supplies. You will be perfectly safe until morning.'

Once she grew used to the idea, Emma thought it might be rather fun to spend the night in a mountain hut instead of a hotel. Kitty also seemed excited. She held her mistress's hand tightly as they trudged through the snow after the dim shape of the coachman and eventually reached the dark and silent log cabin.

'Wait, I shall light the lamp,' he said, striking a lucifer.

Once the light from the oil lamp had spread through the tiny hut it didn't look so bad. There was a wood-burning stove, with a pile of logs beside, a mattress and some blankets, a cupboard containing basic provisions, a kettle and some mugs. The man soon had a fire going with newspaper and the bone dry kindling.

'I shall leave you now, ladies,' the dour coachman announced when they were seated on two small stools near the stove. He nodded at Kitty. 'The kettle will soon boil and then you may make cocoa for your mistress. I shall return in the morning, as soon as I know the situation. Good night.'

Emma thanked him and then turned to Kitty with a smile. 'Well, my dear, this is quite an adventure, is it not?'

'I am glad you are not too upset, Miss Emma. I was afraid . . .'

The girl's words tailed off but it was clear what had been in her mind. Finding Emma in so disagreeable a mood before she had expected her to be angry about this unexpected delay, and to take it out on her.

At once, Emma felt contrite. 'It is all right, Kitty dear, I see no point in railing against the weather! Let us make the most of our situation, shall we? Set out the mugs and put a heap of cocoa and some sugar in each. Look, there is a half bottle of brandy in the cupboard – how delightful! A good measure of that in our cocoa will soon set us right.'

At last the pair were warm enough to take off their heavy cloaks although they remained huddled near the fire. There was something very cosy and intimate about being warm inside, with the cold wind and snow raging outside. Emma felt herself finally letting go of her recent tensions as she sipped her fortified drink.

'Wasn't Florence a beautiful city?' Kitty began, chattily, sensing that the atmosphere was more relaxed. 'I know you did not take to him, but I think it was very fortunate that you had Mr Forbes to escort you, or you would not have seen half the sights.'

Emma knew she had to say something to Kitty once and for all. She seized the girl's hand and looked her straight in the eye. 'Now Kitty, I have already told you that there is nothing between us, so I must ask you not to mention that man's name again.'

Her maid's blue eyes grew round with bewilderment. 'But why, Miss Emma? I do not understand. Is he so bad?'

'I do not wish to divulge what passed between me and Mr Forbes, Kitty. Neither do I wish to think about it. I beg you to forget about him as far as possible.'

'Very well.'

Kitty looked so downcast that Emma put her arm around the girl's shoulders and hugged her close. She looked up at her mistress with a smile. 'I suppose there is a great deal that goes on between a man and woman that I do not yet understand. Sometimes I feel so . . . foolish. I have no idea how I should behave if ever a young man paid court to me.'

Her sigh sounded heartfelt, and Emma felt it was incumbent upon her, as a surrogate mother, to educate the girl a little. 'What is it you wish to know, Kitty? Ask

160

me any question you like, and I shall do my best to answer you plainly.'

'Well, I know how babies are made, and some of the things men like to do to women. But when you talk about your young gentlemen, Miss Emma, your face glows and you look so happy. I find it hard to believe that only men obtain pleasure from the act of love, as I was taught.'

Emma smiled. 'You are quite right. If a woman has an open mind and knows a little about her own anatomy, then she can derive a great deal of pleasure from what other women regard only as a painful duty.'

Kitty was frowning perturbedly. 'What did you mean by "anatomy"? I thought that was only studied by students of art and medicine.'

Emma laughed heartily. 'Oh, Kitty! All I mean is that you should know how you are formed, and what parts of your body may give you the greatest pleasure.' She paused, wondering how to proceed. Kitty's cheeks were flushed with the heat and her hair was tousled, falling loose about her shoulders. She had opened the top three pearl buttons of her white cotton blouse, and beneath it her small but well-formed breasts were rising and falling quite rapidly. She was evidently excited by talking about sexual matters, but now it occurred to Emma that perhaps the best method was not to talk but to demonstrate.

Soon Emma found her own heart was beating excitedly too. For many weeks she had been aware that her feelings for her maid were sometimes more than motherly. The girl's innocence was not unlike that of the young men she had seduced: sweet and trusting. The thought of bringing actual physical pleasure to this young woman who had given her such devoted service, of initiating her into the mysteries of her own body, now seemed more appealing than ever. It would be her way of thanking Kitty for all she had done – and endured – in the employ of her mistress.

Emma got to her feet, looking down at the rosy,

upturned cheeks of her maid, and caressed the girl's glossy locks. 'My dear, do you really wish to have such secrets revealed to you?'

'Oh, yes!' Kitty's reply was fervent. 'More than anything in the world! I long to know what you know, Miss Emma, and to share in your experience.'

'I cannot promise you that!' Emma laughed, stroking her velvety cheek. 'But I can show you how you might acquaint yourself with the sources of pleasure in your own body. Just for this once, Kitty dear, permit me to undress you instead of the other way about.'

The maid stood stock still, trembling slightly, as Emma undid the remaining buttons and removed her blouse. Beneath her stays and the loose cotton camisole the young woman's breasts swelled, with the sharp points of her nipples clearly visible. Emma found she was becoming more and more excited herself as she delicately undid the drawstring ribbon. Where the cotton cloth gaped a shallow cleavage was revealed.

Averting her eyes for the time being she said, affecting a brisk tone, 'Now your skirt and underskirts, Kitty.'

Soon there was only one thin under-petticoat and the loose bodice concealing Kitty's youthful figure. Emma took the girl into her arms and she yielded at once. Slowly she bent her mouth to those pale pink lips, so innocently parted, and then the pair were kissing tenderly, their tongues intertwined. Emma thought she had never felt such soft lips beneath hers nor tasted such sweet saliva.

'Oh, Miss Emma!' Kitty sighed, when at last they drew apart. 'I never knew there could be so much to a kiss!'

'Kissing is an art in itself, my dear,' Emma smiled. 'But let us move over to the bed. I shall put my furs down so we can have a warm soft nest to lie in.'

As soon as she felt the sensual brushing of the furry cloak against her naked skin, Kitty lay back wallowing in the luxurious softness. Emma put out a hand and slipped it into the front opening between her breasts while she kissed her again. The girl's skin was deliciously soft and smooth.

'Oh, that feels divine!' Kitty murmured, already in a voluptuous mood.

'This is only the beginning,' Emma replied. Her voice sounded low and husky. She could feel her pulses racing and, between her legs, there was an insistent throbbing.

'A woman's bosom is very sensitive,' she continued, pulling the camisole over her head. Seeing the breasts fully exposed at last, she could not help exclaiming, 'Oh, what a delightful pair! So perfectly round and full, despite their small size, and with such tender pink nipples. I shall kiss them, and you shall know how wonderful that feels my dear.'

Emma bent her head and took one of the rosy nipples gently between her lips. Almost at once they stiffened with desire. She continued to suck gently for a few seconds then raised her head, saying to Kitty with a smile, 'I think a woman's erotic impulse starts first at the lips and then at the breast. Certainly that is how I would advise any young man to proceed.'

'It is true, I have some strange feelings growing in me, as if I am about to faint. My head feels light and there are some . . . peculiar stirrings below my waist.'

'Tell me, Kitty, have you ever had such "feelings" before?'

Her maid looked thoughtful, striving to remember. Emma stroked her dark curls while she listened. 'Yes, I believe I have. The first time was when I was about thirteen. A man kissed my cheek and when his moustache brushed against me I felt a tingling all over. It was very strange, pleasant and unpleasant at the same time.'

'When did you notice similar feelings again?'

'It was when I fell in love with the boot boy, Adam.'

'Oh, a youthful romance!' Emma laughed, teasingly. 'Do tell me all about it.'

'It was just before I came into your service, so I must have been about fourteen. Adam worked in my aunt's household and he began to take notice of me. He would tease me a great deal, telling me my boots were the dirtiest in the house and it took him twice as long to clean them.'

'And did he make any advances to you, dear?'

'Only once. He caught me in the back passage, near the scullery, and put his arms around my waist. I screamed but no one heard, so he tried to kiss me. I struggled some more and he put his hand on my breast and squeezed. I felt as if all my insides were melting. Then he put his hand under my petticoat and felt my thigh, so I screamed louder and someone came. They gave him the sack, so I never saw him again.'

'And what did you feel when he touched your thigh, Kitty?'

'A tingling, all over. Especially . . .' she blushed, 'you know where.'

'No, Kitty. You must show me. Pretend I am Adam the boot boy. I put my hand up under your petticoat, so, and I stroke your thigh ever so softly, just like this. Now, where does it tingle most?'

Kitty pulled up her petticoat and revealed her naked pudendum. The hair that covered her mons was as dark, thick and glossy as that on her head. It curled prettily, in a perfect triangle. Emma placed her hand over the tightly-furled labia and let it rest there, lightly. 'Here, Perhaps?'

The girl nodded, speechlessly. Emma continued to stroke her thigh with one hand while pressing into the mound of Venus with the other. Slowly Kitty's legs fell apart in languid relaxation. Emma pulled the petticoat right down and cast it away, so that she lay completely naked.

'You have the most delightful figure, Kitty,' she told her. 'Any young man would be overjoyed to be presented with this beautiful sight on his wedding night.'

'Do you really think so, Miss Emma? I always thought I was ugly, what with all that hair.'

'Many men are partial to a thick bush on a woman. And your figure is perfectly in proportion.'

Emma moved up the bed and began kissing her again, but this time she let her hands rove all over the nude torso, caressing the firm little breasts with their taut, straining nipples, then running down to the smooth plane of her belly. She could feel the girl growing aroused in every cell of her body, her breath accelerating and her temperature rising.

A similar process was happening in Emma's own body, driving her on with increasing passion. The novelty of making love with another woman was sharpening all her senses, allowing her to revel in the fresh and familiar tastes and odours, loving the way the girl gasped and moaned as her desire increased, enjoying the sight of a female body so like, and yet so unlike, her own.

Yet above all she loved the feel of smooth, young skin beneath her sensitive fingers. Her male lovers had been good to touch as well, but their bodies had been hard and fretted with hair. Kitty's skin was silken on the surface, her flesh like a soft cushion beneath. As Emma gathered one plump breast to her mouth and flicked her tongue across the madder-rose nipple, a powerful shudder passed through her womb and left her weak with longing.

'Kitty,' she murmured, mindful of her duty to instruct by word as well as by deed. 'Tell me how you feel now.'

'Like I never felt before, Miss Emma. I have no words to describe it. It's like . . . like I was eating a delicious meal and dreaming a wonderful dream, at the same time. And the sun's shining down on me, and my head's all fuzzy like when I've been drinking wine, and' – she made one last leap of the imagination – 'it's as if heaven is just around the corner, Miss Emma.'

Emma couldn't help chuckling at the naive accuracy of her description. 'Well, perhaps we had better proceed towards paradise, then. For it is possible for a woman to have a taste of it, despite what some people would have you believe.'

She let her hand drop casually between Kitty's thighs. The softened labia were parted now, and some gentle probing with her forefinger confirmed what she had suspected, that the crevices within were moistening. Gently she began to stroke the delicate tissues, being careful not to rub too hard, and before long the whole area was opened up to her like a dew-laden rose at dawn.

'Is this good, my dear?' she asked at last.

'Oh . . . Yes, Ma'am!'

'Here, Kitty, is where the seat of your greatest pleasure lies. But it must be handled with care. A moist and soft vulva will soon make your little pleasure-bud grow and then you will feel some strong sensations. If you like what I am doing with my fingers, then I am sure you will love what I am about to do with my lips.'

So saying Emma bent her head and was soon licking the little folds and ridges to an almost continual accompaniment of sighs and moans. Kitty was soon moving restlessly, clearly ready for whatever else her mistress wished to do to her, so as her clitoris became more and more evident Emma moved her forefinger deeper into the entrance to her quim. If the girl was to be deflowered some day it was better that her hymen should be broken beforehand. Most men would never know the difference, but it would make for a happier first night with her husband or lover if that barrier were already breached.

As it was, there was only slight resistance and very little blood. Gently Emma pressed her finger forward until she was right inside, watching Kitty's face for signs of distress, but the girl did not wince or cry out once.

Was this how Napoleon's archaeologists had felt, Emma wondered, when they penetrated for the first time some ancient Egyptian tomb? She was entering a place that had been inviolate since the girl's birth. The thought gave her a special, tender thrill. Her vagina felt soft and wet inside, the thick flesh cushioning her finger tightly. She moved it out a little, then in again. Kitty groaned loudly and began to move her hips in an instinctive rhythm that increased the contact between her vulva and the invading digit.

Emma leaned forward and kissed the girl softly on the lips. She was surprised by the instant fervour of her response. Kitty embraced her mistress eagerly, pulling her into her arms and covering her face with passionate kisses. The latent desire that Emma had been keeping at bay while she focused on the other woman's arousal was now unleashed. She soon replaced her probing finger with her tongue and, while she licked and sucked at the sweet fruit of Kitty's pussy her right hand was equally busy beneath her own skirt, bringing herself to her own fulfilment.

Emma's cry as the first paroxysm quivered through her was stifled by the noise of Kitty's ascent towards an equal bliss. Or perhaps a far greater one, since it was to be her first time. Once she had covertly satisfied her own urgent craving, Emma put all her strength into bringing her maid to her first climax. With one hand she reached up and grasped her straining breast, while with the other she dabbled in the free-flowing juices of her pussy, making sure that she baptised the head of her demanding clitoris at frequent intervals. The fleshy nub was very prominent now, hot and pulsating with exquisite sensation judging by the melodious sounds that were issuing from Kitty's sweet lips.

'Oh, heavenly!' she murmured. 'Delightful! So blissfully delicious I shall faint!'

'Soon, my sweet, soon!' Emma whispered in response.

When the longed-for event did arrive, Kitty was overtaken by surprise. She threw her head back in violent abandon as Emma pinched her nipple quite hard between finger and thumb while frotting her rapidly down below. Then, as the first ripples spread and grew, the girl gave a little scream and exclaimed, 'Oh, this is too much to bear, it is too . . . too . . .'

But there words really did fail her. She turned pink all over and her slim pelvis shuddered with the wild contractions that were sending waves of bliss running freely through her young body. Emma stroked her thighs and kissed her breasts softly until the orgasm finally waned and Kitty sank back onto the soft fur, utterly exhausted and thoroughly sated with pleasure.

For a long time she lay quite still with her eyes closed while Emma took off her dress and corset then lay down beside her in her underclothes. At last Kitty murmured, 'Oh, Miss Emma, I had no idea! No idea at all!'

Emma hugged her close, brushing back the matted hair from her face and kissing her cheek. 'I am glad you now understand what makes a woman prepared to give her all for love, my dear. Yet when you make love with an experienced man you will discover further delights, sensations that will satisfy and fulfil you even more.'

'Impossible!' the girl protested, sleepily. 'I cannot imagine anything more wonderful than what I have just experienced.'

Emma smiled fondly at her. 'Yet consider this, Kitty. Before we entered this hut you had no understanding at all of what a woman's pleasure might consist of. Wonderful as your first climax has been, I am sure that once you meet the right young man your desire will be raised to such a pitch that your eventual satisfaction will be far greater and you will feel that you belong to him, body and soul. Trust me, Kitty, for I know it to be so.'

'Is that how it has been for you, Miss Emma?'

Emma sighed. 'Yes, when I was first married. I was just as inexperienced as you, but my husband-to-be introduced me to the delights of sexual play slowly, over several months, until he finally penetrated me on our wedding night. I had longed for that consummation, and for me, that was the most memorable event of my life.'

'I should like to be married, some day.'

'I am sure you will, Kitty. Sad as I shall be to see you go from my service, I should be delighted if I felt your future happiness was assured. As you have no parents, I regard myself to some degree responsible for your fate.'

'Oh, Ma'am, you are so good to me!' Kitty sighed, snuggling down to sleep.

But Emma could not sleep so easily. In the flickering firelight she contemplated what had happened that night. Had she made a mistake in being so intimate with her maid? It was clear that the situation could not be allowed to continue, or her authority would be undermined. At least she had not permitted Kitty to become free with her own person. As long as she could persuade the girl, and herself, that the incident had been purely educational, simply a private lesson in self-knowledge, then all would be well.

Yet she couldn't deny that she had enjoyed her first full encounter of the Sapphic kind. The contrast between their sweetly innocent love-making and the dark forces roused in her by Daniel Forbes was striking. Had she wished to exorcise that man's ghost by restoring her own innocent delight in the act of love, by seeing it reflected in another? Kitty reminded her so much of herself at that age, and it had given her profound pleasure to initiate her the way she herself had been initiated by Henry. She had previously thought of herself as a mother to Kitty, but now she felt more like her sister. Cuddling up to her Emma pulled the blanket over them both as the fire dulled into embers, and was soon fast asleep.

Chapter Eleven

Mathilda Belfort was a widow in her forties. She had married a Swiss gentleman, a maker of fine chocolate, and with the money he left her had set up an exclusive finishing school where young ladies from France, Germany, Italy and England might further their education. When Emma finally arrived at the elegant chateau on the shores of Lake Geneva, she knew she had made the right decision in going there.

Her feelings were confirmed when Mathilda greeted her with great warmth, kissing her on both cheeks. Although past the first flush of youth, Emma's cousin was still a strikingly good-looking woman with clear blue eyes, hair in which gold still played a large part, and a fresh complexion. She smelt faintly of mignonette.

'My dearest Emma, how delightful to see you! Why, the last time I saw you was on a visit to England, let me see . . . oh dear, it must have been almost twenty years ago! You were a charming little girl then.'

'It is very kind of you to welcome me, cousin Mathilda. I hope I am not imposing on you.'

'Not at all, my dear. As you see, we have plenty of room here and if you wish to stay for more than a few days you might be very useful to me – if you are agreeable, of course. But we will talk of that later. I am sure you are tired, so I will get Roland to show you to your room.'

Emma had been given a most delightful room at the front of the house, overlooking a sweeping lawn that led down to the lake, two colourful parterres, an octagonal Chinese-style gazebo and some statues. Kitty had been put in an adjoining room, but she stayed with her mistress to unpack.

'Kitty, I could become used to this!' Emma smiled, sitting down on the comfortable bed. 'It is so long since I spent the night in a private house. I did not realise how much I had been missing it. There is nothing like home comfort.'

'I agree, Ma'am.'

Kitty seemed so much more contented since her initiation in the mountains. They had spent the previous night in a hotel in Martigny before completing the last lap of their journey. When Emma had insisted that her maid should sleep in the room next door, however, Kitty's disappointment had been so obvious that she decided to give her maid a frank talking-to.

'Now Kitty, I wish you to understand that what happened between us was simply to acquaint you with the secrets of your own body. Some women, once they have experienced what pleasure may be derived from their private parts and in what manner it may be accomplished, enjoy experimenting for themselves.'

'Is that what they call "self-abuse"?' Kitty had asked, anxiously.

'It is what priggish people call it, yes. Those prudes who would prefer to keep our sex in the dark about their own anatomy, and would wish us to endure a man's attentions instead of enjoying them.'

'So it is not wrong, then, to touch oneself down there?'

'I believe not, Kitty. It will relieve frustration and better prepare you for the love of a man. A woman who knows how to pleasure herself may teach her husband or lover to do the same.'

Kitty gave a small, secretive smile. 'Do you mean then, Miss Emma, that I should be able to give myself that kind of pleasure whenever I wished?'

'As long as you are in private my dear, of course. Personally speaking, I find it the best possible cure for insomnia.'

When the girl had come down to breakfast next morning there was such a glow about her that Emma had no need to ask her if she had been 'experimenting'.

Now that they had arrived in Montreux the atmosphere was relaxed and soothing and the air clear and refreshing. Emma was looking forward to hearing what her cousin had in mind. After a brief rest, Kitty helped her into an emerald gown that deepened the hint of green in her eyes. 'You look a picture, Ma'am!' she announced.

'Thank you, Kitty. I hope to make a good impression on Mrs Belfort. I feel that I am somehow representing my branch of the family, albeit a distant one.'

'You are fortunate to have relations, Miss Emma,' Kitty reminded her.

'Yes, of course. But they can be a mixed blessing you know, dear. As Mr Charles Dickens observed, "It is a melancholy truth that even great men have their poor relations".'

'Oh, Ma'am, you surely would not place yourself in that category?'

For a moment Emma was dumbstruck. Was that how Mathilda Belfort would view her? Then she laughed. 'Oh no, my dear! I should not dream of calling upon my cousin if I had the slightest fear of outstaying my welcome, or becoming a strain upon her household purse.'

Even so, Kitty's words had put her into a sober mood. Her hostess welcomed her graciously in the drawing-room, which was stuffed with rather old-fashioned French furniture. A young man stood diffidently by the fireplace. Emma took in his dark-brown curly hair, eyes of the same colour that seemed to smoulder behind long black lashes, a short straight nose and sensually brooding mouth. She knew in one brief glance that he was an extremely handsome youth and her pulse began racing involuntarily.

'Emma, dearest, I am delighted to introduce you to my son, Vincent,' Mathilda said.

He advanced hesitantly, and shook her hand. 'Pleased to make your acquaintance, Mrs Longmore.'

For an instant his eyes flashed fire into hers, but then looked away. She judged him to be in his early twenties at most, but there was a gaucheness about him that made him seem more like an adolescent. Instantly her heart warmed to him. How stifled he must be here, in this genteel backwater.

'Do call me Emma, please,' she smiled. 'Your mother and I are distant cousins, so I suppose that makes us distant cousins once removed, does it not?'

He gave a sardonic smile and his mother broke in with, 'Pour our guest a drink, will you dear. What would you like, Emma – a glass of sherry, perhaps, or some Madeira wine?'

While they drank their aperitifs Mathilda did her best to foster a flow of conversation but her son was not forthcoming. He answered in monosyllables and Emma sensed that there was much tension between them. Whether it was a permanent state of affairs or only temporary she had no idea, but she did hope that her presence was not exacerbating the situation.

At dinner, however, Vincent loosened up a little. He showed great interest in what life was like back in England, his questions bordering on the insistent.

At last his mother explained with a sigh, 'My son longs to return to England, Emma, but his father wished otherwise. Although Vincent went to school at Winchester, Pierre always wanted him to take over the management of Chocolat Belfort when he retired. Alas, my dear husband passed away only four years ago at

173

the age of fifty-eight, but I have carried out his wishes and now Vincent is learning the business at first hand.'

'Is it not possible for him to further his education in England first, Mathilda? Perhaps Oxford . . .'

'Of course it is *possible*!' Vincent muttered. 'Only Mamma will not hear of it!'

'Vincent, do not take that petulant tone!' Mathilda said, sharply. 'I am sorry, Emma, the last thing you will want to hear on your first night at Chateau Bellevue is family bickering. You may be excused, Vincent. We shall take our after-dinner refreshment in the drawing-room.'

Once the two women were alone, Mathilda again apologised for her son's surliness. 'I fear you have caught us at a bad time, Emma. Only yesterday there was a crisis at the factory when Vincent apparently insulted one of the staff. I am afraid he is not taking his rôle as heir to the House of Belfort at all seriously.'

'He is still young,' Emma said, soothingly. 'How old is he, by the way?'

'Just twenty-one. Old enough to be considered a man, although he does not often behave like one.'

'Is he your only son?'

'Sadly, yes.'

'Still, you are lucky to have him.' Emma sighed. 'I have been told that I shall never be able to conceive.'

'Poor Emma!' Mathilda reached out and touched her hand, briefly. 'And your husband, is he resigned to the situation?'

Emma paused. While she had freely described herself as 'widowed' to those she met on her travels, she knew that it would be more difficult to pass herself off in that way to a member of her family. 'I am no longer married, Mathilda. Our marriage was annulled.'

'Annulled? You mean, it was never consummated? No wonder you are without issue, my dear. But you are still young, there is still time . . .'

'No, I fear not. I have a doctor's assurance that I shall never bear children. Still, I have grown used to my fate now and you need not waste your pity on me. I intend to live a full and useful life regardless, I assure you.'

Mathilda gave a tinkly laugh as she poured the coffee into pink and gold cups of Sèvres porcelain. 'My dear, I am sure you will! And maybe you will begin sooner than you think.' She handed Emma her cup with a smile. 'I mentioned earlier that you have arrived at just the right time to help me out here at the school. One of my staff has unfortunately contracted a serious illness and is unable to continue with her etiquette class. I would consider it a great favour if you would be kind enough to step in and fill the breach for a few weeks, just long enough for me to be able to employ someone on a permanent basis. Of course, there is no obligation whatsoever, but your duties would be very light and naturally you would be paid the same salary as Miss Valenti. She took the upper class for two hours a day. For the rest of the time you would be free to amuse yourself.'

Emma had no hesitation in accepting. By good fortune Mathilda's need for assistance and her own desire for employment had perfectly coincided.

For the rest of the evening they talked about the school. Chateau Bellevue had a total of thirty 'gels', as Mathilda referred to them, ranging in age from sixteen to twenty-one. They were in three classes of ten and their curriculum included languages, fashion and deportment, social graces and etiquette, music and dancing, table manners and the duties of a hostess.

'You will be taking the older gels, Emma. I shall fetch Miss Valenti's curriculum which I am quite sure you will find perfectly straightforward. There is nothing in it that a woman of breeding, such as yourself, who has managed a household and entertained her husband's friends and associates, does not already know. I am sure it will be second nature to you.'

Later, when Emma was in her room, she broke the news excitedly to Kitty.

'Oh, Ma'am, you will be the perfect instructress for

175

the young ladies!' she declared, then blushed. They both laughed.

In the morning, Mathilda introduced her cousin to Miss Schmidt who taught the older girls in the morning.

'This afternoon you may take the class for wedding etiquette, Emma,' she suggested. 'That is always a popular topic. Now, I shall get one of the girls to show you round and then take you to the *Salle des Cupidons* where you may observe Miss Schmidt at work.'

Emma found herself filled with trepidation as she made her way to the *Salle des Cupidons* after luncheon and a short walk with Helga Schmidt in the grounds. The German woman had been helpful, but still Emma felt very much on her own as she faced the group of expectant faces who were relying on her to provide them with instruction for the whole afternoon. She decided at once to appeal to their better natures.

'Ladies, I must ask you to bear with me this afternoon,' she began, nervously. 'Although I am delighted to be here amongst you, I must confess that I have never been in this position before and scarcely know how to begin. However, I shall do my best to instruct you in the etiquette that surrounds the most important event in a young woman's life, her wedding.'

As the lesson proceeded, Emma found the girls becoming more responsive and, when she had dictated notes on the basic principles, she hit on the idea of getting each of them to describe her 'perfect wedding'.

It was a stroke of genius! Having hit on the subject dearest to all their hearts there was to be no stopping them as they described their ideal wedding gown, the outfits for the bridesmaids and pageboys, the flowers for their bouquet, the table decorations, the music and, the buffet. Several times Emma had to curtail the flood of detail tactfully so that each girl might have a chance to speak. By the end of the day Emma had managed to create a warm and friendly atmosphere, and had also formed an impression of each girl's personality.

After she had dismissed them Yvette Duval, an attractive French girl with blonde hair and sparkling grey eyes, came up to her. 'Oh, Mrs Longmore, I enjoyed your lesson so much!' she exclaimed. 'What do we do tomorrow?'

The question took Emma by surprise. She had not yet had time to think ahead let alone prepare anything. 'What would you like to do?' she asked.

A mischievous look came over the girl's face. 'Why not . . . the honeymoon?'

Emma repressed a smile, but then she gave it serious thought. Logically it should be the next lesson, yet how many of those girls would be able to take any explicit instruction in such matters? Only a few, she surmised, although Yvette was certainly one of them. A plan began to form in her mind, but for the time being she avoided the issue.

'Well, I suppose I should follow Miss Valenti's curriculum. I need to consult her notes.'

Yvette looked disappointed. 'Oh it is sure to be something dull! Miss Valenti was not like you, Madame. She make us take notes all the time. It was so boring. I, for one, am glad that she is no longer with us and we now have you.'

With that, the girl flounced out leaving Emma in a pensive mood. She sat down at the desk and brought out the former teacher's notes. After 'Weddings' came 'Christenings' and then 'Funerals'. For the class as a whole she must follow the plan, but maybe she could provide some 'extra-curricular tuition' for those girls whom she believed would benefit from it. She would have a word with Mathilda that evening.

At dinner, when her cousin enquired how her lesson had gone, Emma gave an enthusiastic reply. 'Very well, thank you Mathilda. The girls were most responsive and I enjoyed it greatly.'

'Excellent!' Mathilda beamed. 'I knew you would be ideal, Emma dear. You have such a natural manner and positive approach. I am not at all surprised that the girls took to you.'

'Since then, I have been wondering whether I might ask some of the girls to join me for extra lessons. I believe they would greatly benefit, and I should be pleased to give up some of my spare time – without remuneration, of course – to furthering their education.'

'Why, that is most generous of you, Emma. What do you propose to cover in these classes?'

'I am not sure yet,' Emma hedged. 'Some aspects that are not covered by the rest of the curriculum, I suppose. Art appreciation, perhaps, since I have recently visited Paris and Florence.'

'Splendid! I have often wished we could pay more attention to the arts. I suggest you use the *Salle de Vénus* on the top floor for your studies. I think that would be most appropriate.'

'Yes, it certainly would,' Emma smiled, thinking of her real motive in proposing the extra lessons. Perhaps she would invite Kitty to join the girls. She had already shown herself to be ready and eager to learn.

After the following day's lesson on christening etiquette, Emma asked four girls to wait behind. As well as Yvette, she had chosen a German girl with auburn curls and sparkling blue eyes called Lotte Schneider; a dark-haired Italian called Bella Lucci and an 'English rose' with brown hair and hazel eyes called Faith Taylor-Browne. All four struck her as being particularly attractive and intelligent, with an eager appetite for life that endeared them to her.

Once the others had left the room she said, 'Girls, I have chosen you specially because I propose to start a small study group. The classes will be held twice weekly, on a Tuesday and Thursday evening. However, there is no obligation whatever to attend.'

'What kind of class, Mrs Longmore?' asked Faith.

'Before I tell you, I must swear you all to secrecy.' The four girls looked at each other and giggled. 'Please, I am quite serious. Each of you must give your solemn word not to reveal what I am about to tell you.'

'I promise,' Yvette said at once, and the others followed suit.

Emma nodded, satisfied. 'Well, after yesterday's class on wedding etiquette Yvette asked if I were going to instruct you regarding the honeymoon.' The girls giggled again, but this time Emma ignored it. 'Now I am aware that intimate relations between man and wife are not discussed in polite society. However, I happen to believe that young ladies such as yourselves deserve to be better informed in such matters. I am prepared to educate you accordingly, if you so desire.'

Faith gasped. 'You mean you would tell us secrets our own mothers cannot bring themselves to divulge?'

Emma nodded. 'I deplore the fact that women are left ignorant in such matters, and I believe that you four girls are mature and intelligent enough to be able to receive such instruction. If you so desire, of course.'

'Desire!' Yvette gave a sly smile. 'We know all about *desire*, Mrs Longmore! It is what to do about it that we are ignorant of!'

They all laughed, including Emma. 'Then I am able to enlighten you, but I must stress that our classes will be held in the strictest confidence. No word of what happens there must be leaked to others. I am sure you understand that there would be extremely unpleasant consequences.'

The girls were evidently excited at the prospect. Their little cabal had all the allure of an illicit secret society. No one wanted to be left out so Emma arranged to meet them all in the *Salle de Vénus*, the attic room containing a reproduction statue of the Venus de Milo, at eight o'clock the following evening.

'One last point: my younger sister, Kitty, who is about your age, will also attend. Until tomorrow evening then, ladies!'

Emma had thought it best to introduce Kitty as her 'sister' since it seemed more proper. When she mentioned it to her maid, the girl was overjoyed. 'Oh Miss

Emma, I shall be so honoured to join those young ladies!'

Emma smiled. 'Then you must learn to call me plain "Emma". I shall ask the girls to do likewise whenever we meet in private.'

That afternoon Emma dealt lightly with funeral etiquette, observing wryly to herself that she did not wish to 'cast a pall' over the evening's proceedings. She finished the lesson with a brief introduction to addressing the nobility, since she knew that all the girls would at some time be meeting a person of rank if they had not already done so. Indeed, Mathilda seemed to estimate the success of her school by the number of graduates who married dukes, earls, counts or marquises. So in the evening, when she came to begin her first lesson with her 'chosen few' as she liked to call them, Emma began by referring back to that afternoon's lesson.

'Now I dare say that many of you will be hoping to end up as countesses or duchesses one day.' The girls giggled self-consciously – except for Kitty, who would never have dreamed of having such aspirations. 'You are all very attractive girls from well-to-do families, and there is no reason why you should not capture the heart of a noble gentleman if you so wish. However, in order to maintain his interest in you there are many small tricks that a woman may perform.'

'Tricks?' Lotte frowned. 'I do not wish to play tricks. It is not seemly!'

'I think you misunderstand me,' Emma smiled. 'Perhaps the word "secrets" would be more appropriate. You see, a man's interest in a woman is always grounded in the physical. But I am not referring to the more obvious charms such as a beautiful face and comely figure. Have you not sometimes wondered how a man might become besotted with a woman who is, to the impartial eye, extremely plain?'

'Oh, yes!' Lotte laughed. 'An uncle of mine has a wife

180

who is sweet but so ugly, and yet he is absolutely devoted to her!'

'Then you may be assured that she knows the secret of how to please a man. Again, I am not referring to flattering compliments or costly gifts. No, to be blunt ladies, I am talking about pleasing a man in bed.'

Emma saw the girls' eyes widen with curiosity. Some giggled, others blushed, but they all looked extremely interested in what she had to say on the subject.

'I shall be dealing with three main topics during these classes,' she went on, matter-of-factly. 'Firstly, how to become better acquainted with one's own anatomy, so that if one has the misfortune to marry a totally inexperienced man one may subtly guide him. Secondly, how to arouse a man during the courtship phase without compromising one's reputation. And thirdly, how to turn the act of love into an experience that is completely satisfying to both parties.'

Emma noticed a frown on the lovely face of Faith Taylor-Browne, who soon spoke her mind. 'But Mrs Longmore, surely this kind of information is inappropriate for young ladies? I am sure my own mother would be shocked if she knew what you propose to teach us. She once told me that there was one unspeakable thing that happened in marriage which a woman must endure for the sake of perpetuating the line, and it was a wife's duty to perform it uncomplainingly for the honour of the family. I hardly think she would approve of a lady *enjoying* such a base activity.'

Emma sighed. She had expected some such opposition and the whole success of the venture depended on her skill in countering it. Taking a deep breath she explained, 'Faith dear, your mother was probably repeating to you what her mother had told her, and so on back down the ages. Yet, like many other aspects of life, the experience of physical love-making is largely what we make of it. Many women have discovered that it can bring them the greatest imaginable joy . . .'

'Oh, yes!'

Emma turned in surprise to find that Kitty had unexpectedly come to her rescue. Evidently feeling she could remain silent no longer, she began to hold forth. 'I was told the same as you by my aunt, Miss Faith, but I am glad to say that Miss . . . that Emma taught me differently.' Her youthful face was glowing with delight as she continued, 'There is a part of your body – and of mine, and of every woman's – that can bring you more pleasure than you ever dreamed of, if only you know where it is and how to touch it.'

Emma noticed that Yvette was blushing, and guessed that the girl had already, by luck or accident, discovered the secret for herself. She thanked her maid for her testimony, but before she could continue Kitty took her completely by surprise with her next words.

'They say that seeing is believing, don't they? Well, if Emma is agreeable I would be more than willing to demonstrate what I have been talking about.'

'Kitty!'

'No really, Miss Emma, I would not mind. If I can help some other girl to discover the amazing truth for herself I should be very contented. Will you let me show them, right now?'

Emma could hardly believe that demure, innocent little Kitty was actually proposing to perform such an intimate act before others. Yet, seeing the eager curiosity of the other girls, she felt she could hardly refuse. What better way was there to prove her point?

'Very well, Kitty,' she said at last. 'They say a picture is worth a thousand words, but maybe a demonstration is worth a million. Let us arrange things so that you are comfortable and that the girls can all see clearly.'

There was a battered chaise longue in one corner, draped with a paisley shawl. Enlisting the help of two girls, Emma dragged it into the centre of the circle of chairs and bade Kitty lie upon it. She could feel her heart beating excitedly at the prospect of initiating the girls into the secrets of the orgasm. She was also filled with admiration for her maid.

'Come, Kitty dear, lie here and lift up your petticoats,' she smiled. 'I shall first give a brief introduction to anatomy.'

Emma invited the others to come closer and examine Kitty's exposed pudendum so that she could describe the various parts. It was clear that none of them had the slightest idea how they themselves were made, and their response was most encouraging.

'I had no notion that a woman's parts were so complex,' Faith declared, in wonder. 'I thought we just had a hole down there.'

'So did I,' confessed Lotte. 'Now, when I am alone I shall take my hand mirror and look at myself down below.'

'I recommend that you each do the same,' Emma said. 'But now Kitty will show you how you may pleasure yourselves.'

Smiling with anticipation, Kitty pulled her labia delicately apart with one finger and, with the other, began to gently rub the top of her clitoris. The girls gazed in fascination as her tissues began to swell and moisten. Soon Kitty's face became flushed and her expression was one of intense concentration.

'How does it feel, Kitty?' Bella asked after about a minute of increasing friction.

'Beautiful!' Kitty gasped. 'My whole body is warm and throbbing with life. I can feel the waves of desire growing and the crisis is not far off.'

'Crisis?' Lotte repeated, puzzled.

'Yes, indeed. Perhaps I should explain, for Kitty will find it increasingly difficult to speak and we do not want to interrupt her rise towards ecstasy. You see how flushed she is, how her hips and breasts are thrusting upwards? That tells me that she is near the summit of her pleasure, that peak of thrilling experience that men and women alike can reach if only they know the route.'

Emma glanced briefly through the window. In the distance she could see the alpine peaks rising to the sky. She had spoken at some length to an elderly mountaineer whom she had met in the hotel at Martigny, and now she knew she had found her metaphor.

'You see, it is a little like mountaineering. As you rise up the side of a mountain you become more and more exhilarated. When you reach each plateau the view seems a little more spectacular, and your own achievement in arriving there that much more worthwhile. At the same time the air becomes rarer, you gasp for breath and feel light-headed, yet a burning desire urges you on towards the peak. You strain at the last, long to get there and yet find the going hard, but all the while you are filled so intensely with the pleasures of nature and your own immense satisfaction at scaling the heights. Then, at long last, you make the first stumbling steps onto the topmost peak and find yourself in another world, one where you may wallow in your new discovery with pure delight. You stay there on the height for a while, bathed in sunlight and silence, admiring the incredible beauty of the world. Then, when you have had your fill of ecstasy, you begin the slow descent back into normal life again.'

'Look at Kitty!' Lotte exclaimed. 'I think something is happening!'

She was right. Kitty had reached that exalted peak of excitement and was beginning to moan and shudder as the exquisite thrills spread through her entire body. Emma looked at the faces of the spectators, and saw contrasting emotions at play. Yvette was giving a secretive smile confirming what Emma had guessed, that she had scaled those heights already. Lotte was looking incredulous, and a little afraid. Faith was frowning with faint disapproval yet was clearly fascinated, and Bella was looking envious.

'Why did she shake so?' Lotte asked, when Kitty had relaxed again and was lying in a languid pose.

'The intense sensations of the climax come in waves,' Emma explained. 'But quite honestly, ladies, I could employ a thousand metaphors to describe this miracle and yet come nowhere near the truth. The only way to understand it is to discover it for yourselves.'

Faith looked shocked. 'You mean . . . we should do as Kitty has just done, to ourselves?'

'Why not?' Emma smiled. 'Then you will discover why it is that men and women have fallen deeply in love throughout the ages. For I believe that without this most ecstatic experience love between the sexes, however sincerely expressed, is merely friendship.'

'Between the sexes?' Lotte repeated, thoughtfully. 'But if we may enjoy this wonderful experience on our own why should we bother with a husband?'

Emma smiled. 'Ah, my dear girl. Perhaps if women were all of private means and could give birth like the Virgin Mary none of us would need men!' Everyone laughed. 'But seriously speaking, you may take my word for it that however delightful self-pleasuring seems, once you have tasted the joys of conjugal bliss you will find they greatly surpass it. Provided that you can educate your husband or lover in the art of love-making, of course. Alas, few men of breeding know instinctively how to please a woman in that way.'

By now Kitty had recovered from her blissful swoon and was sitting up with her skirts decorously arranged once more. Judging that the young ladies had received quite enough instruction for one lesson, Emma reminded them of their vow of secrecy and dismissed them.

'I think that went well, do you agree Kitty?' she asked her maid, once she had returned to the privacy of her room.

'Oh yes, Ma'am.'

'It was largely thanks to you, of course. I am very glad that you were there to back me up, my dear.'

'It was nothing, Miss Emma. Only my way of thanking you for instructing me first.'

Emma kissed her on the cheek, but was careful not to take it any further. It would not do for Kitty to become too attached to her mistress in that way. It occurred to

Emma that when they returned to England she should perhaps seek out some suitable young man for Kitty to marry. Much as she disliked the idea of losing her personal maidservant, she would like to see Kitty comfortably settled and enjoying married life.

Before she went to sleep that night, Emma reflected on how pleasant it was be entirely in the company of her own sex. She had enjoyed that evening's class very much and believed that the four girls she had chosen for special instruction would prosper greatly once they graduated from the school and entered society. Paradoxically, however, Emma's own faith in men had been severely tested by her unfortunate encounter with Daniel Forbes. Emma felt as if her self-confidence had been sapped, and she needed a period of withdrawal from mixed society to enable her to forget the past. Well, she had certainly chosen the right place in which to do that.

Chapter Twelve

After a week of teaching at the Chateau Bellevue Emma was glad to have some time to herself at the weekend. On Saturday morning she had left Kitty in the company of the other servants and was strolling along the wooded walk that ran alongside the lake, when she heard footsteps on the gravel behind. It was Vincent Belfort.

'Oh, Emma! I am so pleased to find you,' he began, his brown eyes gleaming at her in a most disconcerting fashion. 'I have been so wanting to talk with you, but this is the first opportunity I have had.'

'Well, Vincent, you may accompany me on my walk,' Emma said, her curiosity roused. 'What was it you wished to talk to me about?'

'It is a little difficult,' he began. 'I know that you will naturally want to side with Mamma, but I had hoped you would see my point of view as well. You see, I had such a wonderful time in England, and made such good chums there. Here, I feel like a fish out of water. I am not cut out for commerce, Emma. It bores me absolutely. I long to go to London and study law.'

'Have you told your mother?'

'Yes, but she will not hear of it.'

'Maybe you could find someone influential to plead

your case, Vincent – someone who knows you and your mother well. A godfather, perhaps?'

'My godfather lives in England.'

'Why not write to him? I am sure he would be sympathetic.'

'Then may I ask you a favour, Emma? Would you help me compose such a letter?'

'With pleasure, dear boy!'

'Oh thank you! Thank you!'

To Emma's surprise he gave her a fervent kiss on the cheek. His lips were soft and warm, rousing in her dangerous instincts. Detaching herself from his arm on the pretext of going over to the parapet to view the lake, Emma said, 'I will not side with you against your mother, Vincent. Please remember that. It is for your godfather to put your case, not I.'

'I understand that, Emma, but I know you also understand me. That is true, is it not? I sensed it that first evening.'

Emma smiled enigmatically, but would not be drawn. She refused to discuss his prospects but after luncheon they met again, as arranged. It was gloriously sunny and Vincent suggested they should go to the summer house.

'It is so peaceful there, and quite private. I do not wish Mamma to see us together, you understand.'

'Of course.'

The summer house was delightful. Built in the style of a Chinese pagoda, it had pink climbing roses around the door and balcony so that the place was filled with the homely buzzing of bees. Inside it was simply furnished with bamboo chairs and settee, a table and a Chinese rug. Vincent opened his writing case and filled his pen from the inkwell, then took out a sheet of paper. 'So, Emma, how shall I begin?'

They worked for almost half an hour on the letter before Vincent declared himself well pleased with it. At the end, he took her hand and raised it thoughtfully to his lips, saying, 'I cannot thank you enough, Emma dear.'

His eyes were looking deep into hers with an expression she had seen in young men's eyes before, and Emma felt her heart begin to race. He was certainly attractive to her and, in other circumstances, she would not have hesitated to proceed in the manner he so obviously desired. However she was Mathilda's guest, and already risking her hostess's displeasure by her unorthodox instruction of some of her 'gels'. It would not do to put herself in double jeopardy at Chateau Bellevue.

On Monday evening Emma met her select group of girls once again. They were chatting excitedly together when she arrived, and Emma guessed what had been happening since their last lesson. The four shared a dormitory at the top of the house, away from the others, which gave them every opportunity for practical experimentation.

'Well, ladies, I hope you have all done your preparation for this evening's lesson,' she began, with a twinkle in her eye. 'I would like to have a progress report from each one of you, starting with Yvette.'

The girl's face was glowing as she spoke. 'Oh, Miss Emma, I have made such discoveries about myself. I find that if I think about . . . certain things I can more quickly get to that glorious mountain peak of which you spoke.'

'Ah yes, of course! I forgot to mention the important rôle played by the imagination in these matters. Did you find yourself day-dreaming while you explored your body?'

'I did indeed,' Yvette confessed. 'I have a favourite scene that I love to think about.'

'Would you be prepared to share it with us, Yvette dear?'

'Yes, I think so. It begins in my stable, at home. I have always loved to ride, and one time I was riding fast on Maître Jacques, my favourite stallion, when I felt

189

a warm tingling in the place between my thighs. After that I used to bunch my night-gown between my legs at night and pretend I was riding him in bed. The faster I rode, the more excited I became.'

'You are not the first young lady to become excited on horseback, Yvette.' Emma smiled. 'But pray continue.'

'Sometimes I dream that I am riding bareback, not side-saddle but astride my darling Jacques. I am wearing no clothes and behind me, also naked, sits . . .' she blushed. 'Well, a man I have always considered most handsome. So, I imagine that while I ride my beloved horse, this man is right behind me with his hands upon my breasts. He is feeling my nipples, which have grown big, and I can feel his . . . well, his parts prodding into my buttocks as we ride. But most of my pleasure comes from the rough feel of my horse between my legs as we move up and down. After a while we begin to trot, then to canter and then to gallop. When we are going as fast as we can, I start to feel the most wonderful sensation I have ever felt.'

'Thank you for sharing that with us,' Emma said. 'How about you, Bella?'

Bella smiled. 'Yes, I did succeed . . . in the end. But not without the help of my friend.'

'Really?' Emma was intrigued. It seemed that these bold young ladies had already taken their experimentation farther than she had expected.

'I did try, but no matter how hard I rubbed myself I just felt uncomfortable, even sore.'

'You were probably trying too hard. But you said someone helped you?'

'Yes.' She smiled shyly at the German girl. 'In fact, Lotte and I helped each other. Shall I tell them, Lotte?' Her friend nodded. 'Very well. We were alone in the dormitory while the other two girls were having their music lesson. We talked about what Kitty had shown us and decided to try ourselves. When I had difficulty,

Lotte said she would help me by rubbing some of her face cream into me down there. She said I was too dry.'

Emma nodded. 'It can happen, especially if you are nervous or tense. That is something to remember on your wedding night, ladies. The application of a little cream or oil can work wonders.'

'As she gently rubbed me with the rose-scented cream I felt very good. I lay back and she went on and on until I began to feel really hot and it was very pleasant indeed. Then, quite suddenly, I felt the most extraordinary quivering in the central part of me. I cannot describe it, but those who have felt the same will know.'

'And you, Lotte?' Emma prompted. 'Did you have a similar experience?'

'Oh, *Ja!*' Lotte said, emphatically, and everyone laughed.

But then Faith suddenly blurted out, 'It is all very well for you others, but I would not lower myself to do such a thing!'

Emma looked at the English girl. Her hazel eyes were clouded and her lips formed a pout. 'Is that so, Faith dear?'

'I think that what you are telling us to do is wrong!' she declared, sulkily.

The others gazed at her in dismay, but Emma stayed calm. 'I am sorry you feel like this. As I said at the beginning, there is no obligation to attend these classes. If you would like to leave you are free to do so, although I must ask you to respect your vow of secrecy.'

'I am not surprised you swore us to secrecy. You knew that what you were doing was wrong!' the English girl exclaimed, her pretty face marred by an ugly expression.

Emma adopted a soothing tone. She knew that she must remain sweetly reasonable or all would be lost. 'I happen to differ in my opinion, Faith, but you are entitled to yours.'

'Oh, you have an answer to everything, Mrs Longmore! But if Mrs Belfort knew what you were teaching us pure and innocent young ladies she would have forty fits!'

'That is unfair, Faith!' Yvette exclaimed. 'We are none of us so innocent as you suppose. Remember how we used to talk in the dormitory after lights out, wondering what would happen on our wedding night? We were all dying to know about such things, including you. It is hypocritical of you to deny it.'

'To know is one thing, to do is another!' Faith sniffed. 'I think you are all dirty girls. I shall ask to move to another dormitory. And I certainly shall not attend these disgusting classes any longer!'

With that she flounced out, leaving Emma feeling that she had seriously misjudged the girl's character.

'Do not worry about Faith,' Lotte said. 'I think she is jealous because she could not make herself have the same lovely feelings that we had, and yet she was too proud to ask for help.'

Even so, Faith's outburst had dampened Emma's enthusiasm. She began to talk about how men are aroused but although she described the male erection, and the tell-tale distortion it made in a gentleman's apparel, she felt disinclined to go into further detail.

'Next time we shall discuss the kiss,' she said, before dismissing them. 'From the formal salutation on the hand to the peck on the cheek, and beyond.'

But would there be a 'next time'? Emma could not help feeling perturbed as she returned to her room with her maid.

'I think that Faith Taylor-Browne has a bad case of sour grapes,' Kitty exclaimed, as she unbuttoned Emma's gown. 'You should not worry about her, Ma'am. I always thought she was a prig.'

'Then you have better judgement than me,' Emma said, ruefully.

It was not pleasant to have the girl glowering at her throughout the lesson on calling and card-leaving that she gave the following afternoon. Emma did her best to pretend all was well, but when Faith refused to answer

192

a question in a surly tone several of the other girls, who were not amongst the select few, looked puzzled.

After dinner, Mathilda took Emma aside. 'I am very pleased with the way you have settled in here,' she began. 'Are you happy, Emma?'

'Oh yes, thank you. Your girls are quite charming, and I enjoy teaching them immensely.'

'Then would you care to stay? I confess I have not yet advertised Miss Valenti's post, so if you would like to take it on a permanent basis . . .?'

'Oh, you are too kind! But that was never my intention, Mathilda. I thought I would stay here for a month at most, then return to England.'

'Well it is entirely your choice, Emma dear, but I hope you will give my proposal your serious consideration.'

Emma was flattered, but the idea of remaining indefinitely at Chateau Bellevue did not appeal. To be shuttered up in an all-female environment, having little contact with the outside world, was not the life she had envisaged for herself. Mathilda was disappointed, but said she would advertise immediately.

On Sunday night Emma decided to retire early, ready for the rigours of the next day. She rang the bell, but Kitty did not appear. She waited a few minutes then tried again. Still no reply. Emma took off her own clothes and put on her night-dress. She was used to Kitty brushing her hair last thing at night. Wondering what could have become of her, she rang again and this time Kitty entered looking flushed.

'Did you ring earlier, Ma'am? I am so sorry. I was asleep.'

'Asleep?' Emma repeated, in surprise. The girl's eyes slid guiltily away from hers.

Suddenly Emma laughed. 'Oh, you naughty girl! I know just what you must have been doing when I rang!' Kitty looked bashful as she began brushing Emma's hair. 'Even so, you must not let your personal pleasure interfere with your duty to me, my dear. I shall overlook it just this once, but next time you must be patient and wait until a more appropriate time.'

'Yes, Miss Emma,' Kitty replied. But in the mirror her mistress could see a secretive, almost smug expression on the girl's face that disconcerted her.

When she went to bed that night Emma was still in a state of semi-excitement after the events of the day. The minute she closed her eyes she imagined a scene of debauchery that soon forced her to place a hand between her restless thighs, so that she might squeeze them hard against it. The scenario that was unfolding seemed to have been stimulated by the girls' accounts of their first orgasmic experiences.

Emma could see herself mounting the stairs that led to the dormitory occupied by her chosen girls. As she drew near to their door she heard noises coming from within, sighs and moans of a sensual nature. She paused, imagining that they were pleasuring themselves in the way Kitty had showed them, and an urge to spy on their covert activities came over her. Gently she turned the handle and opened the door a crack. The room was illuminated only by night lights, but she could plainly see what was happening and had to smother a gasp. Instead of her pupils practising self-pleasuring, or even experimenting upon each other, she saw that they had introduced a new participant into the proceedings.

For there, lying completely naked on the floor upon an improvised bed of pillows and eiderdowns, was Vincent Belfort!

Emma felt the urge in her loins grow strong as she examined the detail of the scene in her mind's eye. She parted the soft petals of her sex and found her hardening bud, then proceeded to rub it gently while her fantasy unfolded. In her imagination, the intrepid Vincent had found a way to satisfy all three girls at once (Faith, needless to say, was quite out of the picture). While Yvette straddled his chest Vincent, with his head supported by a pillow, was able to reach her pussy with

194

his tongue and was giving excellent service to her demanding clitoris. To one side sat Bella on a pillow, her legs spread wide so as to give Vincent's thrusting fingers full access to her hungry quim. Being near to each other, it was natural that the two girls should be kissing affectionately and gently fondling each others' breasts, thus increasing their own exquisite pleasure.

However the third of the girls, Lotte, was by no means left out. In fact, hers was perhaps the most delightful position of all, for she was directly behind Yvette and in sole charge of Vincent's magnificent penis. At first she licked and sucked upon it, helping it to reach its full dimensions. Then, when she judged him ready, she tentatively lowered herself down onto the upward thrusting shaft and eased the glans into her, inch by glorious inch. Emma watched a smile spread across the girl's face as she managed to accommodate its full length and girth.

Soon all of them were united in one, pulsating rhythm of love-making, for while Lotte glided slowly up and down the axis of her pleasure, Yvette was gently thrusting her hips back and forth so as to gain maximum stimulation for herself from Vincent's eager tongue. At the same time Bella was squirming in abandon as she felt his fingers deep inside, wringing every ounce of sensation from the experience and gasping wildly as she did so. The three girls were moaning uninhibitedly with intense feeling as they rode towards their climax.

Emma, too, felt the crisis approaching as she envisaged the three girls and Vincent all in their throes at once. She could hear the sweet feminine cries and the deeper groans of the young man as they mingled in climactic accord, and then the whole scene was blotted out as her own orgasm broke upon her, thrilling her through and through with a blessed, tingling warmth. She lay for a while with the sheets thrown back and her nightgown pulled up to her waist, luxuriating in the afterglow, then drifted gradually into a deeply satisfying slumber.

* * *

The Café du Lac was situated at the opposite end of town from the Chateau Bellevue. At a table on the terrace, overlooking the lake, was a well-dressed Englishman pretending to read a newspaper. At last a young woman in a hooded blue velvet cloak arrived, and sat down at his table. He ordered her a lemonade then asked, 'What news do you have for me, Faith?'

She looked back nervously over her shoulder. 'Well Sir, at the last meeting I attended the other girls related, in great detail, the filthy things they had been doing.'

'Are we speaking of self-abuse, perchance?' he enquired, coolly.

The girl blushed and nodded. 'I hardly know how to speak of it.'

'There is a sovereign for you if you tell me all. I need to know such details before we can bring a prosecution. Such a place of iniquity should be cleaned up before more innocent minds are corrupted, do you not agree?'

'Yes, I suppose so,' Faith said, dubiously. 'But there is nothing wrong with the school in general, I assure you, just that wicked Mrs Longmore.'

'Do not fear, I shall make sure that only Mrs Longmore is dismissed. So, what have your classmates been doing that has so shocked you?'

Faith's voice lowered to a whisper. 'They have been . . . abusing themselves in a most lewd manner. Mrs Longmore's younger sister showed them how to do it, and they all practised in the dormitory at night. I thought they were well-brought-up girls, but Mrs Longmore has ruined them. Now they are unfit for marriage to any respectable man.'

'Hm. I hope there are no men involved in these "lessons", are there?'

Faith looked shocked. 'Oh no! At least, not yet. Heaven alone knows what that dreadful woman has in store for those poor girls in future. I am afraid I had to leave the class, Sir. I could not allow myself to be soiled in mind and body.'

'That is a pity. I was counting on you to furnish me

with more details, but I think we have enough evidence already. Here is your money. Now I think you should go back before your absence is noticed. Thank you for your help, and I can promise you that something will be done about the situation soon.'

'Thank you, Sir. I do hope so, for the other girls' sake.'

Once Faith had left the café a smile spread over Daniel Forbes's face. So Emma was initiating young girls into the joys of love, as well as young men – what a woman! He had never met anyone like her. She was not mercenary, like a whore, nor was she a debauchee, concerned only with her own pleasure. She seemed to have a kind of reforming zeal, as if it were her duty to educate the young of both sexes in the pleasures of the flesh, counteracting ignorance and superstition. He couldn't help but admire her.

Yet there was more to it than that. Daniel stared out at the still waters of the lake, deep in thought. He had believed that his fascination with Emma Longmore would end once he had tricked her into letting him have his way with her. It was true that he had felt an extraordinary revitalisation when he took her incognito in the cloister of Santa Croce, but instead of that being the end of the matter it now seemed like only the beginning. He had become more obsessed with her, not less. He wanted to take her while she was fully aware of him, he wanted her to know her lover's identity. More than that, even, he wanted her to want him.

Was this a self-destructive path he was following? Daniel downed his schnapps in one go but sat on, vacantly staring. He could not forget that look in Emma's eyes when he was being driven away into the Florentine night. He had seen the lightning flash of recognition, indicating that she had known him for what he was, her seducer. Did she despise him? He would not blame her if she did. That was why he was skulking on the edge of this town, paying a priggish schoolgirl to spy on her. It disgusted him, but he was in the grip of something uncontrollable and he had to see it through to whatever end might be in store for him.

Only three of the girls assembled in the Salle de Vénus on the following evening, as Kitty had asked to be excused on the grounds of a headache. Emma, not knowing how much longer she would be staying at the Chateau Bellevue, decided to go straight to the heart of the matter.

'Tonight I shall deal with the subject of sexual intercourse,' she began. 'There are many things a man should know about this but, sadly, he may prove to be as ignorant as most women. It is up to you ladies to educate your future husbands in the art of love-making.'

'How shall we do that?' Lotte asked, bluntly. 'Do we have to give him a lesson, like this?'

The others laughed. 'No, I think there are better ways,' Emma said. 'For example, you may guide his hands or lips to your breasts before he attempts to breach the nether region.'

'But what if he insists?' Bella asked.

'Well then you may have to explain briefly, "Husband, if you delay your entrance for a few minutes and make me desire you a little more, then it will be so much easier for us both." No considerate husband would refuse his wife in such circumstances.'

'One thing I have always wished to know, Emma,' Lotte said. 'How long does this act of intercourse last?'

'The longer the better, from a woman's point of view,' Emma smiled. 'However, you should not expect miracles, especially on your wedding night. Generally speaking, the older and more experienced a man becomes, the longer he can last. That is to say, anything from ten minutes to an hour or more. But what you should remember, ladies, is that while you are making love time has no meaning. A minute can seem like an hour, or vice-versa.'

Suddenly Emma felt immensely sad. She was realising how much she missed the lovemaking of her husband, the fond coupling of two people who knew each other well and had all the time in the world together. Would she ever experience that kind of love again?

'And shall we feel the same pleasure with our husbands that we feel by ourselves?' Bella asked, eagerly.

'Well, that depends . . .' The girls were eagerly awaiting her reply. Emma did not wish to give them false hopes, but she also felt obliged to give them realistic expectations. 'A skilled lover will progress from kissing to fondling of the breasts and beyond, taking note of the woman's responses,' she began. 'If he sees that you are becoming more eager he will intensify his labours, or else surprise you with some new titillation. The ways in which a man may arouse his wife are many and varied, and the good lover will employ everything that his imagination can produce.'

'There are certain things that make me feel good,' Yvette volunteered. 'The touch of silk on my skin, the light brushing of a feather. Any man who desires me will soon find me ready and willing if he employs such means.'

'Exactly!' Emma beamed. These young ladies were learning fast. It was remarkable how their animal sensuality was reasserting itself after years of repression.

Suddenly the door of the room burst open and Mathilda entered, a worried frown on her face. She asked, peremptorily, 'Mrs Longmore, where is your maidservant?'

'In her room I imagine, Mathilda. She was complaining of a headache.'

From behind the headmistress, the slight figure of Faith Taylor-Browne emerged. Her face was contorted with gloating excitement. 'Then she is lying!'

'Faith tells me she knows where the girl is, but she would not reveal more until I fetched you. Please, dismiss your class at once and come with us.'

Emma was filled with trepidation. She had the uneasy

feeling that Faith was about to discredit her. But what had become of poor Kitty? Faith led them downstairs and out into the garden, where a glorious sunset was incongruously in progress.

As they went, Mathilda talked to Emma in a low voice. 'Really, my dear, I haven't the faintest idea what this is all about. Faith said you were attempting to pass your maidservant off as your sister. Is that so?'

'Only for propriety's sake, Mathilda. I thought she might benefit from attending some of my lessons.'

'Well, this girl has a bee in her bonnet about something, that's for sure. Where on earth is she taking us? Oh, good Lord! The summer house?'

As her feet followed the other women's across the lawn, Emma felt her heart beating faster in her chest with foreboding. Faith paused at the door and motioned them to approach, with a finger to her lips. The three women peered in through the ornate lattice window.

Mathilda uttered a gasp, and Emma felt her heart give a painful lurch. For there, perfectly visible from their vantage point, were two figures lying together on the Chinese rug. They were both naked, and Emma recognised her maid immediately by her dark, tumbling curls and pretty, uptilted breasts.

'Vincent!' Mathilda gasped, identifying the other party just as easily. She put a hand to her forehead. 'Oh, I fear I shall faint!'

While Faith fanned the headmistress with her handkerchief, Emma found she could not tear her eyes away from the scene. Still oblivious to the onlookers, Vincent was stroking Kitty's soft parts between her wide-open thighs while his lips toyed with the erect buttons of her nipples. As Emma watched, he got onto his knees and was preparing to make his entrance. His sturdy organ was poised in readiness, its pink head twitching eagerly while he inserted his finger into Kitty's opening to make sure she was ready for him. His self-confident air suggested to Emma that this was by no means his first time.

A part of her was almost pleased that Kitty was having her first experience with a man, yet she knew that the circumstances were altogether wrong. Only yesterday afternoon that young man had been apparently interested in her! Then, remembering how Kitty had not answered her bell, she realised that the girl had probably been with Vincent on the previous evening, too. She felt cheated and betrayed – by both of them.

Suddenly she came to her senses. 'I will stop them!' she told a still swooning Mathilda, and going up to the door she flung it open.

'Vincent! Kitty! What do you think you are doing?' she called. 'Get up off the floor!'

The pair looked up, shamefaced, and Vincent scrambled for his clothes while Kitty grabbed the edges of the rug and rolled herself up in it.

'Do not be foolish, Kitty. Put your clothes on at once!' Emma ordered her. 'Mrs Belfort is outside in a fainting fit because of what she has just seen. You will have some explaining to do to your mother, Vincent. Now get dressed and come back to the house.'

Five minutes later they were in Mathilda's study. Faith had been thanked for her vigilance by the headmistress and dismissed, but she had asked Emma to hear the erring couple's account of themselves.

'Was this your first . . . encounter with this young lady, Vincent?' Mathilda began, severely.

He hung his head. 'No, Mamma.'

'Then where and when?' Emma snapped.

'On Sunday, while you were at dinner. I asked her to meet me in the summer house at ten o'clock because I had a message for her mistress.'

'For Emma?' Mathilda raised her eyebrows. 'And was this true, or was it just a ploy Vincent?'

'A ploy I suppose, Mamma.'

Mathilda threw Emma an exasperated look. 'I cannot apologise enough, my dear. I thought my son had learnt his lesson after that last unfortunate episode . . .' She hesitated. 'You may as well know about it now. I

201

am afraid that Miss Valenti, your predecessor, was not "indisposed" as I made out. She had been carrying on an extended liaison with my son, and had . . . suffered the inevitable consequences.' The headmistress began to choke into her handkerchief. 'Pardon me, Emma. I cannot speak of it without becoming upset.'

Emma put her arm around the other woman's shoulders. 'Never you mind, Mathilda. I am sure this is all very distressing for you, but you need continue no longer. I think we know enough of the facts. It is up to you what steps you take to punish your son, but I believe that my maidservant was equally to blame. Come with me, Kitty. We shall return to my room.'

She led Kitty upstairs in icy silence. There was a dull anger burning in her breast, but she also recognised that her wrath was tinged with jealousy. How dare the girl give in to that man, when Emma herself had displayed the appropriate self-control and spurned his tentative advances!

'Kitty, I am ashamed of you,' she began immediately she had closed the door. 'You have behaved in a most unseemly fashion for a lady's maid and I am obliged to chastise you. Remove your petticoats, if you please, and bend over the side of the bed.'

It was the only way she could think of to punish her maid.

'Oh, please Miss Emma, do not spank me as if I were a child!' Kitty's eyes were large and frightened as she stared at her mistress.

'Would you rather be dismissed from my service, then?'

'Oh, no Miss Emma!'

'Then you must take your punishment. You have acted like a child, like a spoilt child who is easily led when sweetmeats are offered, and so you will receive a good hiding. Do as I say and take off your petticoats.'

Reluctantly Kitty did as she was told and bent in trepidation over the bed, lifting her skirt to expose her plump little behind. Emma found her slipper, but before she administered the first blow she felt obliged to give her maid a lecture.

'When I introduced you to physical pleasure, I did not expect you to behave in an improper manner, unbecoming to a lady's maid,' she began. 'You have let me down very badly, Kitty. A lady's reputation and that of her servants are closely linked. Heaven knows what Mrs Belfort thinks of me now.'

'I am sorry, Ma'am. I became carried away. Mr Vincent was so very . . . persuasive.'

'Persuaded you to deceive your own mistress, you mean. Shame on you, girl!'

With that Emma brought the slipper down hard on the exposed pink buttocks. Kitty whimpered a little. Emma spanked her again and again, finding the sound of soft leather on softer skin not unpleasing. She could hear Kitty moaning quietly as the pace increased and yet she did not seem to be in pain. As she got into her stride, Emma felt quite exhilarated. Each time she raised her arm her nipple pressed tight against its confines and grew rigid, while beneath her skirts she could feel her swollen lips rubbing against each other as she tensed her thighs. The exertion was making her pleasure button swell and harden, and soon she was tingling all over from head to toe. After a dozen or so strokes, however, her arm became tired and she stopped, with a dizzying rush to her head. She was sure she had punished the girl enough.

Kitty peered round, her face flushed, but made no attempt to get up from the bed or pull her clothes down. 'Is that all?' she asked, but Emma was surprised to hear a faint note of disappointment in her tone.

'Yes, I think so.'

'Do you really feel you have punished me sufficiently, Ma'am? After all, I admit that my misdemeanour was grave. I do not believe I have been thrashed thoroughly enough yet, Miss Emma.'

There was a look on her face that disturbed Emma. It was a sly, vixenish look. She felt she was seeing a side of Kitty that she had never noticed before. Suspecting that her maid had been enjoying the physical chastisement just as much as she had enjoyed delivering it, she decided not to pursue that dangerous line of approach any longer or her authority over the girl would surely be undermined. Instead, she made a decision.

'That was one half of your punishment, Kitty. The other half unfortunately must involve myself, although perhaps I deserve it. I believe I have been foolish in trusting you not to abuse the knowledge I gave you.'

'Oh, Miss Emma!' Kitty protested, but was silenced with a look.

'I should have known that if I regaled you with stories of sexual conquest and introduced you to the pleasures of the flesh that you would sooner or later wish to try them out with a male partner. Well, you have brought disgrace on us both and we shall be obliged to leave this place as soon as possible.'

'No, please Miss Emma, let us stay a while longer!' Behind Kitty's plea was a note of genuine anguish.

'I cannot think why you object so strongly. You knew that our stay here would be temporary. We will be leaving a little earlier than scheduled, that is all.'

The girl looked so miserable that Emma suspected some hidden motive, but she dared not question her more closely. Dismissing her coldly, she sat down at her dressing-table and opened the atlas she had brought with her to plan their route back to England.

Chapter Thirteen

*I*t was a sunny September afternoon and Russell
Square was full of nannies airing their charges and
old ladies walking their dogs. On a seat under a plane
tree sat Kitty, reading Mrs Gaskell's biography of
Charlotte Brontë. Her heart went out to the lonely
authoress, who had longed for wider experience and
fallen hopelessly in love with a man she had met while
abroad. She knew just how poor Charlotte must have
felt. Her own love for Vincent Belfort had also been
cut off in its prime, and now she thought about him
every waking minute, but most of all on her afternoons
off.

Along with her shattered dreams Kitty was nurturing
a growing resentment of her mistress. Since they had
returned to London, Emma had become caught up in
her new project and the closeness that used to exist
between her and her maid had faded. A house had
been rented in Bloomsbury and Emma had begun to
advertise in the journals of the Women's Suffrage Move-
ment as an 'educator of the daughters of forward-
thinking women'. In consequence she now held daily
classes with up to a dozen young ladies, from which
Kitty was strictly excluded. She had been reduced to
the status of a mere maidservant and, although Emma

was always civil towards her, Kitty missed the old friendship and intimacy.

The girl sighed as she read how Charlotte's letters to Monsieur Heger had not been answered after her return to Haworth. Kitty had thought of writing to Vincent but she had no doubt that any correspondence would be intercepted and destroyed by his mother. Was he missing her too? During their passionate encounter Vincent had murmured over and over again that he was utterly enamoured of her. She had known from the start that they were right for each other. Their bodies had been so perfectly attuned that their minds and hearts had been bound to soar in equal harmony.

The print on the page before her began to blur as Kitty recalled their first love-making in the summerhouse. Vincent had known exactly how to rouse her, using his lips and hands in a way that showed he was no novice in the art of love. Even now, as she thought about it, warm tingles were creeping down from her breasts to her thighs, making her ache with desire. She could recall it all in detail, although over two months had passed since then.

She remembered how Vincent's first kiss had been exquisitely slow and sensitive, keeping her hungry for him and only giving her more when she was ravenous. Even then he'd teased her with his tongue, now entering her mouth, now withdrawing. She'd been obliged to take his hand herself and put it on her straining breast, and then he'd stroked and softly pinched her rigid nipple over the layers of her blouse and corset and chemise for an interminable length of time before Kitty's patience finally gave out and she begged him to feel her warm, throbbing flesh.

With a beautiful smile Vincent had finally unbuttoned and unlaced her, revealing one pale breast. He spent a while exclaiming over its charming shape, and gently caressing the sensitive slopes before bending his lips to kiss her where she longed to be kissed. At once Kitty felt warm spirals of satisfaction pass through her, but the gratification was short-lived. Vincent had been paying so much attention to her left breast that the right one was becoming consumed with jealousy! It clamoured to be given equal treatment, and she began pulling at her clothes in an almost frantic fashion until her lover scolded her in a friendly way and took over, his lips following where his fingers went. Then, with her bosom fully exposed, Kitty relaxed while he licked and caressed her into a state of blissful near-oblivion.

Even so, she had been aware of a growing need for stimulation down below. Her thighs moved restlessly beneath her petticoats, and she could feel the moist unfolding of her parts. Deep inside the primal need was asserting itself, and she wanted to know whether Vincent felt it too. Her hand crept to his fly, and when she found his erection fully developed Kitty let out a deep sigh, savouring her first direct experience of phallic power.

'Do you want to see it?' Vincent had whispered, and she'd croaked her assent. He unbuttoned himself and pulled it out, urging her to look.

For a few seconds Kitty had stared down at the enormous pink head, staring back up at her with its blind eye, and thought she had never seen anything so extraordinary. To think that such a huge and strange creature remained hidden beneath men's apparel while they talked and did business, ate and drank, rode in carriages and attended church, pretending to be completely oblivious to its presence! Suddenly she saw the male sex in an entirely different light. Each and every one of them harboured a huge secret that they were obliged to conceal, for social reasons, for most of their life. No wonder they sometimes behaved strangely, or went off the rails!

'You may hold it if you wish,' Vincent had whispered.

In awe Kitty reached out, finding it warm and friendly to her touch, like a baby animal. He'd let her fondle its velvety smoothness, feeling it twitch against her palm and watching a small white pearl of liquid emerge from the slit at the end, until he cautioned her not to proceed.

'Let him go where he wants to,' he had murmured, as if his organ had an identity of its own. Vincent's fingers began parting the fleshy divide of her vulva and found it already open, inviting him in. With a sigh he positioned himself between her thighs, pausing only to give her mouth and nipples a taste of his eager lips. Then, for a while, he simply nudged her with his member. Kitty felt the hard, round head plugging her entrance while all around the most wonderful sensations teased her flesh. She recognised the hot itch from her self-pleasuring, and knew that this time her experience would be a new adventure in sensuality, taking her to places that she had never known before.

Then, when she felt she could bear the suspense no longer, Vincent had finally slid his way into her. Kitty had welcomed the intruder with an involuntary embrace of her interior flesh, clasping the hard length of him as easily as she had done with her hand. At the same time she was filled with a glorious warm contentment, such as she had never known before. At last she knew what women throughout the ages had known, knew what men longed for, were even prepared to die for, and with the knowledge came a new sense of power over her own destiny.

That first time Vincent had made three or four strong thrusts and then pulled out of her, so that his seed should spill on the floor. Seeing her disappointment, he'd explained that he had no wish for her to 'suffer consequences' but that he would continue to make love to her until she was satisfied. He tenderly caressed her still-throbbing parts in the same way that she did when she was alone, but this time it was accompanied by soft mouthing of her breasts and lips and within a few seconds Kitty found herself soaring into a climax of such exquisite and tender sensitivity that when she came down from it her eyes were filled with tears.

'My dear, beloved sweetheart,' he'd murmured, into

her matted hair. 'Next time we shall continue for longer, I promise you.'

Kitty had dashed back to her room, found her mistress ringing for her and then, despite her still-damp crotch and racing heart, was obliged to brush Miss Emma's hair as if nothing had happened. Yet all the while she wanted to sing and laugh and cry at the same time. All she could think of was her lover, and all she could hope for was that they would meet again soon. Yet, when they had their second chance, instead of making love for longer and with even greater passion as she had hoped, their meeting had been cruelly and ignominiously cut short.

The crunch of footsteps on the first fallen leaves brought Kitty back to her present, sadly bereft, state. Despite everything Vincent still loved her, she was quite sure of that. They were like Romeo and Juliet, she thought ruefully, 'star-crossed lovers'. Would Fate ever let them meet again?

A shadow suddenly fell across her page. Kitty looked up, startled, and was amazed to find Daniel Forbes smiling down at her. She blushed in confusion, not knowing how she should behave, but he smilingly tipped his hat and gave a bow.

'Kitty, my dear, how delightful to see you again after all this time. How are you?'

'Very well thank you, Sir,' she mumbled, still unsure of herself.

'Would you mind if I sat beside you?'

Kitty could hardly refuse. She moved up nervously although there was plenty of room on the bench. Aware that she would get into trouble if her mistress knew she had been speaking to this man, Kitty prayed that he would not ask her anything about Emma Longmore.

But, surprisingly, he seemed more interested in her.

'Did you enjoy your travels around Europe?' he asked, in a kindly way.

'Oh yes, thank you.'

'And which city pleased you most, Kitty?'

She wanted to say 'Florence', but remembering that for some reason Emma had broken off her relationship with this man there she thought better of it. Instead she said, 'Paris, I think.'

'Really?' he sounded genuinely surprised. 'I had thought you would say "Montreux". I believed that was where you found your greatest happiness, but perhaps I was mistaken.'

Kitty stared at him incredulously. Was he hinting at her short-lived affair with Vincent? Surely not. He could not possibly know about it. Nevertheless, she did give him a rueful smile.

'Well, it is true,' she conceded, warily. 'Montreux will always have a special place in my heart.'

He took her small hand between both of his large, gloved ones and forced her to look straight into his dark eyes. Kitty felt an excited tremor pass through her, making her believe she was on the verge of some great discovery. 'Tell me, my dear, is this your afternoon off?' he asked, gravely. She nodded. 'What time does your mistress expect you back?'

Kitty shrugged. 'She will be busy this evening, with one of her classes, and only needs me at bedtime. I doubt whether she will notice what time I return so long as I am there by ten o'clock or so.'

'Excellent!' Daniel beamed. 'Then I have a wonderful surprise for you, Kitty. There is a certain person who longs to meet you. He has travelled all the way from Montreux . . .'

'Vincent?' Kitty asked, tremulously, her heartbeat thudding loudly in her ears.

'The very same! He has come to London to study law, and I have given him lodgings in my house. I am sure he would be delighted to see you again, if you wish to see him?'

'If I wish!' she exclaimed, laughter bubbling up in her throat like champagne. 'Oh, If only you knew, dear Mr Forbes! It is what I have been wishing for, night and day, ever since we were forced to part.'

'I suspected as much. Well, let us waste no more time. I left Vincent reading some dry tome on jurisprudence and I am sure he would welcome the interruption! It is not far, we may walk from here.'

Kitty had never felt so excited, and as they walked through the streets of Bloomsbury she plied Mr Forbes with questions. 'But how did you find out about me and Vincent?' she asked, hurrying along beside his longer stride.

'Let us say I had an "informant" at the Chateau Bellevue,' he smiled, mysteriously.

'But the last time we saw you was in Florence! Did you follow us to Montreux?'

'Yes, when I eventually found out where you and your mistress had gone. I had my own reasons for wishing to track you down, which I must ask you not to pry into. When I heard of the circumstances leading up to your sudden departure I confess that my heart went out to you. Young love thwarted is always a poignant story, but to be able to reunite a pair of pining lovers brings warm cheer to the heart.'

'Oh Sir, how shall I ever thank you?'

'I may think of something,' he murmured under his breath. Then aloud, 'It is nothing, Kitty. My reward shall be the sight of both your faces when you gaze into each others' eyes once more. Prepare yourself, my dear, for we are almost there.'

They stopped before a large house in Brunswick Square. Kitty followed Daniel Forbes up the stairs to the first floor drawing room, where she was told to wait. Too nervous to sit down, she paced by the window until at last the door opened and her beloved Vincent stood there in all his glory, as flushed and excited as she was.

They flew into each others' arms and he proceeded to cover her face with kisses.

'Oh, my darling Kitty, I have so longed for this moment!' he sighed.

'And I, dearest Vincent! After our last disastrous meeting I truly believed I would never set eyes on you again, and yet – here we both are! What a wonderful man Mr Forbes has turned out to be! It is to him alone that we owe all this bliss. But where can he be? I want to thank him again, now that I have you in my arms again and know this is real life and not just an empty dream.'

'Dear Kitty!' Vincent kissed her on the forehead. 'I think he knew that we would wish to be alone. He has ordered tea for us and then, when we have caught upon each others' news, I think he would not mind if I took you to my room.'

'You mean . . .?' Kitty was wide-eyed. She had not hoped for such an opportunity so soon.

Vincent kissed her passionately on the mouth, and his lips said it all. When the parlour maid brought in the tea, they broke apart for a few minutes but as soon as she had gone they were back in another embrace.

'Shall we go straight to my room?' Vincent whispered.

'Well, I think I would like some tea,' Kitty smiled, mischievously. 'With one of those delicious-looking macaroons. And perhaps a slice of that pound cake.'

'Oh, Kitty!' Vincent said, with mock disappointment. 'And I thought you were hungry for me!'

'Oh I am, I am! But I need to eat so I may have the energy to keep up with you!'

They passed a quarter of an hour in similar affectionate banter, then Vincent took her by the hand. 'Come, Kitty, I want to feast my eyes on your beautiful body once again. Let us go where we shall not be disturbed.'

While they walked up the top staircase, Daniel was already waiting in the dressing-room next to Vincent's quarters. He was comfortably seated in an armchair close to the party wall and beside him, on a small table, was a flask of brandy. Hearing the pair enter the room next door he removed a small oval painted portrait from the wall and revealed a two-way mirror, a device which afforded the onlooker an excellent view of the proceedings without being seen himself.

Smiling to himself, Daniel took one more swig from the flask and settled down to enjoy the spectacle. This girl, he mused, was the pretty little fly he would use to lure Emma Longmore into his web. She was already so grateful to him that she would do almost anything in return, and after an hour or two of carnal delight she would be even more eager to meet her lover again. As for Vincent . . .

Daniel almost laughed aloud when he recalled how he had posed as one of the staff at Winchester – the divinity teacher, no less! – in order to persuade that trumped-up chocolatier's widow that her son should train for the Bar.

'I was just passing through Montreux on my way to Rome, Madame Belfort,' he had simpered, 'and I thought I would enquire after one of my favourite ex-pupils. It was clear to all of us at Winchester that Master Belfort was destined for a glittering career in any of the professions, so I was wondering which path he had finally fixed upon. Medicine, perhaps? Or the law?'

How easily the old trout had swallowed the bait, hook and all! It had gone perfectly according to plan, and now he had this pair of turtle-doves just where he wanted them: embroiled with each other again, and deeply in his debt. He watched them almost fondly as they fell upon each other, deep in the throes of lust, and began to undress. When the girl's plump breasts first appeared, their rosy tips hard with desire, Daniel felt a corresponding hardening in his member and unbuttoned his fly to release it. Then, as her dainty black vee was revealed, the tight pubic curls concealing pink lips that must already be moistening and flushing in readiness, Daniel put his hand to his shaft and gave it a few strong tugs.

He continued to watch as Vincent went straight into his willing accomplice with his firmly extended phallus, making her thrash around and roll her eyes like a demoness. The boy was mouthing at her nipples now, making them as red and wet as his tongue, while he cupped her delightfully taut buttocks with his hands. Clearly on their previous encounters they had established a fine physical rapport, for the girl was thrusting her hips in time with his while she reached beyond the plunging root of his sturdy member in order to tickle his balls. Through the wall Daniel could hear their moans and cries as they reached a crescendo and his right hand worked automatically upon his own erection, bringing him closer and closer to the brink. Yet it was an absent-minded procedure, for although what he saw with his eyes seemed to be directly stimulating his member, his thoughts were far away.

Emma Longmore! She was almost at his command now, and yet he must proceed with the utmost caution. He watched Vincent bend his lips to Kitty's mouth while the pace of his copulation quickened, but in his mind's eye it was himself and Emma that he saw there, *in flagrante delicto*, with her urging him on deeper and deeper inside her softly undulating quim. He wanted her to be as willing and eager for him as that trollope was for her paramour! Daniel gave his penis a last, savage tug and the seed spilt from him, hot and searing, like liquid fire spilling from his veins. He groaned with the torment of it, eternally unsatisfied, knowing that only *she* could bring him what he craved.

The pair next door were done for the time being. They'd had their little deaths and were now lying in each others' arms like figures on a tomb. Daniel replaced the portrait in disgust. How jaded he was by the pleasures of the flesh, regardless of whether they were someone else's or his own! Was that why he had spun his pursuit of Emma Longmore out, chased her through four countries playing 'cat and mouse' all the way? Well, some day soon it would have to end, one way or the other. And that love-struck hussy in the next room was the one who would help him bring the affair to its conclusion.

* * *

Emma sat in the drawing-room of her house off South-ampton Row drinking tea, but her mind was far from her cup of Earl Grey and the little box of crystallised fruits, given to her by a grateful student, which she was absently consuming. The success of her venture in educating the daughters of progressive women was undeniable. She now held a class every morning and afternoon during the week, with extra tuition on two nights besides. The scope of her syllabus had been considerably widened to include politics, anthropology and history as well as modern manners, and what went under the euphemistic title of 'marital and pre-marital etiquette'.

Not all of the mothers knew exactly what their daughters were learning in Mrs Longmore's establishment, but the girls had been carefully vetted and not accepted until Emma was quite sure that she was not harbouring another viper in her nest. To her great delight two of her students from the Chateau Bellevue had followed her to London. Both Yvette Duval and Bella Lucci had managed to persuade their parents that they wished to perfect their English, and that the best way to do that was to attend classes in England. Now they were invaluable in helping with the other girls, in giving confidence where it was needed and showing by their example that worldly knowledge and experience were still compatible with beauty, charm and intelligence.

Furthermore, these two young ladies were soon to be introduced into polite society by Lady Brendan, an old acquaintance of Emma's. They were attending their first embassy ball soon, and she had high hopes that they would attract the attention of some wealthy and influential gentlemen. They might, in time, work their way into the upper echelons of society, perhaps even into the exclusive coterie of the Prince of Wales! Although Emma had no such ambitions for herself she knew that she would enjoy bathing in the reflected glory if any of her students managed to reach those exalted heights. To think that young women whose minds she had moulded with forward-looking ideas would be influencing those who held positions of power in the land. Why, an educated and well-bred courtesan might change the course of history with her pillow-talk!

Emma rang the bell for Kitty to clear away the tea-things. The girl entered looking vague and distracted. Once Emma would have enquired after her maid's health, but lately she had been in the habit of ignoring her. In a sudden fit of conscience she decided to become her old, friendly self for once. 'Kitty, dear, is anything wrong? I have been so busy these past few weeks that I feel I have neglected you somewhat. Is everything here to your liking?'

'Oh yes, Ma'am, thank you. Everything here is perfectly fine.'

Was Emma mistaken, or did she hear a sarcastic note in the girl's voice. She decided to pursue it further. 'And how do you find London? I have noticed that you always go out on your free afternoons. Do you find somewhere pleasant to visit? The British Museum, perhaps?'

Her efforts at making conversation were sounding forced. Emma felt annoyed with herself for letting her relationship with Kitty deteriorate. She had ceased to be angry with the girl for her behaviour in Montreux, but the old warmth had gone from their relationship. Perhaps it was time to mend fences. She still needed loyalty from her staff – now more than ever.

Kitty looked embarrassed, arousing Emma's curiosity. After hesitating for a few seconds she said, 'Well, Ma'am, I usually take a book to read in the square. It was while I was there, the other day, that I fell into conversation with . . . a young gentleman.'

Emma stiffened automatically, but then realised that she was being unfair. The wretched girl must think that her mistress would frown on any contact she had with the opposite sex, but that was far from the truth. It would have been the height of hypocrisy to introduce her to the pleasures of the flesh then forbid her to enjoy them with a young man. Although the unfortunate circumstances surrounding her liaison with Vincent had earned Emma's disapproval, she was by no means hostile to her forming a new relationship now that they were in London.

'Well, Kitty, I am pleased to hear it.' The girl visibly relaxed a little. 'Tell me more about him.'

'He is studying law, and lives not far from here. He has invited me to tea on Sunday, but I told him I could not come without a chaperone.'

Emma caught her drift at once. 'My dear, I should be delighted to accompany you. What is the young man's name?'

Kitty averted her eyes, saying hesitantly, 'His name is . . . Vernon. Vernon Lamont.'

Emma decided to ignore the girl's obvious apprehensiveness. She recalled her own trepidation on introducing Henry to her parents for the first time and felt a warm glow of compassion. Since Emma was *in loco parentis* with regard to her orphaned maid then Kitty must be undergoing similar feelings, wondering if her beau would meet with approval, afraid that – for whatever unimaginable reason – he might not.

Emma went up to the girl, who was staring absently out of the window, and put one arm around her thin shoulders. 'Kitty, dear, do not fret. I am sure I shall like your new admirer very much. A chance meeting in the square – how romantic! Perhaps he had often gazed upon your sweet face from afar before he plucked up the courage to approach you. I am looking forward very much to meeting this young man.'

Emma was trying her best to sound enthusiastic, but somehow it was not ringing true. For some reason, Kitty remained diffident and anxious. Giving her maid a last hug, she allowed the girl to clear away the tea things and depart.

A few days later the two women set out across Russell Square, each dressed in their Sunday-best outfits. It was a sunny afternoon and Emma was in good spirits, although Kitty still had that air of nervous expectancy about her. Well I am determined to like this new beau of hers even if he has a squint and a hunchback, Emma thought. She wanted to make up for the girl's previous disappointment, and for what she now regarded as her own harsh and unsympathetic treatment of her.

'Here we are,' Kitty announced as they reached a tall, elegant town house. The door was opened by a man-servant who ushered them upstairs and into a light and airy drawing-room.

'Well, this is very nice,' Emma declared, looking round. 'Is this the young gentleman's family home, or does he lodge here?'

'He . . . he lodges here, Ma'am.'

Kitty seemed more agitated then ever. What on earth was worrying the girl? She began to imagine all kinds of hideous deformities or social disadvantages that her unfortunate suitor might possess. Well, if he and Kitty were sincerely in love she was determined that she would put no further obstacles in their way.

As Emma stood gazing out at the trees of Brunswick Square she thought she heard the sound of a door quietly opening, but before she could turn around she was being pulled away from the window, with both arms pinioned behind her back and a thick blindfold was being slipped over her eyes. She uttered a scream and, on the verge of fainting, exclaimed, 'Kitty! What is this? Help me, for God's sake!'

Then her maid's voice could be heard saying, agitatedly, 'You will not hurt her, Sir? Promise me you will do her no harm!'

'I promise!' came the guttural reply. 'Now go to him. He awaits you in his room.'

Emma felt weak and dizzy. Half collapsed, she allowed strong arms to support her and lead her trembling from the room.

'Who are you? Where are you taking me?' she gasped, but there was no reply. All she knew was that she was being led into another room in the house. Her captor partly untied her wrists but Emma's relief was short-lived for she was straightaway made to lie down on a bed and her wrists were tied to the posts. She struggled this way and that, but could not free herself and a dreadful suspicion overtook her. She knew of only one man in the world who was capable of treating her this ruthlessly. A demon whose lust knew no bounds, and who was relentless in his pursuit of her. Had that fiend tracked her down once again?

'Daniel Forbes?' she cried, weakly, almost choking with disgust as she spat out the name.

He gave the low chuckle that she recognised at once. With unexpected gentleness he untied her blindfold and she saw him standing there in a black quilted dressing-gown, smiling down at her in the lamplight. Despite Emma's terrified state she could not help noticing the look in his eyes. To her amazement, they were filled with a tender warmth and wonder, and his mouth was curved into a soft, sweet smile. Daniel Forbes was gazing at her in what could only be described as adoration, as if she were the most beautiful creature he had ever seen.

Chapter Fourteen

'Why have you done this to me?' Emma breathed, straining at her bonds. She found she could no longer look Daniel in the eye. The contradiction between his rough treatment of her and the unutterable tenderness of his expression was horribly confusing.

'Because I knew of no other way to make you listen to me,' he replied. 'If I had not blindfolded you I believe you would have shunned me at once, then tried to flee. If I had not tied your hands you would have attempted to scratch my eyes out. Admit it, Lady Longmore!'

Emma winced as he used her title. So he had somehow discovered that. What else did this obsessed man know of her background? Try as she might to think straight and keep her wits about her, Emma felt shocked and utterly confused.

'I do not understand,' she told him, near to tears. 'Why can't you leave me alone? You had your way with me in Florence – was that not enough?'

Daniel's expression grew pained. 'Emma, do you really think that was all I wanted of you? It is true that I was consumed with lust for you, that I would stop at nothing to possess you. But afterwards my longing for you only intensified and I felt ashamed of my treachery.

Knowing how susceptible you were to innocent young men I played upon your weakness – '

'*My* weakness!' Emma's fiery spirit revived as she addressed him scornfully. 'Surely a man who follows a woman halfway across Europe, has no right to call the object of his adoration "weak". You followed me like a fawning lap-dog!'

To her surprise, Daniel gave a hearty laugh. 'Oh my dear, I have never been awarded that title before! Lap-dog, indeed!'

'I have known some of those creatures to be vicious and spiteful,' she told him, tartly.

'*Touché.* But if you must liken me to some canine, at least choose a more noble and untamed creature than that. How about a wolfhound? It better describes how I feel when I look at you – wild and predatory. Yet I know that you have the power to tame me.'

'Tame you? I have no desire to have anything to do with you. So if you will pretend, at least, to be a gentleman and kindly untie me I shall return home. Any more of this nonsense and I shall shout and scream loud enough to bring this house down.'

Daniel sat down on the bed beside her, near enough for Emma to see the sadness in his eyes. He spoke softly to her, and she felt her heartbeat falter despite her anger. 'Oh, my dear, if only we could be friends! I know that you have mistrusted me from the beginning, probably with good reason. Yet if you knew the depths of my feeling for you perhaps you would be more forgiving.'

She remained silent, locked into her own troubled thoughts. Impulsively he bent forward and kissed her cheek. Emma turned her head away in disgust, but the spot that his lips had touched continued to burn. For several minutes Daniel just sat looking at her, a fleeting shadow-play of emotions passing over his handsome features. Then he said with a sigh, 'Very well, Emma, I shall release you now. I forced you once, but I'll never do so again. You will come to me willingly, or not at all.'

Emma lay there in tight disapproval while he untied her. She began to rub the chafed skin but Daniel swiftly seized both her hands and planted a kiss on each wrist. Annoyed, Emma pulled her hands free and sprang from the bed. He shrugged, a half smile on his face.

'Do not attempt to do anything like this again,' she warned him, as she made for the door. 'Or, I warn you, there shall be dire consequences.'

'I can think of no worse consequence than never to set eyes on you again.'

Emma stared, unwilling to believe he was speaking in earnest, but the look he gave her said that he was. Even so she forced herself to shun him, flung open the door and began to hurry across the landing towards the stairs. Quickly she descended to the hall and went straight to pull back the latch of the front door. After a moment's struggle she managed to open it and slipped out into the pleasant autumn air. Emma hurried along the pavement until she was quite sure she was not being followed, then slowed her pace. She felt as if she had just escaped from prison.

Yet did not even released prisoners feel some slight nostalgia for what they had left behind? As she walked through the familiar streets to her rented home, Emma could not get the image of Daniel Forbes's sad eyes out of her mind. Good heavens above, was it possible that a victim of deception could forgive her deceiver, or even pity him?

Only if she had secretly desired his deception of her, Emma concluded. Remembering her feelings in the cloister of Santa Croce she could not pretend that she had been taken totally against her will. She had wanted that 'priest' to believe that he was ravishing her, had wanted him to feel the guilt that he induced in others, wanted to show him that he was a man like all other men. The fact that he had turned out to be someone she knew could not alter the fact that she had revelled in dark and forbidden pleasure for a while. She had fully intended to seduce a virgin priest, to trick him into sating his lust. How could she then condemn a man for tricking her in return?

As soon as she was indoors, however, Emma's thoughts turned to the trickery of her maid. This time the girl could not be so easily forgiven. Kitty had lured her to that house, she was sure of it. Before the event she had been as nervous as a highly strung filly. But what hold did Daniel have over the girl to force her to do such a thing?

Emma awaited Kitty's return with mounting fury. When at last she heard Jones admit her saying, 'Nice walk this afternoon, Miss Kitty?' she flung open the door of the drawing-room and said, icily, 'Will you wait in my study please, Kitty? I need to speak to you immediately.'

'Yes, Ma'am,' she muttered, her head hung low. Jones gave them both a quizzical look but said nothing and returned to the kitchen. While Kitty made her way slowly to the study on the first floor, Emma did her best to compose herself. She was so furious that she feared she might strike the girl if she confronted her straight away.

But as soon as Emma entered the room Kitty flung herself at her mistress, sobbing. 'Please forgive me, Ma'am! He made me do it!'

'*Made* you, Kitty?'

Emma bade the girl get up and sit on a chair in proper fashion while she did likewise. When they were facing each other Emma questioned her closely. 'Now tell me from the beginning, Kitty. Where and when did you meet Mr Forbes?'

'In the square, Ma'am. He told me that a certain person wanted to see me and I went with him to his house. I did so long to see him again, and – '

'This "certain person" – is he the young man I think he is?' Dumbly, Kitty nodded. 'I see. So for "Vernon

Lamont" we must substitute Vincent Belfort. Is that correct?'

Kitty burst into tears. 'Oh Ma'am, I never meant any harm! He swears he loves me, and I love him. It was terrible the way things went for us. Now he is in London studying for the Bar, but when he finishes we plan to marry if he can get his Mamma to agree to it.'

Emma gave the girl her handkerchief and waited for her to dry her eyes and blow her nose. Then she said, more in sorrow than in anger, 'I wish you had not deceived me, Kitty. If I had known about this then Mr Forbes would have had no hold over you, I presume. Was it because he threatened you in some way that you agreed to dupe me into going to his house?'

'He never threatened me, Miss Emma. But it was him who brought me and Vincent together again. Vincent lodges in his house, you see. I thought he wouldn't let me see him again if I didn't do as he asked.'

'Oh Kitty, Kitty!' Emma put a hand to her brow. 'I cannot find it in my heart to be hard on you, my dear. I feel I have been too harsh in the past, causing you to become afraid of me.'

'Then you will not punish me for what Mr Forbes made me do?'

'Not this time. And if you wish to continue seeing Vincent I shall not prevent you. Except that I hope you are being careful . . .'

'Oh yes, he is very good in that way.'

'Very well Kitty, you may go to your room now. But leave the salts with me, please. I have a headache.'

After Kitty had left, murmuring eternal gratitude, Emma drew the blinds and lay down on the chaise longue in her study. It had been an extremely taxing afternoon and she needed to rest and collect her thoughts. Behind all the duplicity that she had been subjected to, Emma detected one sole passion: desire. For some reason she had evoked it disastrously in Daniel Forbes and it seemed that Vincent had done the same with poor Kitty. Yet why did such attraction so often become an unholy power struggle between the sexes? It still irked her to think that Daniel had lured her into his house in that grotesque fashion, and ended up having the last word. Sometimes she wondered whether the game was worth the candle.

After drifting into an uneasy slumber, Emma awoke with an outrageous plan in her head. She examined it carefully, but knew that she would not rest until she had carried it out. She would need Kitty's assistance, but the girl would no doubt be only too pleased to help. Emma rang the bell and soon her maid appeared, fresh-faced and eager to do her bidding.

'Sit down please, Kitty, and tell me when you next intend to visit your Vincent.'

'On my afternoon off, if it pleases you Ma'am.'

'It pleases me very much since I have a task for you to perform, one that will even the score between me and that dastardly Daniel Forbes.'

Seeing her mistress in a lighter mood, Kitty's brows shot up in amusement. 'Really, Ma'am?'

'Yes. You may tell that scoundrel that your mistress will be at home to him that evening at six o'clock. When you have seen your young man, you will bring Mr Forbes here and between us we shall wreak our joint revenge on him.'

Kitty giggled. 'How on earth shall we do that, Miss Emma?'

'Never you mind. I have three whole days to work out the details, then I shall let you know. He shall not go scot free, I can assure you.'

On Thursday afternoon, Kitty set out for the house in Brunswick Square. Emma watched her go from an upstairs window, filled with such a heady sense of anticipation that she could feel herself growing hot and aroused. Was this what was meant by the 'lust for revenge,' she wondered?

During the intervening hours, Emma reflected on her history with Daniel Forbes. It seemed to be full of contradictions. In many ways he had been courteous and friendly towards her, and she could not deny that she had enjoyed his company on occasions. She had been fascinated by him, too. Yet always she had been wary of him, suspecting that something disreputable lurked below the surface of his civilised veneer. Even when he had taken her to the Jockey Club, with its salacious atmosphere and lewd performances, he had behaved like a perfect gentleman. But now it irked her to think that all the while he must have been secretly revelling in the knowledge that he had deceitfully violated her.

Emma knew she should feel that the man had some obscure power over her, but it felt more like the reverse. He had told her she had him in her thrall. She had never been faced with such paradoxical emotions before. It was almost as if he wanted to be her slave, wanted her to take control of his desires and mould them to hers. Well, tonight she would see how it felt to be in that position. It was high time.

Kitty arrived promptly at six-fifteen and ushered Daniel into the drawing-room. Emma wanted to treat him just as he had treated her, so when she gave Kitty the signal they both rushed in together. Everything went according to plan: while Emma swiftly bound his wrists behind his back with a tight cord, Kitty slipped a blindfold over his eyes.

Daniel made no attempt to struggle but said, wryly, 'So, I am to be given a taste of my own medicine, ladies. Lead me, as a lamb to the slaughter. I am in your fair hands.'

Emma was disconcerted. Remembering how terrified she had been when given the same treatment, she grew angry. 'You mock us now but soon you will be begging for mercy. Help me to take him out of this room, Kitty. We shall have him exactly where we want him.'

They led him, stumbling, into Emma's bedroom where they laid him face down on the bed and stripped off his lower garments, then tied his ankles to the brass foot-rail. As previously instructed, Kitty handed her mistress the short riding crop with a smile. Emma could feel her blood grow hot as she took the whip and raised her arm above the slack, pale buttocks.

'Now, we shall see if you can take your punishment like a man!' she cried, her voice hoarse with anger.

Filled with sudden exhilaration, she brought the leather down hard on his bare behind. It struck the skin with a satisfying whack, and she saw him flinch with the pain. For a moment her hand wavered as pity began to creep in, but she had only to remember that he had twice taken cruel advantage of her and the powerful urge to strike returned.

'There!' she exclaimed, as a second stroke lashed across his bare skin, swiftly followed by a third. There was soon a criss-cross pattern of red stripes, yet Daniel lay with gritted teeth taking it all in abject silence. Emma found her resolution waxing further. She had wanted him to cry out with pain, to beg and plead with her to stop the torment, yet it was obvious that he would not give her that satisfaction. The more obdurate he became, the more she was tempted to wreak sterner vengeance upon him, to wring some sound from his silent form.

Kitty tried to stay her hand. 'No, Miss Emma, surely you have punished him enough!' she protested.

'Kitty, please leave the room!' The girl hesitated. Her mistress added with a smile, echoing Daniel's previous words to her, 'I promise I will do him no harm.'

When Emma was alone she raised the leather once again in her right hand, enjoying the surge of power it gave her. To be so entirely in control of the situation, to have him lying before her in naked abandonment, was filling her with a subtly erotic pleasure. Her breasts felt tight beneath their restricting garments, but beneath the loose skirts her pussy was plump, soft and warm. By contrast she was aware of the hard centre of her desire thrusting hungrily between her swelling lips and clamouring for satisfaction. Every time she brought down the lash she pressed her thighs together and felt the delicious tingling increase.

Preparing to resume the scourging, Emma took a deep breath and looked down at Daniel's prostrate body. His strong thighs, the long sweep of his spine and his broad shoulders were all sunk in submission. His buttocks were latticed with red, but where his skin was untouched it was creamy white and delicate, a silky covering over the developed muscles and tough sinews beneath. The sight of his passive male nakedness, evoking the still beauty of a Florentine *David*, suddenly brought her to her senses and she let her hand drop to her side.

Emma had the feeling of awakening from a nightmare. What on earth was she doing? Her lust for him had been dark and dangerous, revealing a side of herself hitherto unsuspected. How could she have enjoyed inflicting physical pain on this man? He might have afforded her emotional and mental torment but he had never harmed her. There must be something beastly in her if she could become aroused by her own cruelty in that fashion.

Shamefacedly Emma fumbled with the knots that tied his ankles to the bedposts, but she left his hands and eyes bound. Daniel gave a low groan and spread his thighs apart, showing the dark sac between them. Overcome with remorse, Emma went to her dressing-table and found the cold cream containing extract of marigold that she used to heal cuts and rashes. She dipped in her finger and returned to the bed, where she placed a blob of cream in the centre of each buttock.

Daniel winced, grunting, 'What the devil, woman?'

'Ssh, it is a cool salve. Just lie still and you shall feel better soon.'

Lightly Emma smoothed the cream into his inflamed skin. When she had finished with his posterior she smoothed the excess cream over his shoulders, feeling the taut musculature beneath her fingers. A strange sadness had possessed her and she hardly knew what to do or say, but the rhythmic stroking of his warm flesh was comforting.

At last she reached up and untied the knot that secured the blindfold. 'Turn over,' she said. 'I want to see your face.'

But when he did so it was not his face that drew her attention. To her astonishment his organ was fully extended and stood up from the neat mat of black hair like a blazing beacon. Emma could not help but stare at it. Tall and thick, with its shiny bulb of dark pink neatly slit, his member quivered slightly under her gaze. She put out her hand and curled her fingers around its solid girth. For several seconds she just held it while he watched her, neither of them saying a word. The thought came into Emma's head, unbidden: 'With just a few thrusts of this lively creature he pierced my heart and soul, once and for all!'

Silently she hitched up her skirt and petticoats then knelt astride him. His face stared up at her, unblinking, shadowed in the mellow half-light. Emma could feel the dull throb of her sex as she let the distended glans nudge in between her nether lips, but Daniel's face remained impassive, almost monk-like in its abstracted meditation. Soon she had lowered herself to take the whole of the head into her opening, baptising it with her warm juices. She felt her empty vagina contract with desire for him, longing to be completed by his flesh, but still she kept control of the probing bulb at her entrance.

It came to her suddenly that this was the power she wanted over him, not that other, crude and shameful dominion. He had taken her once with no thought for her pleasure, but now she would make him service her for as long as she wished. She would use his living flesh in the same way that she might make use of an inanimate dildo, purely to serve her needs. Emma drew back a little and began to rub herself against the smooth solidity of his shaft, letting it slide between her softly swollen lips until it reached the solid nub beneath her mons, wriggling sensually to maintain the stimulating contact. Soon she could feel the urgent thrilling of her nerves that signalled her approaching climax.

When her orgasm eventually arrived it was accompanied by a flood of euphoria that seemed to lift her up on a tidal wave of pure energy. She was dimly aware of Daniel far below her, his pole the axis of her being round which she spun and pivoted like a dancing star. While it lasted, the heady sensations had her completely under their spell so that she felt elated, omnipotent, but when they began to fade a world-weariness overtook her, bringing her back down into a post-coital *tristesse* such as she had never before experienced. The urge to make further use of Daniel's captive flesh had completely dissolved, and she lay face down on the bed beside him, utterly spent.

For some time she lay insensate, drained of all feeling. When she did become aware of her surroundings again she felt a hand gently stroking her hair. Turning her head she expected to find that Kitty had returned but instead, to her utter confusion, she found that the person caressing her was Daniel!

'What . . .?' she exclaimed, sitting up in alarm. Her suspicions were confirmed at first glance: both his hands were free.

He smiled at her consternation. 'Perhaps I should have told you that I count escapology amongst my many talents,' he explained, fully the old, suave Daniel again. 'It is a skill that I have found invaluable several times during my life.'

'But I tied the rope so tightly!'

'There are few bonds tied by men, let alone women, that I cannot slip out of within a few seconds.'

Emma stared at him as the truth sunk in. 'Then why did you not escape straight away? Why did you allow me to inflict pain upon you, to use you however I wished?'

He smiled and drew her up into his arms until she

230

felt his lips pressed to her forehead. 'My dear Emma, there is much you have to learn about me. Physical pain I have trained myself to endure, even to find pleasure in. I have also acquired considerable control over my body in other ways, although I must admit you tested me to the limit just now. But the kind of emotional torment that comes from knowing I cannot have you is the most unbearable I have ever known.'

'*Have* me? But you took me yourself, in Florence. You have had me, Daniel.'

He gave a harsh laugh. 'Do not mock me, Emma. I used you, and just now you used me in return. We have not possessed each other in the way I desire more than anything in the world. I suppose, however, that you consider that you have evened the score between us.'

Emma stared up at him from the warm crook of his arm. She was utterly confused. All she knew was that she needed to be alone with her tangled thoughts, to try and make some sense of them. 'Yes, I suppose so. And now that you are free to go I hope you will do so at once.' She got up and walked away from the bed, turning her back on him. 'Go, please!' she repeated. 'I shall not trouble you again.'

His laugh echoed round the room like the sharp cry of a bird. 'You trouble me every waking hour, Emma Longmore!' she heard him say, softly. The bed creaked as it was relieved of his weight, and she heard him step towards the door. 'And every sleeping one, too!'

Steeling herself not to turn round, Emma heard the door close; first with relief, but then with a terrible, aching emptiness.

Chapter Fifteen

*O*ver the next few days Emma felt utterly split in two. Her normal self continued to go about her daily business, educating her young ladies with her usual enthusiasm and running the household efficiently. But all the while the hidden part of her, that puzzled interminably over things and was subject to radical changes of mood, was going over and over what had happened between her and Daniel Forbes.

Emma simply could not make sense of it. At one time she'd thought of him as some kind of devious puppeteer, pulling her strings. But then she remembered how he had spoken so abjectly of his desire for her, and how he'd let her overpower him. Sometimes she was filled with anger when she thought of him, at other times she pitied him. Yet the one thing that she could not deny was the attraction between them. Emma had never met anyone that roused her curiosity as much, kindling a desire to know him better. But at some deeper level she was afraid that if she once let herself come too close to the secret heart of him she would be consumed, like a moth in a candle flame.

Emma was worried about Kitty still being in contact with the man. She gave her maid orders to be polite to him, but never to try and arrange any further meetings between him and her mistress. Then one day the girl announced, 'Vincent is moving into lodgings near Temple Bar, with two fellow students,' and Emma sighed with relief. Now she could put Daniel Forbes out of her mind forever.

Fortunately there was a convenient distraction on the horizon. Yvette and Bella were attending the Ball at the French Embassy in honour of the coming-of-age of the Ambassador's son, and Emma was to go as their chaperone. Although the occasion was a relatively informal one with no royalty present, there was much to do. Gowns had to be made for the three of them, and new shoes and accessories purchased. On the great day itself, Kitty was kept busy arranging their hair in elaborate coiffures. Emma was so pleased with the results, for her maid had excelled herself, that she gave the girl a present of an emerald dress ring as a token of her gratitude.

'Oh, Ma'am, it is so beautiful!' Kitty exclaimed, enthralled. Then she looked at her mistress with a charming smile and added, 'But not so beautiful as you, Miss Emma. I declare I have never seen you look more lovely.'

It was true, Emma thought as she surveyed herself in the pier-glass before leaving. She did look perfectly alluring in the peacock blue silk gown, cut low across the bosom with a small cascade of diamonds winking in her cleavage. A peacock feather was cunningly wrought into her chignon, and another decorated her reticule.

The carriage dropped them off in Kensington, as near as possible to the grand mansion that housed the Ambassador and his family. After depositing their cloaks, the three ladies moved on into the saloon where guests were mingling in anticipation of their entrée into the main ballroom. There Emma caught the eye of Lady Brendan, who greeted her warmly.

'My dear Emma, how good to see you again.'

'It was very good of you, Elizabeth, to obtain invitations for my two young protégées. It is their first social event in London, and they have both been looking forward to it tremendously.'

'We shall each present one of them to his Excellency. Perhaps you would care to take Yvette under your wing? He is sure to be more interested in her, since she is French.'

'Of course,' Emma smiled. 'But I hope both girls will have an equal chance of handsome and attentive dancing partners.'

'Do not worry, my dear, I shall do my best to secure dances for both of them with the birthday boy, Jean-Paul himself!'

The women laughed, but then a hush fell over the room as a pageboy announced the first of the presentations. Emma found her heart racing as she took her place amongst the glittering throng. It reminded her of her own introduction to Society soon after she married Henry. How long ago that now seemed!

Although Emma was very nervous as she approached the Ambassador and his family, he turned out to be such an ordinary little man, bald and podgy with twinkling eyes, who chatted so amiably with Yvette about her home town, that she soon felt quite at ease.

Once the dancing began Emma was delighted to find that her two charges had no lack of partners and were on the floor almost continually. She sat chatting with Lady Brendan, admiring the ball gowns and the handsome escorts. Suddenly, however, she had such a shock that she almost spilled her champagne. Approaching their table with a confident smile was the man she had thought never to set eyes on again.

Quashing the urge to rush to the ladies' retiring room, Emma sat rigidly on her flimsy chair staring at Bella and Yvette, who were whirling gaily around the ballroom without a care in the world. As Daniel Forbes greeted her friend, she felt her colour heightening. He was deliberately avoiding her eye, and yet she could feel the electric tension in the air between them.

'Lady Brendan, how delightful to see you. And your

charming daughter? What, two grandchildren? You scarcely look old enough . . . Yes, please do.'

Then came the dread words, 'Emma dear, I should like to introduce you to a friend of my late husband.'

She turned in trepidation, unable to avoid the inevitable any longer, but found she could not raise her eyes higher than the jewelled pin that secured Daniel's cravat. Elizabeth concluded, proudly, 'Lord Merton, Earl of Harfield.'

Emma's startled eyes met his. Darkly ironic, they glittered brighter than the diamond at his throat. His smile widened as he bowed and then kissed her limply proffered hand.

'I am . . . pleased to make your acquaintance,' she replied, stiffly, afraid that he would perceive the frantic pulsing in her wrist.

A part of her felt several miles removed from the scene as she heard her own name mentioned, followed by Daniel saying, 'Delighted to meet you, Lady Longmore. I wonder if you would do me the honour of the next dance?'

Emma squirmed in her seat. She could hardly refuse in front of her friend. Besides, she was surprised to find that she actually wanted to dance with him. It would give her the opportunity to let him know just what she thought of his duplicity!

When the music changed Emma rose from her seat and allowed 'Lord Merton' to lead her onto the dance floor. She could feel his hand burning into her back where it rested, and her own hand tingling where it was clasped in his. To be this close to him, surrounded by people who knew nothing of their past, was oddly exciting. She was soon feeling short of breath, and not only from the exertion of dancing.

'So, Lord Merton, I see you at last in your true colours,' she murmured, as he pulled her close during a turn. 'I rather think that you have been sailing under false ones.'

'Not at all, my dear Lady Longmore,' he replied,

smiling suavely. 'Forbes was my mother's family name I feel at liberty to adopt either cognomen, according to circumstances.'

'Even so, Lord Merton of Harfield is a little more respectable than Daniel Forbes, manufacturer of ladies ndergarments, do you not agree?'

He gave a soft laugh, to which Emma found herself responding with a smile. 'Not if you knew my reputation, my dear! But my alter ego is not entirely fictional I can assure you. The Harfield estate in Yorkshire does contain a factory producing high-class underwear for ladies and I am, in theory at least, its proprietor.'

They ceased talking then, but Emma continued to marvel at the man's nerve. It seemed he was a born dissimulator. How many times had he deceived other women, she wondered, relying on his considerable charm to see him through? She could not forget that he had told her he was besotted with her. Had that been a falsehood too? Yet now, feeling their bodies move in perfect accord, weaving through the others on the floor as if they did not exist, Emma was inclined to believe that there was something special between them, something genuinely fine and rare like an old brandy.

As the dance drew to its close, Daniel whispered in her ear with beguiling urgency, 'Please, Emma, let me talk to you. There is much that I wish to explain, but we cannot talk freely here. Tell Elizabeth Brendan that you are indisposed, and I have kindly agreed to see you home. She may take charge of your two young ladies and bring them safely to your door.'

'Daniel, I cannot . . .'

'I promise that I shall not take advantage of you Emma. I wish to talk, that is all. Please grant me one more chance to give an account of myself, I beg of you Then, if it is your wish, I promise never to so much a acknowledge you in public or private, again.'

Emma stared into his eyes, seeing how painful it was for him to make such a promise. She knew he was being sincere, and her heart was torn in two. How could she refuse him? If she spurned him now she would be acting as callously as if she were to refuse a dying man his last request.

'Very well.' She sighed. 'I shall tell Elizabeth I am unwell and you may take me home.'

It was embarrassing having to lie to her friend, who started to prattle about summoning a doctor, but Emma managed to hint that the nature of her indisposition was a 'female disorder' and Elizabeth at once became discreet.

'How kind of Lord Merton to accompany you,' she simpered. Then, beneath her breath, she murmured, 'Are you sure he does not have an ulterior motive, my dear? I feel I must warn you that he has something of a reputation, where women are concerned.'

'Do not fear, Elizabeth, I am perfectly able to take care of myself. I have made my way around Europe accompanied only by my maid, remember?'

'Forgive me, dear. You look so beautifully feminine in that gown that one forgets you are of an intrepid disposition!'

Emma began to think she would never get away, but at last she crossed the ballroom on Daniel's arm and, once she had collected her cloak, was whisked out into the night. They rode in silence in the cab, but as it swayed through the dark streets Emma felt herself becoming sleepy and rested her head on his shoulder. It was so comforting that she soon fell into a doze.

She awoke when the cab jolted to a halt, and was embarrassed to find that she had her head in Daniel's lap. 'Oh, I beg your pardon!' she muttered, sleepily.

'Not at all, it was a most pleasant journey!' he smiled, as he helped her out.

Emma took him up to the drawing-room and unlocked the Tantalus, bidding Daniel to take his pick of the liquors on display. He poured himself a tumbler of whisky but she declined all alcohol, being afraid of its effects. Tonight, of all nights, she was determined to remain as clear-headed as possible. It was difficult enough being alone with him in her house again, reviving not only memories of what had happened between them on the last occasion but also the attendant feelings. Already she could feel her body tautly aroused, from the straining tips of her breasts to the hard little bead that nestled in the topmost nook of her vulva.

'So, Daniel, explain yourself if you can,' she ordered him, once they were seated in facing arm chairs. 'Are we to play lords and ladies, or shall we be plain Emma and Dan?'

'Do not mock me, please! I can stand most things, but not your ridicule.'

'But is our situation not ridiculous? You have chased me for weeks on end across several countries pretending to be an underwear salesman, and now I discover that you have a seat in the House of Lords and a country seat besides. In addition, you seem uncommonly well acquainted with the European underworld and, I dare say, with the London one too. Yes, Daniel Forbes-Merton, Earl of Harfield, I believe you *do* have some explaining to do.'

He set down his glass and took her hand. 'Then please be patient, dearest Emma. I shall begin with a little of my family history. I was born the second son of the Earl and I confess that as a youth I led a profligate life. When my elder brother was killed in a riding accident and I succeeded to the title my parents had already died, and I had no one to keep me in check. I allowed the estate to run down, and squandered much of the family fortune on gambling and vice. I am deeply ashamed of my behaviour, Emma.'

'So you should be!'

'Indeed.' His eyes grew as troubled as a stormy sea. 'But there has always been a dark side to me, a part that craved sensation. I have tried drink, opium, gambling, women. Such distractions satisfied me for a time but then I felt jaded and debauched. I travelled extensively but never found peace of mind.'

'Why are you telling me this?'

'Because when I saw you for the first time I had a glimpse of a new possibility, a new path for me. I dreamed of finding someone who could help me make something fine of my life instead of wreck it. Someone who could redeem me from my life of sordid self-seeking.'

'I?' Emma stared at him, feeling shaken. 'But you do not know me, Daniel. You do not know what I have done, what I have been . . .'

'I know that, like me, you have seduced young innocents. I know that, like me, you are familiar with many aspects of life which respectable gentlefolk shun completely. I know that you are, like me, a seeker after sensation.'

Emma shuddered. He had painted such a black picture of himself, and now he was painting a similar portrait of her. The trouble was, she recognised it as a true likeness.

'That is why we could be so good for each other, Emma. We could reclaim our lost innocence together, by sharing all our dark experience and neutralising it. I have no idea whether you understand what I am saying, but I feel compelled to say it. Perhaps words are inadequate.'

'I think I have some inkling,' Emma replied, staring at him intently. She was fighting a strong urge to offer whatever comfort her arms might afford him. Could it be that their bodies were somehow wiser than their petty minds?

She reached out and took his hand. He smiled, gratefully. 'Your sympathy would be enough for me, Emma, if I were a pure soul. But I fear that I need a more gross absolution. I cannot blame you for wanting to keep away from me. I suppose I am, as Lady Lamb said of Lord Byron, "Mad, bad and dangerous to know". And, not even possessing his poetic talent, I suppose that makes me more or less worthless.'

'*Worthless!*' Emma half rose from her chair in indignation. 'What a terrible thing to say about anyone, even oneself! Do you suppose that God made any man in vain?'

'Ah, God! Well, there is another problem. You see, I am not quite sure that I approve of the Almighty. If he exists, that is. And as for his Church . . . Well, as you may have observed, I do a passable impersonation of a renegade priest.'

'Oh, you *are* wicked!' Emma chuckled.

'That is what I have spent the last ten minutes attempting to convey, my dear, so I am gratified that you have finally taken the point.'

'I meant delightfully wicked, the kind of wicked that makes women weep with laughter, not with sorrow.'

'They may laugh at first, but you may be sure they will weep later.'

'Really?' Emma grew suddenly very serious indeed. She could feel herself being inexorably drawn towards this man, recognising in him a kindred spirit that she could not ignore. Was she, too, storing up tears for herself if she gave in to her impulse? But if she restrained herself, if she let him go now and bade him never to darken her door again, would she regret it for the rest of her life?

Daniel saw her hesitation and rose to leave. 'Thank you for your indulgence, Lady Longmore.' He gave a bow. 'I shall detain you no longer.'

'No, please!' Emma threw her arms around him to prevent him leaving. 'It has gone too far between us, I cannot let you go now. Hardly a day goes by when I do not think of you. I puzzle over what has happened since we met, and can make no sense of it. You are like a tormenting conundrum in my life that I can never solve.'

'Ah!' He kissed her cheek, his lips like ice to her fire. 'Some things cannot be understood by the mind, only by the soul. And the soul perceives them only through the body.'

'Then speak to me that way,' she begged him. 'Show

me, tonight, exactly why you have such a hold over me that I can never forget you.'

Daniel looked down at her with a kind of pained indulgence, apparently wrestling with conflicting thoughts. Then he heaved a long sigh and took her hand, leading her from the room into the dark corridor and up the stairs. Emma waited while he lit the lamps in her room, hovering in a limbo between fear and eroticism. When he turned to face her she felt a trembling, like wind over grass, brushing her nerve-endings lightly. Her skin felt eerily sensitised to his presence, like one who perceives a ghost through some sixth sense.

'Emma,' he breathed, in an almost formal tone, approaching her slowly with arms outstretched. 'You have never looked more ravishing than you do now. But the splendour of your gown merely hints at the greater beauty beneath.'

So saying he bent to kiss the exposed white skin of her bosom. His mouth brushed her as lightly as insect wings, making her shudder with intense desire. From the waist down she was weak as water. Sensing her frailty, Daniel put his arm around her waist and held her suspended while he continued to press his warm lips to her neck and cleavage. Emma felt close to swooning, but knew that she must keep a grip on herself so that she could clearly register whatever was about to happen between them. She had a feeling that, somehow, her fate depended on it.

Daniel moved her over to the bed and began to unfasten her gown. Emma helped him until she was reduced to her underwear. Soon she felt the accelerated thudding of her heart as his fingers untied the laces and unhooked the stays, bringing her nearer and nearer to a state of complete vulnerability. His fingers hardly fumbled once, testimony to much practice, and she found herself wondering how many other women he had led along this path. Was she to be just one more, merely the latest in a long line of conquests? She had staked her heart on it that she was not.

Looking into his eyes for reassurance, Emma was amazed by what she saw there. His expression was adoring, almost fawning. As one of her breasts came free of its frilly covering, she heard him gasp and then softly press his lips to the tip of her nipple. The tickling lightness of the contact made her gasp in turn. She wanted him to take the whole of it into his mouth, to suckle strongly and satisfy the ache in her womb, but he merely removed the rest of her upper garments and let her lie in her under-petticoat until he was ready for her.

Emma lay back against the pillows and watched him undress himself, admiring the firmly-muscled arms and shoulders with their light freckling, then his deeply moulded chest with the dark hair emblazoned across it like a spread-eagle. His body was familiar to her now and she found herself anticipating the moment when her eyes would see again that proud phallus rising from his loins, as hot and keen for action as a soldier held long in suspense. For the first time she had a sense of the nobility of a man's body, a feeling that neither Henry's somewhat flabby physique nor the boyish figures of her other lovers had been able to evoke.

'I took you roughly once, with no thought but for my own satisfaction,' he told her. 'This time everything will be different. I am yours to command, Madame!'

The dark centre of his eye caught the light, flashing like a warning beacon. She remembered their last encounter and wondered if she should play the cruel mistress again, but thought better of it. Tonight she would wallow in sheer bliss, challenge him to seek out her secret foibles, her private *penchants*. She would let him play upon the sensitive instrument of her body and see what sweet music he could get out of her.

Emma watched him slowly lift his shirt over his thighs to reveal the object of her desire. It grew like an exotic flower in a mossy bed, straight and tall with its

242

purple lotus-head in full bloom. Below she could see the elongated sac that held his seed. Although she would not have protested if he had come into her straight away, Emma knew that it was to the advantage of both of them to wait for as long as was endurable.

She uttered a sigh as he approached the bed and then felt him raise the hem of her cotton petticoat until he could reach the silk and lace of her garter. Slowly he rolled it down her thigh, over her knee and down her leg until he slipped it off her foot. Emma felt the sheer silk of her stocking rumple then caress her thigh as it slid down, rucking at her knee. Daniel gently pulled it down to follow the path of her garter, pressing his lips to her knee in the process, and soon one leg was completely bare.

Instead of stripping the other one, Daniel began to play with the contrast between them. First he kissed her naked ankle, then her stockinged one, apparently relishing the two different sensations. He passed his hands up both shins at once, letting Emma feel the slight pull of the mesh against her skin on the one leg and the faint clamminess of his palm on the other. He massaged both her feet at once, working the silk between one set of toes and his little finger between the other, tickling her mercilessly until she squirmed and squealed.

'Relax!' he cooed. 'Enjoy it all, my sweet. Tantalising pleasure and exquisite pain are but two sides of the same coin.'

His roving hands passed up her thighs, bypassed her overheated pussy and met again on her belly, beneath the ruffles of her underskirt. His stroking there was soothing, calming the nervous flutterings within, but after a while Emma longed for him to move elsewhere. She sighed with relief when he hitched himself up the bed in order to place a kiss on her yearning lips. Pressing his mouth lightly to hers so that she could feel his moustache brushing just beneath her nose, he let his tongue penetrate just a short way within, licking

243

along the underside of her lips in a way that sent shudders of electric current through her. She flicked his tongue with the tip of hers, challenging him to enter further, but he desisted and soon retreated, leaving her wanting more, always more. Wryly, Emma reflected on his expertise in arousing desire in women. He seemed to know her body better than she did!

Daniel slipped back down the bed again and put his head beneath her skirt. Emma hoped he might pause at the sweet delta that was already beginning to overflow with her juices, but instead he moved on up to the smooth roundness of her stomach. His tongue dipped into her navel and delicately swirled around in the tiny hollow, while his hands stroked her thighs.

Looking down her body, all Emma could see was the great white tent of her petticoat and, beyond it, Daniel's long back and firm, pale buttocks. No longer streaked with red, they rose between her outstretched legs like cool marble mounds. She wanted to reach out and touch them, imagining how she might clutch them with eager hands as they heaved up and down upon her, but for the moment she would lie still and savour the subtler pleasures of having her belly teased with his tongue. Now he was kissing all around the central hollow, brushing the top edge of her pubic vee, his moustache making a rough contrast to the smooth coolness of his lips and tongue. Emma could feel thrilling little eddies moving beneath her skin, setting up a circular motion within, spiral waves of arousal that made her aware of the empty ache in the centre of her body that longed to be filled.

'Oh, Emma, your body is the temple where I worship!' Daniel exclaimed, on coming up for air. He began to pull down her last remaining garment and soon had her completely naked. She enjoyed watching his eyes as they roved freely over her supine figure, taking in every detail. It was easy to believe that he was indeed worshipping her with his eyes, for his gaze spread a radiance everywhere and almost had the power to warm her without the aid of touch.

Daniel moved down the bed again and began to kiss her toes, one by one. Emma had to quell the urge to laugh as his moustache hairs tickled her, but she restrained herself and was soon revelling in the voluptuous pleasure that his ministrations afforded her. Emma had often remarked how there seemed to be some mysterious connection between her nipples and her clitoris, but now she discovered that the same was true of her toes. The more Daniel licked and sucked upon them, the stronger became the tingling current that spread up her legs and between her thighs, flooding her sensual bud with a throbbing vitality.

'Oh, you fill me with such impossibly irresistible sweetness!' she sighed voluptuously.

She looked at him down the length of her body. His hair lay darkly matted over his forehead, curling slightly around the ears. His brows were straight and thick over his jet-black eyes that gleamed softly at her now, full of frank enjoyment.

How well I know his features, Emma thought wonderingly. Then she murmured to him, 'Come here, I want to kiss you.'

Reluctantly he relinquished her dainty toes and came up the bed again. She had commanded him and he must obey. At first Emma was content to place feather-light kisses on his brow and cheeks, but soon she craved deeper contact and pressed her tongue against his lips, willing him to let her enter. Daniel groaned as their tongues met, furled around each other then fought a little, tip to tip. While their kiss grew more passionate, she felt him cup both breasts from beneath, squeezing the heavy contours as they lay in his palms and just brushing her erect nipples with his thumbs. The combined effect of his hands and lips was sending her wild with desire and her thighs shuttled restlessly back and forth, rubbing her labia together.

Knowing how much she hungered for him, Emma

tried to reach down and touch his rampant organ but he removed her hand at once. 'Not yet,' he whispered. 'We are not ready enough for each other. I want you near to dying for me before I will give you that satisfaction.'

'You enjoy tormenting me, then?'

'Only because one must suffer for one's art, my dear. I prefer to approach love-making as an artist, and I deeply regret that my first intimate act with you was that of a clumsy artisan. I am so grateful to you for giving me this opportunity to prove that I can behave quite differently.'

Emma smiled and lay back passively once more, relishing the tender stroking that was calming her thighs. Softly he kissed the brown curls of her mons, burying his nose in her scent, then moved his lips over her stomach again in a spiral path until he reached her right breast. Fastening his mouth over one turgid nipple he seized the other and began to pinch it quite firmly, so that her bosom thrust eagerly against him. Emma could soon feel his hardness rubbing against her thigh with equal enthusiasm, and despite Daniel's declared intention to hold back she wondered exactly how long he would be able to maintain his resolve.

Down her side in one long sweep went his right hand, ending in a flourish over her pubis. Emma let her thighs fall open, hoping that he would take the hint and begin to venture into her secret recesses. He spent some time skirting round it but finally, to her great relief, he gently probed in between the damp lips. At first his touch was tentative, almost excruciatingly so, but as her secretions began to flow more readily his fingers grew bolder.

Emma issued a loud moan as she felt his index finger slip easily inside her and his thumb press hard on the swollen nub of her desire, sending her into an upward spiral of yearning. She moved against him, slowly at first but as his digit penetrated deeper she quickened her pace until the throbbing outside was transformed into a series of stronger pulsations within, and she gasped with the ecstatic delight of her sudden climax. Vaguely she could hear him crooning encouragement as the fierce rhythm swept her higher and higher. Then, when she was approaching her peak, he held her tightly as the spasms shook through her again and again.

'Oh, my sweet, my dearest!' she heard him murmur as she sank into his arms, utterly spent. Emma felt she had been cleansed through and through by purifying fire. She had the strangest urge to laugh and cry at the same time but instead she snuggled up to him like a child, pressing her breasts to the warm bulk of his chest.

'Daniel . . .' Emma began, tentatively.

'Ssh! This is only the beginning,' he replied.

At first she was unsure what he meant, but sensing his own urgency she felt her lust begin to return and knew that her desire was matched by his. This time he let her touch his manhood, while he continued to kiss her breasts and stroke her stomach and thighs. Emma took the thick rod between both palms and rolled it gently. She bent down and kissed its bulbous head, licking along the salty groove. The skin was warm as velvet, yet beneath it she could feel that the shaft was strong as steel. The thought of it sinking into her own flesh and pounding away urgently produced a tiny, excited fluttering in the pit of her stomach.

Emma widened her mouth to take in the glans, letting her tongue move around the groove beneath. She heard Daniel grunt as she took in more of the shaft, her lips tracking across the protruding veins. While she slipped the penis in and out of her open mouth Emma was delicately rolling his balls with her fingers, feeling them moving around independently in their sac. Now she was lying on her stomach facing his feet and Daniel was kneading her buttocks with both hands, exciting her more keenly from time to time by slipping a finger into the deep crack between them where the skin was very sensitive.

Then she felt his finger slip down further, into the warm moistness of her front crevice. This time Daniel did not tease her but let his digit roam right into her entrance, where she was already meltingly soft and ready for him. He dabbled there for a while, producing little suction noises that excited her immensely, yet she was in too awkward a position to benefit wholly from the stimulation. With a low moan she removed her lips from his straining erection and turned around, pleading with her eyes to be given the licence she longed for. He lay with a distant smile on his face, scarcely seeing her through the dark glaze that covered his pupils.

Emma straddled him, easing the great head of his penis between her labia so that it fitted snugly into the humid recess. For a while she remained delicately poised above him while she gyrated slowly, maintaining the titillating contact between his glans and her clitoris. She was looking down upon his transformed features, marvelling at the way his face looked so open and guileless, a far cry from the world-weary sophisticate that she had taken him to be. Was it possible, after all, that what he had said was true and she was able to restore to him his lost innocence?

Suddenly she was filled with a hunger that demanded instant fulfilment, an urge to take and be taken that would not be brooked. Emma plunged down the full length of his flesh, her own flesh quivering with erotic delight as she took him wholly into her well-primed vagina. Once inside, she let the walls close round him in a deeply satisfying embrace, eliciting an 'Aah!' of satisfaction from Daniel. She leaned forward and kissed his open mouth, letting her tongue meet his in lazy salutation, then moved back so that she could begin to ride him. She rose and sank in a slow rhythm at first, relishing the length of him as, inch by inch, she familiarised herself with his pulsating penis. For the lips of her sex were as sensitive as her mouth or fingers in detecting every vein, every ridge, every wrinkle of that mobile skin.

Emma sensed that Daniel was far away, immersed in some blissful heaven that she still hovered outside, but once she began to quicken the pace her own arousal increased until she could feel the world recede and a new realm of pure sensuality come into focus. Now when she bore down upon him she could feel him thrust upwards in response, rubbing against the humming generator of her pleasure. That great wand of his was transforming her consciousness and creating expanding ripples in the liquid centre of her being.

Suddenly Daniel pulled her over to one side and knelt over her, reversing their position. Emma groaned as she felt him penetrate her more deeply than before, allowing gravity to help him reach every far corner of her expanded quim. Each time he plunged into her she could feel the increasing fire of his passion, and found that she longed for his fulfilment even more than she desired her own. Emma knew instinctively that they were coming close to the same ecstatic consummation, and that when it happened they would be indissolubly welded together, but now she was not afraid. She had at last recognised that this man, unlikely as it seemed, was her destiny.

So, when it finally happened, it was a sweet relief to be able to abandon herself to him completely. As the orgasmic wave swept over her it swept away all doubt, all fear, all suspicion. Emma felt a tide of love wash through her, cleansing her of petty emotions and elevating her beyond superficial distinctions of personality so that Daniel ceased to be alien to her and became her other self, a shade darker perhaps but made of the same basic stuff. She knew him right through to his heart's core, and in knowing him gained a greater knowledge of her true self. At last she was able to give up her petty independence and drift beyond the boundaries of their two bodies into a perfect melding.

When the great cataclysm finally subsided Emma was struck by how small a part the physical seemed to have played. They had gone beyond mere flesh and blood in a way that she had never experienced before. Lying in Daniel's arms she felt perfectly fulfilled, perfectly at ease, and knew beyond all doubt that he felt the same. For many minutes they lay without need of speech, communicating through touch and breath alone.

Then, when Emma felt herself beginning to drift off, she heard him whisper, 'Emma, can you ever forgive me?'

'What for?' she asked, sleepily.

'For having the temerity to love you.'

She laughed, taking his head between her hands and kissing his mouth and eyes with tender passion. 'Only if you allow me to punish you for your impudence whenever I wish.'

He grinned, his handsome face taking on its old devilish cast in the waning candlelight.

'Your wish, my darling Emma, is my command. And since I know that our desires perfectly coincide I think there shall be no need for further conflict between us. What say you, my love?'

But Emma, who had let her hand stray once more, already had at her command that part of him which she most desired. And, needless to say, it was obeying her wish absolutely.

BLACK
lace

NO LADY
Saskia Hope

30-year-old Kate dumps her boyfriend, walks out of her job and sets off in search of sexual adventure. Set against the rugged terrain of the Pyrenees, the love-making is as rough as the landscape.

ISBN 0 352 32857 6

WEB OF DESIRE
Sophie Danson

High-flying executive Marcie is gradually drawn away from the normality of her married life. Strange messages begin to appear on her computer, summoning her to sinister and fetishistic sexual liaisons.

ISBN 0 352 32856 8

BLUE HOTEL
Cherri Pickford

Hotelier Ramon can't understand why best-selling author Floy Pennington has come to stay at his quiet hotel. Her exhibitionist tendencies are driving him crazy, as are her increasingly wanton encounters with the hotel's other guests.

ISBN 0 352 32858 4

CASSANDRA'S CONFLICT
Fredrica Alleyn

Behind the respectable facade of a house in present-day Hampstead lies a world of decadent indulgence and darkly bizarre eroticism. A sternly attractive Baron and his beautiful but cruel wife are playing games with the young Cassandra.

ISBN 0 352 32859 2

THE CAPTIVE FLESH
Cleo Cordell

Marietta and Claudine, French aristocrats saved from pirates, learn that their invitation to stay at the opulent Algerian mansion of their rescuer, Kasim, requires something in return; their complete surrender to the ecstasy of pleasure in pain.

ISBN 0 352 32872 X

PLEASURE HUNT
Sophie Danson

Sexual adventurer Olympia Deschamps is determined to become a member of the Légion D'Amour – the most exclusive society of French libertines.

ISBN 0 352 32880 0

BLACK ORCHID
Roxanne Carr

The Black Orchid is a women's health club which provides a specialised service for its high-powered clients; women who don't have the time to spend building complex relationships, but who enjoy the pleasures of the flesh.

ISBN 0 352 32888 6

ODALISQUE
Fleur Reynolds

A tale of family intrigue and depravity set against the glittering backdrop of the designer set. This facade of respectability conceals a reality of bitter rivalry and unnatural love.

ISBN 0 352 32887 8

OUTLAW LOVER
Saskia Hope

Fee Cambridge lives in an upper level deluxe pleasuredome of technologically advanced comfort. Bored with her predictable husband and pampered lifestyle, Fee ventures into the wild side of town, finding an outlaw who becomes her lover.

ISBN 0 352 32909 2

THE SENSES BEJEWELLED
Cleo Cordell

Willing captives Marietta and Claudine are settling into life at Kasim's harem. But 18th century Algeria can be a hostile place. When the women are kidnapped by Kasim's sworn enemy, they face indignities that will test the boundaries of erotic experience. This is the sequel to *The Captive Flesh*.

ISBN 0 352 32904 1

GEMINI HEAT
Portia Da Costa

As the metropolis sizzles in freak early summer temperatures, twin sisters Deana and Delia find themselves cooking up a heatwave of their own. Jackson de Guile, master of power dynamics and wealthy connoisseur of fine things, draws them both into a web of luxuriously decadent debauchery.

ISBN 0 352 32912 2

VIRTUOSO
Katrina Vincenzi

Mika and Serena, darlings of classical music's jet-set, inhabit a world of secluded passion. The reason? Since Mika's tragic accident which put a stop to his meteoric rise to fame as a solo violinist, he cannot face the world, and together they lead a decadent, reclusive existence.

ISBN 0 352 32907 6

MOON OF DESIRE
Sophie Danson

When Soraya Chilton is posted to the ancient and mysterious city of Ragzburg on a mission for the Foreign Office, strange things begin to happen to her. Wild, sexual urges overwhelm her at the coming of each full moon.

ISBN 0 352 32911 4

FIONA'S FATE
Fredrica Alleyn

When Fiona Sheldon is kidnapped by the infamous Trimarchi brothers, along with her friend Bethany, she finds herself acting in ways her husband Duncan would be shocked by. Alessandro Trimarchi makes full use of this opportunity to discover the true extent of Fiona's suppressed, but powerful, sexuality.

ISBN 0 352 32913 0

HANDMAIDEN OF PALMYRA
Fleur Reynolds

3rd century Palmyra: a lush oasis in the Syrian desert. The beautiful and fiercely independent Samoya takes her place in the temple of Antioch as an apprentice priestess. Decadent bachelor Prince Alif has other plans for her and sends his scheming sister to bring her to his Bacchanalian wedding feast.

ISBN 0 352 32919 X

OUTLAW FANTASY
Saskia Hope

On the outer reaches of the 21st century metropolis the Amazenes are on the prowl; fierce warrior women who have some unfinished business with Fee Cambridge's pirate lover. This is the sequel to *Outlaw Lover*.

ISBN 0 352 32920 3

THE SILKEN CAGE
Sophie Danson

When university lecturer Maria Treharne inherits her aunt's mansion in Cornwall, she finds herself the subject of strange and unexpected attention. Using the craft of goddess worship and sexual magnetism, Maria finds allies and foes in this savage and beautiful landscape.

ISBN 0 352 32928 9

RIVER OF SECRETS
Saskia Hope & Georgia Angelis

Intrepid female reporter Sydney Johnson takes over someone else's assignment up the Amazon river. Sydney soon realises this mission to find a lost Inca city has a hidden agenda. Everyone is behaving so strangely, so sexually, and the tropical humidity is reaching fever pitch.

ISBN 0 352 32925 4

VELVET CLAWS
Cleo Cordell

It's the 19th century; a time of exploration and discovery and young, spirited Gwendoline Farnshawe is determined not to be left behind in the parlour when the handsome and celebrated anthropologist, Jonathan Kimberton, is planning his latest expedition to Africa.

ISBN 0 352 32926 2

THE GIFT OF SHAME
Sarah Hope-Walker

Helen is a woman with extreme fantasies. When she meets Jeffrey – a cultured wealthy stranger – at a party, they soon become partners in obsession. Now nothing is impossible for her, no fantasy beyond his imagination or their mutual exploration.

ISBN 0 352 32935 1

SUMMER OF ENLIGHTENMENT
Cheryl Mildenhall

Karin's new-found freedom is getting her into all sorts of trouble. The enigmatic Nicolai has been showing interest in her since their chance meeting in a cafe. But he's the husband of a valued friend and is trying to embroil her in the sexual tension he thrives on.

ISBN 0 352 32937 8

A BOUQUET OF BLACK ORCHIDS
Roxanne Carr

The exclusive Black Orchid health spa has provided Maggie with a new social life and a new career, where giving and receiving pleasure of the most sophisticated nature takes top priority. But her loyalty to the club is being tested by the presence of Tourell; a powerful man who makes her an offer she finds difficult to refuse.

ISBN 0 352 32939 4

JULIET RISING
Cleo Cordell

At Madame Nicol's exclusive but strict 18th-century academy for young ladies, the bright and wilful Juliet is learning the art of courting the affections of young noblemen.

ISBN 0 352 32938 6

DEBORAH'S DISCOVERY
Fredrica Alleyn

Deborah Woods is trying to change her life. Having just ended her long-term relationship and handed in her notice at work, she is ready for a little adventure. Meeting American oil magnate John Pavin III throws her world into even more confusion as he invites her to stay at his luxurious renovated castle in Scotland. But what looked like being a romantic holiday soon turns into a test of sexual bravery.

ISBN 0 352 32945 9

THE TUTOR
Portia Da Costa

Like minded libertines reap the rewards of their desire in this story of the sexual initiation of a beautiful young man. Rosalind Howard takes a post as personal librarian to a husband and wife, both unashamed sensualists keen to engage her into their decadent scenarios.

ISBN 0 352 32946 7

THE HOUSE IN NEW ORLEANS
Fleur Reynolds

When she inherits her family home in the fashionable Garden district of New Orleans, Ottilie Duvier discovers it has been leased to the notorious Helmut von Straffen; a debauched German count famous for his decadent Mardi Gras parties. Determined to oust him from the property, she soon realises that not all dangerous animals live in the swamp!

ISBN 0 352 32951 3

ELENA'S CONQUEST
Lisette Allen

It's summer – 1070AD – and the gentle Elena is gathering herbs in the garden of the convent where she leads a peaceful, but uneventful, life. When Norman soldiers besiege the convent, they take Elena captive and present her to the dark and masterful Lord Aimery to satisfy his savage desire for Saxon women.

ISBN 0 352 32950 5

CASSANDRA'S CHATEAU
Fredrica Alleyn

Cassandra has been living with the dominant and perverse Baron von Ritter for eighteen months when their already bizarre relationship takes an unexpected turn. The arrival of a naive female visitor at the chateau provides the Baron with a new opportunity to indulge his fancy for playing darkly erotic games with strangers.

ISBN 0 352 32955 6

WICKED WORK
Pamela Kyle

At twenty-eight, Suzie Carlton is at the height of her journalistic career. She has status, money and power. What she doesn't have is a masterful partner who will allow her to realise the true extent of her fantasies. How will she reconcile the demands of her job with her sexual needs?

ISBN 0 352 32958 0

DREAM LOVER
Katrina Vincenzi

Icily controlled Gemma is a dedicated film producer, immersed in her latest production – a darkly Gothic vampire movie. But after a visit to Brittany, where she encounters a mystery lover, a disquieting feeling continues to haunt her. Compelled to discover the identity of the man who ravished her, she becomes entangled in a mystifying erotic odyssey.

ISBN 0 352 32956 4

PATH OF THE TIGER
Cleo Cordell

India, in the early days of the Raj. Amy Spencer is looking for an excuse to rebel against the stuffy morals of the British army wives. Luckily, a new friend introduces her to places where other women dare not venture – where Tantric mysteries and the Kama Sutra come alive. Soon she becomes besotted by Ravinder, the exquisitely handsome son of the Maharaja, and finds the pathway to absolute pleasure.

ISBN 0 352 32959 9

BELLA'S BLADE
Georgia Angelis

Bella is a fearless, good-looking young woman with an eye for handsome highwaymen and a taste for finery. It's the seventeenth century and Charles II's Merrie England is in full swing. Finding herself to be the object of royal affections, Bella has to choose between living a life of predictable luxury at court or following her desire to sail the high seas – where a certain dashing young captain is waiting for her.

ISBN 0 352 32965 3

THE DEVIL AND THE DEEP BLUE SEA
Cheryl Mildenhall

A secluded country house in Norfolk is the setting for this contemporary story of one woman's summer of sexual exploration. Renting a holiday home with her girlfriends, the recently graduated Hillary is pleased to discover that the owner of the country estate is the most fanciable man in the locale. But soon she meets Haldane, the beautifully proportioned Norwegian sailor. Attracted by the allure of two very different men, Hillary is faced with a difficult decision.

ISBN 0 352 32966 1

WESTERN STAR
Roxanne Carr

Maribel Harker is heading west, and she's sure grown up since the last wagon train moved out to California. Dan Cutter is the frontiersman that Maribel's father has appointed to take care of his wilful daughter. She is determined to seduce him – he is determined not to give into temptation. Thrown together in a wild and unpredictable landscape, passions are destined to run high!

ISBN 0 352 32969 6

A PRIVATE COLLECTION
Sarah Fisher

Behind an overgrown garden by the sea, a crumbling mansion harbours a tantalising secret: a remarkable collection of priceless erotica belonging to a fading society beauty and her inscrutable chauffeur. When writer Francesca Leeman is commissioned to catalogue the collection, she finds herself becoming embroiled in a three-way game of voyeurism and mystery.

ISBN 0 352 32970 X

NICOLE'S REVENGE
Lisette Allen

Set against the turmoil of the French Revolution, opera star Nicole Chabrier faces a life of uncertainty now that angry hordes are venting their wrath on the aristocracy. Rescued by a handsome stranger and taken to a deserted palace, Nicole and her insatiable lover, Jacques, seek a reversal of their fortune using charm, sexual magnetism and revenge!

ISBN 0 352 32984 X

UNFINISHED BUSINESS
Sarah Hope-Walker

As a financial analyst for a top London bank, Joanne's life is about being in control. But privately, her submissive self cries out to be explored. She has tried to quell her strange desires, but they insist on haunting her. There is only one place where she can realise her desire to be dominated: the *Salon de Fantasie*, run by her enigmatic Parisian friend, Chantal. Soon, the complexities of Joanne's sexuality begin to take over the rest of her life.

ISBN 0 352 32983 1

CRIMSON BUCCANEER
Cleo Cordell

Fiery noblewoman Carlotta Mendoza is cheated out of her inheritance by the corrupt officials of Imperial Spain. But help is at hand in the form of a rugged young buccaneer who introduces her to a life of piracy and sexual adventure. Carlotta is determined to make her enemies squirm with shame as she takes her revenge.

ISBN 0 352 32987 4

LA BASQUAISE
Angel Strand

The scene is 1920s Biarritz. Oruela is a modern young woman who desires the company of artists, intellectuals and hedonists. Jean is her seemingly devoted lover who will help her to realise her wildest dreams. But when she is accused of murdering her cruel father, Oruela's life is thrown into turmoil. Bizarre characters play games of sexual blackmail against a background of decadence.

ISBN 0 352 329888 2

THE LURE OF SATYRIA
Cheryl Mildenhall

Satyria is a mythical land of debauchery and excess: a place where virtuous maidens dare not venture. When Princess Hedra's castle is threatened with invasion, she takes refuge in this land and finds plenty of virile suitors willing to make her feel welcome. When she is captured by the leather-clad King of Satyria, her lascivious talents are really put to the test.

ISBN 0 352 32994 7

THE DEVIL INSIDE
Portia Da Costa

One morning, the usually conventional Alexa Lavelle wakes up with a dramatically increased libido and the gift of psychic sexual intuition. In order to satisfy strange new desires, she finds herself drawn to an exclusive clinic where an enigmatic female doctor introduces her to some very interesting people. A world of bizarre fetishism and erotic indulgence is about to unfold.

ISBN 0 352 32993 9

BLACK
lace

WE NEED YOUR HELP . . .
to plan the future of women's erotic fiction –

– and no stamp required!

Yours are the only opinions that matter.

Black Lace is the first series of books devoted to erotic fiction by women for women.

We intend to keep providing the best-written, sexiest books you can buy. And we'd appreciate your help and valued opinion of the books so far. Tell us what you want to read.

THE BLACK LACE QUESTIONNAIRE

SECTION ONE: ABOUT YOU

1.1 Sex (*we presume you are female, but so as not to discriminate*)
Are you?

Male	☐
Female	☐

1.2 Age

under 21	☐	21–30	☐
31–40	☐	41–50	☐
51–60	☐	over 60	☐

1.3 At what age did you leave full-time education?

still in education	☐	16 or younger	☐
17–19	☐	20 or older	☐

1.4 Occupation _____

1.5 Annual household income
 under £10,000 ☐ £10–£20,000 ☐
 £20–£30,000 ☐ £30–£40,000 ☐
 over £40,000 ☐

1.6 We are perfectly happy for you to remain anonymous;
but if you would like to receive information on other
publications available, please insert your name and
address

_____

_____

_____

_____

SECTION TWO: ABOUT BUYING BLACK LACE BOOKS

2.1 How did you acquire this copy of *The Seductress*?
 I bought it myself ☐ My partner bought it ☐
 I borrowed/found it ☐

2.2 How did you find out about Black Lace books?
 I saw them in a shop ☐
 I saw them advertised in a magazine ☐
 I saw the London Underground posters ☐
 I read about them in _____
 Other _____

2.3 Please tick the following statements you agree with:
 I would be less embarrassed about buying Black
 Lace books if the cover pictures were less explicit ☐
 I think that in general the pictures on Black
 Lace books are about right ☐
 I think Black Lace cover pictures should be as
 explicit as possible ☐

2.4 Would you read a Black Lace book in a public place – on
a train for instance?
 Yes ☐ No ☐

SECTION THREE: ABOUT THIS BLACK LACE BOOK

3.1 Do you think the sex content in this book is:
Too much ☐ About right ☐
Not enough ☐

3.2 Do you think the writing style in this book is:
Too unreal/escapist ☐ About right ☐
Too down to earth ☐

3.3 Do you think the story in this book is:
Too complicated ☐ About right ☐
Too boring/simple ☐

3.4 Do you think the cover of this book is:
Too explicit ☐ About right ☐
Not explicit enough ☐

Here's a space for any other comments:

SECTION FOUR: ABOUT OTHER BLACK LACE BOOKS

4.1 How many Black Lace books have you read? ☐

4.2 If more than one, which one did you prefer?

4.3 Why?

SECTION FIVE: ABOUT YOUR IDEAL EROTIC NOVEL

We want to publish the books you want to read – so this is your chance to tell us exactly what your ideal erotic novel would be like.

5.1 Using a scale of 1 to 5 (1 = no interest at all, 5 = your ideal), please rate the following possible settings for an erotic novel:

Medieval/barbarian/sword 'n' sorcery ☐
Renaissance/Elizabethan/Restoration ☐
Victorian/Edwardian ☐
1920s & 1930s – the Jazz Age ☐
Present day ☐
Future/Science Fiction ☐

5.2 Using the same scale of 1 to 5, please rate the following themes you may find in an erotic novel:

Submissive male/dominant female ☐
Submissive female/dominant male ☐
Lesbianism ☐
Bondage/fetishism ☐
Romantic love ☐
Experimental sex e.g. anal/watersports/sex toys ☐
Gay male sex ☐
Group sex ☐

Using the same scale of 1 to 5, please rate the following styles in which an erotic novel could be written:

Realistic, down to earth, set in real life ☐
Escapist fantasy, but just about believable ☐
Completely unreal, impressionistic, dreamlike ☐

5.3 Would you prefer your ideal erotic novel to be written from the viewpoint of the main male characters or the main female characters?

Male ☐   Female ☐
Both ☐

5.4 What would your ideal Black Lace heroine be like? Tick as many as you like:

Dominant	☐	Glamorous	☐
Extroverted	☐	Contemporary	☐
Independent	☐	Bisexual	☐
Adventurous	☐	Naive	☐
Intellectual	☐	Introverted	☐
Professional	☐	Kinky	☐
Submissive	☐	Anything else?	☐
Ordinary	☐	_____	

5.5 What would your ideal male lead character be like? Again, tick as many as you like:

Rugged	☐		
Athletic	☐	Caring	☐
Sophisticated	☐	Cruel	☐
Retiring	☐	Debonair	☐
Outdoor-type	☐	Naive	☐
Executive-type	☐	Intellectual	☐
Ordinary	☐	Professional	☐
Kinky	☐	Romantic	☐
Hunky	☐		
Sexually dominant	☐	Anything else?	☐
Sexually submissive	☐	_____	

5.6 Is there one particular setting or subject matter that your ideal erotic novel would contain?

_____

SECTION SIX: LAST WORDS

6.1 What do you like best about Black Lace books?

_____

6.2 What do you most dislike about Black Lace books?

_____

6.3 In what way, if any, would you like to change Black Lace covers?

_____

6.4   Here's a space for any other comments:

_____

_____

_____

_____

_____

Thank you for completing this questionnaire. Now tear it out of the book – carefully! – put it in an envelope and send it to:

Black Lace
FREEPOST
London
W10 5BR

No stamp is required if you are resident in the U.K.